THE UNLIVED

PETER ELLISON

Copyright © 2026 Peter Ellison

All rights reserved. No part of this publication may be reproduced, distributed, or transmitted in any form or by any means, including photocopying, recording, or other electronic or mechanical methods, without prior written permission of the publisher, except in the case of brief quotations used in critical reviews or as otherwise permitted by copyright law. For permission requests, contact Fano Press at fanopress.com.

This is a work of fiction. Names, characters, places, and incidents are either the product of the author's imagination or are used fictitiously. Any resemblance to actual persons, living or dead, events, or locales is entirely coincidental.

ISBN: 979-8-9954407-0-3

Published by Fano Press

Edition: 2026.3

We are not human beings having a spiritual experience. We are spiritual beings having a human experience.

PIERRE TEILHARD DE CHARDIN

PART 1

1

Eleven years. That was Dr. Cunningham's number, give or take. Zach Hayes was twenty-eight years old and he did not intend to die at thirty-nine. His telomeres were shortening. Dr. Cunningham had used the word "manageable." Zach had booked the flight to Lisbon the same day.

He was walking down Avenida da Liberdade in downtown Lisbon, trying not to stare. This was his first trip to Portugal and nothing was what he'd expected. He'd expected Europe. What he found felt like South America: the palm trees, the parching sun, the old buildings in the Hispanic style lining up both sides of the avenue. The street was named after the 1974 revolution that had ended forty years of dictatorship. Forty years. The old establishment had accepted democracy only once its own interests were taken care of. Some things were universal.

The western side of the avenue was flanked with a string of old mansions, whose proud stucco facades were losing a hopeless battle against the outrage of time. Even though the business day had started, most of the window shutters were still pulled down and would remain so for most of the day, an ancient form of air conditioning the capital was not about to abandon. Behind those windows he imagined armies of young lawyers looking after the interests of the upper echelons of Lisbon society. Right in front of the most prestigious law firms in the country a construction worker was tearing apart the sidewalk with his jackhammer. Shiny little inch-wide tiles, that had been assembled in pre-revolutionary times to make the most exquisite mosaics, would fly left and right. Unfazed, the worker would clench his jaws and hammer on. Passers-by, used to the absence of fence or signs, would simply cross the street and walk on the safe side. No such thing as liability suits in Portugal.

Zach was finally approaching the end of the avenue and the mansion that housed the Fundação do Leste e Sul. The building didn't look conspicuous at all. A bit larger than the other houses on the Avenida, its facade appeared just as decrepit and tired as the other buildings. Hardly the seat of power Zach was expecting to find. Otto Krueger, his mentor, was waiting for him outside.

"Zach! I'm glad you could make it. I was getting worried. What happened to your driver?" said Otto.

"Once I figured out the Fundação was a five-minute walk from the hotel I decided to walk here. This is my first trip to Portugal you know. I wanted to take a look for myself" Zach replied. "Where is Igor? I thought he was going to join us?"

"No, he couldn't make it, said he had other commitments this week."

"Other commitments? I thought..."

Otto cut him off.

"Zach, we're going to be late with Dr. Oliveira. We should go in. He's expecting us in a few minutes."

Zach made a mental note of how Europeans were much more inclined to be worried about protocol and social forms, and Otto was no exception. After two knocks on the massive gate, a Malaysian butler opened a small door with a distressing squeal.

"Mr. Hayes, Mr. Krueger, Dr. Oliveira is expecting you. Please follow me."

Inside, his eyes needed a moment to adjust. The mansion had been a disappointment from the street, just another faded stucco facade. Inside was a different country. Wealth didn't announce itself here; it accumulated. It dripped from the chandeliers, pooled in the Persian rugs, pressed itself into every painting on every wall. The butler, Jamal, led them through a series of rooms arranged by century: late medieval first, crying Madonnas facing down rows of silver crucifixes, then a navigator's library with an astrolabe on the table as if someone had just set it down. Zach had grown up with nothing on the walls. He understood immediately that this was the kind of money that didn't need to explain itself.

Zach and Otto found Dr. Oliveira in the following room. Dr. Oliveira's office consisted of a large study with an imposing mahogany desk in the middle and a pair of French doors on the side opening onto an atrium. Dr. Oliveira, a short bald man with a thin mustache and square gold-rimmed glasses, was looking at them.

"Gentlemen! It is my pleasure to meet you. Please take a seat," said the host with a formality that shattered any illusion of friendly hospitality Zach might have had. A bottle of

Vinho Verde was sitting on a silver tray with three crystal glasses. Dr. Oliveira waved his hand before Jamal could reach the tray. The butler promptly left the room.

"How is your trip to Portugal so far? Did you get a chance to do some sightseeing in Lisbon?"

"Not much, we just arrived last night, you know," replied Otto. Zach wasn't sure what to say.

"What about you, young man? Otto's been singing your praises... I hear you're a talented software engineer? Founded your own quantum encryption startup with Otto's support, took it public last year. Very impressive, not many people can say they've accomplished as much as you have. And you're not even thirty!"

"Couldn't have done it without Otto..."

Oliveira's easy smile disappeared. His expression turned more serious. He stared at Zach, as if taking his measure.

"You must be courageous too. Coming here to raise money for your business... I assume Otto told you about our investors. Or was it his choice, and perhaps he forced you to come here?"

Something shifted in Zach's chest, not quite anger, not quite fear. He'd walked into a thousand rooms where people had underestimated him. This felt different.

"No, I came here of my own free will. As a matter of fact Otto didn't say much about the Fundação. What do you guys do?"

Oliveira ignored his question and pressed on.

"Your own free will... Do you realize there is no such thing as free will?"

"What do you mean?"

"Think about it, Mr. Hayes. We are just machines, information processing machines. We react to stimuli. A leads to B which leads to C. Free will is nothing but a metaphor, a device by which we train our judgement. Wise choices are rewarded, poor choices are not, and in the process we learn. I can see the impact of my choices reinforced every day, for instance with this foundation, just as I know you will too. The question is, what will you learn by coming here?"

"Interesting take, I don't think I've ever thought about it, to be honest."

Satisfied he had imparted to his audience this nugget of wisdom, Oliveira beamed with pride and shifted gears promptly.

"What can I do for you? Mr. Krueger indicated you had some important matter you needed to discuss with me, Mr. Hayes."

Zach Hayes looked his host straight in the eyes and started his pitch.

"Well, it sounds like Otto brought you up to speed already Dr. Oliveira. As you know Quantum Technologies, the company I founded, is a leader in quantum encryption. We secure more online transactions in more secure ways than any other players. The market is particularly active, however, and we will need more liquidity to tide us over and keep sales growing. I assume you researched our stock price recently, and if so, you must know there is a ton of upside..."

Once his pitch was done Zach paused and stared at Oliveira. The good doctor looked out the window into the atrium. After a few minutes of silence, Oliveira turned toward Zach.

"All right, the foundation will help you," he replied, using the royal third person. He called the butler while lifting a finger, indicating he wanted his guests to remain seated.

"Jamal, would you please get Mr. Silverinha on the phone," said Dr. Oliveira.

Zach noticed the phone sitting on the desk, and suddenly felt in a very foreign land. A land where no self-respecting official would ever touch a phone dial, where the measure of power was the ability to summon armies of support staff to dial the phone for you. A young democracy, as Zach reminded himself.

On Jamal's signal, Oliveira lifted the handset and uttered a few short sentences in Portuguese. He turned back to Zach while holding the phone.

"Mr. Hayes, we can wire the funds tomorrow but I would expect a significant discount over your current stock price. I need to justify this to our investment committee. Something in the range of a forty percent discount would be appropriate," said Oliveira.

Zach didn't flinch. This was a steep discount, but they would be able to structure the transaction so no one would find out. And the alternative, telling public markets he had previously traded on insider information, would be much worse. No, this was going to be presented as a private transaction where the foundation was effectively purchasing Zach's stock. Zach would have to sell a bit more because of the discount to get the thirty million cash he needed, but he would just have to deal with it.

"Make it thirty percent, and we'll work with it," he shot back.

Oliveira spent a few more minutes on the phone, then hung up and faced his guests. The old man, Zach thought, was hiding a smile.

"Our attorneys will work on the paperwork this afternoon. We will wire the funds tomorrow."

Oliveira set the handset down and folded his hands on the desk.

"The foundation's investors are making a bet on you, Mr. Hayes. Please do not disappoint them."

A pause.

"I would hate for you to have to meet their people in person."

2

Walking out of the Fundação building Zach was blinded by the parching sun. As his eyes were adjusting to the light Oliveira's words were still ringing in his ears. *Do not disappoint them...* He and Otto set off toward the hotel. Not a word was said. Their pace was brisk, both were silent.

Zach's phone buzzed. An unknown number, no name. The text had been sent twelve minutes ago, right as the meeting with Oliveira had started.

It went well. Safe travels.

He stopped to stare at it. The coincidence was puzzling. Otto had already walked on. He was half a block ahead, hands in his pockets, moving fast. Zach looked back at his phone, then up at the street around him. Tourists, locals, a man selling newspapers. Nobody paying any attention to him. He pocketed the phone and started catching up to Otto. Wrong number, probably.

They stopped at a traffic light to let throngs of over-caffeinated drivers whiz by. Next to him was an old

Portuguese lady, dressed in black from head to toe, her face all leathery and hardened by decades of sun exposure. She turned to him and asked:

"*Você vai me ajudar a atravessar a rua?* Will you help me cross the street?"

Without a word, Zach smiled and grabbed her arm gently. She reminded him of his mother, of a time that had been harder in some ways and simpler in others.

His mind drifted.

It had been a sunny Friday. A younger Zach had just finished his shift at the coffee shop, and was on his way to the hospital. He felt so excited! Earlier this afternoon he had received a letter in the mail informing him he was accepted into the Baltimore Coding Academy. This was his golden ticket! He couldn't wait to see his mother and tell her about it. He couldn't wait to learn about her treatment either. The last few months had been difficult. Community college and working at the same time were harder than he had expected. His mother's health had been slipping. She used to be so strong but this year had been tough on her. She had been in the hospital five times in the last six months.

At least he felt confident they would take care of her at Mercy Medical Center. When he was sick in school, Ms. Nancy the nurse had always taken care of him. She would give him antibiotics if he needed them, so they wouldn't have to buy them. His mother had told him she had a new doctor, a young guy. He couldn't wait to learn about him! He assumed and hoped this doctor would identify new treatment options for her... There were so many more options today, he remembered reading about genetic therapies, about CRISPR, and more. There had to be an option that would work for his mother.

He arrived at the hospital. By now he knew Mercy's lobby like the back of his hand; the medical center was practically a second home. The tired yellow paint on the walls, the crackling concrete right above the edge of the baseboard, the fluorescent lights... Part of him dreaded these visits because the hospital was depressing and old, but part of him loved coming here because he figured his mom was taken care of. Linda was at the front desk. She recognized him.

"Hey Zach, good to see you again! You're here to see your mom?"

"Yes, Linda! How are you today?"

"Great! She's in room 409, but you knew that already... Tell her I say hi!"

He walked to the elevator bank in the back of the lobby, trying to avoid a very old lady on her walker with her husband hanging onto her. He wondered who needed the walker more: the wife with her iron grip on the aluminum handles, or her husband who was pretending he didn't need any help but clearly did. Zach pressed the button for level four. The elevator creaked on the way up; he was pretty sure the door shouldn't shake that much, but he didn't care, the only thing on his mind was making sure his mom was okay.

Room 409. He'd been here so many times the number had become a part of him, the way your own phone number lives in your fingers. He pushed the door open. She was smaller than he remembered, and he'd only seen her a few days ago. The bed seemed to be getting larger each visit, or she seemed to be getting smaller, he could never tell which. He sat down next to her and took her hand, careful around the IV.

"Hi mom! How are you feeling?"

As soon as she saw him, her face lit up.

"Hi Zach, how was your day? You look excited, tell me about your day at school!"

"Today's been amazing! But first I want to learn about your new treatment, how is it? Are the nurses nice to you, do you like them?"

"They're all right, I'll tell you what's going on but tell me about you first, I can tell something is going on... What's the news?"

He told his mom about the Coding Academy scholarship and how excited he was. As he described the program to her, how the curriculum worked and what the academy meant to him, he could see something in her face: pride, and something else, something strained. As he stared at her more he started noticing how pale she actually was, and how far her eyes had receded into her face. Realizing how self-centered he had been he stopped and asked her:

"Are you okay mom? You look tired; do you want to take a nap? I don't need to talk; I can simply stay here next to you."

"No, I can't sleep. We should probably talk about what's happening to me, things have changed here, and I need to tell you what's going on."

"What do you mean?"

His mom leaned over to the nightstand and took a long sip of water from the cup sitting there. She was so weak she almost spilled the cup over, but he caught it in time.

"Mom! You're ok? Tell me what's going on," he said, with increasing worry in his voice.

"Well, this whole thing started back six months ago... I went to see Dr. Cunningham because my back was causing me grief again; I figured he would give me some pain killers, maybe run a test or two. You know how he always takes care of me, right?"

He nodded. Dr. Cunningham was a ray of hope in mom's otherwise harsh daily routine. He had always been there for her. His mom did everything she could, so Zach would have what he needed for school. Life wasn't easy, especially when she took that second job, back when he was thirteen. But she always made sure he had what he needed for school. And yes, it meant a twelve-, thirteen-, fourteen-hour workday doing back-breaking work as a warehouse clerk, juggling multiple jobs, but she never complained about it.

Once he visited her at the warehouse when he was fourteen. It was bring-your-child-to-work day, and she wanted to show him what the world was like after school. They walked through a gigantic warehouse filled with all sorts of things, from pillows to books to vitamin bottles. Workers were hurrying everywhere, with a device in hand. He asked mom what the device was for.

"This device does two things, Zach. First it tells you what you need to grab together in a box, then it also tells you how much time you have to complete the job."

"What do you mean mom? How can the device know how much time? Why does it tell you?"

"Well, it's something called productivity, and it's not really the device, it's my boss telling me to work faster through the device"

"Ah, okay mom".

He didn't truly understand what his mother had told him, but she said it in a way that seemed to make sense to her, and there was so much going on around them, he was already distracted by something else. As they were talking he could feel in his chest the low frequency whir of robots going by around them, like ballet dancers at the opera, or so he imagined. These robots seemed low, perhaps a foot high, and went from one shelf to another. At any point in time there would be a dozen robots lifting a shelf and taking its cargo to another part of the giant warehouse across which they happened to be walking. The level of activity was astounding and fascinating at the same time.

At break time Zach's mom had taken him to the break room to grab a snack and go to the bathroom. He was so excited! He had skipped breakfast that morning since they needed to get up unusually early, and he was definitely ready for some Chex Mix and a Mountain Dew. This was basically his school routine, and he was happy to re-enact it in this unfamiliar environment. As he approached the snack machine, he noticed something was different. Instead of bags and bars the items were all boxed, smaller, different. As he walked up to the machine he realized the machine was stocked in an utterly different way: Advil, Tylenol, Aleve...

"Mom, these are all medicines! Where are the snacks?"

"Well, son these are the snacks we use here. People would rather have painkillers than a snack."

"Why?"

"Well, after you work here, you'll realize work can be painful. Genuinely painful. So, people want and need painkillers to do their jobs. And they need their job, so they can pay the rent, and put food on the table."

His mom had smiled at him, so matter-of-fact about it that he'd filed it away and moved on to the Mountain Dew. He was fourteen. He hadn't wanted to understand. Today, a few years later, sitting in room 409, he understood everything.

"What did Dr. Cunningham say? Did he give you medication for your back?"

"Yes he did, he always does. But this time he didn't really give it away. He couldn't, not those pills, I needed to pay for it somehow."

"Mom, you are talking in riddles, what do you mean?"

"I have cancer, son. Hodgkin's lymphoma. Something called LFS. I didn't understand that part, the doctor tried to explain it."

She paused, smoothed the blanket with her free hand.

"Dr. Cunningham gave me medication for it. The good kind. But it was expensive, the kind they track every pill of at the pharmacy. So I paid what I could. Then I told them I'd pay the rest. Then I couldn't."

She looked at the window.

"They garnished my salary."

He was stunned. At least this explained why his mom stopped buying soda and switched to water a few months ago.

"What about insurance mom? They can't take this away from you, they have to cover you!"

"First they said the treatment wasn't proven. Then they said it was a pre-existing condition. Then they said I'd hit my lifetime maximum."

She said it quietly, like reading from a list she'd memorized a long time ago.

"Remember when I switched jobs? I dropped the insurance for a few months. I couldn't keep up with the payments. That was enough for them."

A long pause.

"I got tired of fighting, son."

His eyes filled. So did hers.

"So what are we going to do, mom?"

"We're going to go home, son. Dr. Cunningham gave me something for the pain. I just want to be in my own bed now. It doesn't make sense to be here anymore."

She squeezed his hand once.

"I want to be comfortable."

He didn't ask what came next. The answer was in the room with them already, had been for a while. He held her hand and didn't say anything, because there was nothing left to say that wasn't already understood between them. They were poor. That was the whole story. That had always been the whole story.

3

Zach's mother died at home, alone, on a Tuesday. He was at the Coding Academy when it happened. She had seemed fine that morning. She always seemed fine, right up until she wasn't. She was the kind of woman who would encourage you out the door even when she could barely stand.

"This is your future, son. You better go to your classes. Don't you worry about me, I'm fine. I've been fine my whole life!"

"OK mom, I'll be back this afternoon. There's soup in the fridge, call me if you need me. I love you!"

As he came back to the house, he noticed an ambulance and a police cruiser parked in front of their building. He understood right away the ambulance came for them, but he was hoping it wasn't the case. He climbed the stairs two at a time. Their apartment door was wide open, a deputy standing in the frame. He pushed past him. He never made it to the bedroom. The gurney was in the living room, navigating the tight space between the sofa and the TV stand. His sofa, the one he slept on, and on it a white sheet, strapped down over something that was no longer moving. He stopped. The room he had lived in his whole life looked completely different with a body in it. The officer turned to him:

"Are you her son? Your mom called 911, said she wasn't feeling well. Sorry we couldn't make it in time."

He was speechless, staring at the white sheet. He wanted to lift what was now a shroud, but was too stunned to act on his impulse.

"Son, we're taking her to Mercy Medical Center. Do you have family to stay with? How old are you?"

"Um, I'm nineteen, sir..."

He lied, without even blinking. Shocked as he was, he was keenly aware that if he told the officer he was in fact seventeen the policeman would have to place him with a foster family. There was no way, no way, he was going to let that happen. His mother wouldn't want that for him either.

"I'll sleep here tonight, I'll be fine, don't worry. And no, we don't have family, it was just her and me."

"Okay, well here is my contact info, you call this number if you need anything. We're taking your mom to the hospital morgue for now, you'll have to contact them tomorrow to make plans for her funeral."

The officer looked at him with a somber smile. He felt sorry for him. Zach couldn't tell if he saw through his lie, but he was acting as if he didn't.

"Thank you, sir"

"Bye now. Guys, let's go!"

And just like that, it was over. A million thoughts rushed through his mind.

What am I going to do? How am I going to pay the rent? Food? I need to find a job and a place to stay, what are my options? How come mom died like that? I knew she was in bad shape, but she looked fine this morning, how did I miss this? If we had the money, mom would still be alive. Working all these years at the warehouse wore her down. Hitting the vending machine for painkillers instead of getting proper care wore her down. Not being able to afford a proper treatment wore her down. The whole system did her in. Does this mean I am now all alone? Will the police come back when they realize I lied about my age?

He grabbed a bowl of cereal, poured some milk he found in the fridge and plopped himself down on the old sofa. He turned on YouTube on his laptop. As the video stream started, he realized three things: this laptop was now his only and most prized possession, he needed to complete his coding training more than ever, and he was going to need money to survive.

The following morning he went to the Coding Academy as he always did. The building was a few blocks from the house, in an old warehouse which had been converted into a tech incubator, all exposed bricks and industrial steel. As he walked into the main room he saw Ashley, looking stunning as always.

"Hey Ashley..."

"Hi Zach!"

"Um..."

His voice trailed, he wasn't sure what to say. On a normal day his crush on Ashley would have prevented him from saying much more, but today was different. He had nothing to lose. He was sad but also angry at the system that failed his mother. And more than anything he had a deep-seated fear of not having food or a place to stay for much longer. His survival instincts were kicking in.

Ashley was one of the few girls in the program. Unlike him she came from a normal family with money, or so he thought. She always talked to him with poise, with kindness in her eyes. She made him feel like she cared about him. She seemed kind. He figured it wouldn't hurt to ask.

"My mom died yesterday."

"What??"

"My mom died yesterday during classes. She called 911, but they didn't make it in time. When I came home, they were getting ready to take her away."

"Oh my gosh! Are you okay? I can't believe it!"

"Am okay, I just won't be able to stay at the house much longer. I'm pretty sure the landlord will kick me out..."

He was too embarrassed to tell her it was because he had no money to pay the rent, and no one to turn to, no relative, no one who would take him in or pay his rent.

"No way! What are you going to do?"

"Well... I was wondering..."

Overcome by burning shame, he sensed her eyes on him like a thousand needles. He couldn't look her straight in the face. He remembered she had a place of her own as she had mentioned it to him.

"Well I was wondering if there was any way I could stay at your place for a few days... just so I can find a new place..."

There he had said it; he finally mustered the courage to give her a short glance. Her mouth was slightly open, her expression now changed and motionless.

"Oh, Zach, I don't know... Um... It's that, you know... I'm not sure I can do that."

His heart sank. Before he was able to say anything, Brad showed up. Brad was everything he hated yet wanted to be. Like Ashley, he was poised, came from a family with money too, as was obvious from his clothes and expensive laptop. He walked with the confidence of someone who's never been worried about shelter, food, or love. He walked like he downright *owned* this place. But Zach could code faster than him.

"Hey Ash, you okay? You look worried," he said, walking up to Ashley without so much as a glance toward Zach.

"Hey Brad! It's nothing. Did you finish the assignment they gave us yesterday? Can I compare notes with you?" she asked, as if her discussion with Zach had never taken place.

Zach thought she might like him enough to help him when he genuinely needed it. As he watched the two of them walk away, apparently engrossed in their discussion and ignoring him altogether, he realized he never stood a chance with her. He came from nothing, had nothing but his wits. Brad came from something, and had everything. There was no way she was going to do anything with him or for him, Zach thought, at least not until he made something of himself.

4

A few months later Brad called Zach after their graduation from the Coding Academy. Zach was working on his social-media-powered game when he wasn't at the call center working his shift. He figured, since so many silly games seem to be selling, why couldn't he come up with his own game, and make money that way? This would beat answering customer service calls with other inner city kids, and asking for permission every time he wanted to go to the bathroom... He was home debugging his application and couldn't believe how insecure the social media authentication API was when Brad texted him.

"Yt? I had an idea I wanna talk to u about..."

"Sure"

"Can I call? Be easier to discuss live"

"OK"

Zach's phone rang and Brad's name flashed across the screen.

"Hey man, what's up"

"Hey Zach, long time no see! Um, I've been thinking... you know, ever since we graduated from the Academy, I've really focused on getting my infosec startup off the ground"

Zach smiled. Yes, information security was always a hot area, but there was no way Brad would ever be able to do anything about it. He simply wasn't skilled enough to handle it. He had never been. Zach always thought he attended the Academy so he could go after Ashley. He truly didn't have the demeanor or the intensity of a good coder. Zach always thought Brad was a fake. He was enjoying the conversation though. Now he was calling him for help. How interesting.

"Anyway, I'd love to get you involved somehow. We just raised some friends and family money and need to put together our first demo. I know what I want to do, but you know how it is, I need some help actually doing it."

I bet you do, thought Zach.

"Okay, what are we talking about?"

"Well, let's meet in person, it'll be easier that way. Can I meet you in an hour at the Starbucks by the Academy?"

"Um, sure, why not?"

By the time Zach arrived at Starbucks Brad was already there, sitting at a table in the back. He seemed so happy to see Zach. Brad hadn't changed. Still the same, a rich kid from the suburbs, poised and blissfully unaware of his shortcomings.

"Hey man, so good to see you!"

"Hey Brad..."

Brad jumped right into the meat of the topic.

"You wouldn't believe how busy I've been since we were together"

The irony of "being together" wasn't lost on Zach. Back at the Academy there had never been "togetherness". There had only been a gigantic gap between the rich kids who hung together, like Brad and Ashley, who had it easy and were never that motivated in the first place, and the few poor kids like Zach for whom the Academy was a lifeline, an opportunity to run away from a world filled with chaos and desperate needs. Zach was pretty sure Brad had never had to worry about his mother's medication or paying the rent.

"Anyway, information security is all the hotness right now, and we have a great concept and the money, and all we need is to flesh it out"

"Well, call me a skeptic, but everybody thinks they have a great concept, Brad."

"No, really Zach, let me explain. People have been monitoring web traffic for decades. Back in the early days of deep learning people were training AI algorithms to watch for certain patterns in the http requests between, say, your cable router and the local gateway, and classify these requests as legitimate or not. If the pattern between all the available variables looked normal, traffic would be allowed to go through. If something looked weird, like a mismatch between the router's settings and the traffic request, then traffic would be presumed an illegitimate request from a spammer, hacker etc, and be blocked and set aside for review by a human."

"I know. Tell me something I don't already know..."

He couldn't believe Brad would even be into that kind of topic. He started paying attention.

"But there were always a number of problems with that approach... First, training these AI algorithms is hard and labor-intensive. Just when you think you're done, patterns change on you and you need to retrain your AI. Then as both traffic volumes and the complexity of routers continued to increase, the sheer number of patterns to be matched exploded exponentially. People tried to recycle algorithms and neural network components using transfer learning, but it actually hasn't been that effective. It's become so complex, operators are starting to lose out again to the bad guys."

"Okay, and you think you can solve it because..."

He couldn't help but have a tinge of sarcasm in his voice. Brad was better at this than he expected but this was an impractically hard problem, and there was no way he or his buddies were solving it.

"Well, see I told you we raised money from friends and family, right? It's actually more than friends and family... Ashley's dad works at NIST, and we also have a grant from them, which means we have access to some of their quantum computing resources as well."

NIST was the National Institute of Standards and Technology, a state-of-the-art computing research institution funded by the federal government. The problem he was trying to solve was mind-bogglingly hard with conventional computing power, but if he had access to NIST's 256-qubit quantum server this would become a whole different ball-game! You could use it to solve the traffic classification problem by applying sheer brute force.

While quantum computing had been in commercial use since the mid 2020s, it was not yet mainstream. Quantum computing had effectively made traditional encryption obsolete, which had threatened to put at risk all online transactions. Any skilled hacker with enough quantum resources could steal a credit card number on every transaction. As a result the US government and NIST, in coordination with their Chinese counterparts, had taken control of the technology and regulated its use. Getting access to quantum computing resources was hard, you had to be credentialed. Definitely a hard game for kids like Zach. But with Brad's connections, that was a whole different story! He was definitely getting excited.

"No way! That's a game changer, man..."

"Yes it is."

Brad grinned, beaming with pride.

"So..."

"So, we need to hire good people, and of course I thought of you," Brad replied.

His eyes locked into Brad's. Brad's idea was incredibly exciting but there was no way Zach was going to work for this douchebag. He simply didn't trust him. Brad was going to use him, claim all the credit and then push him aside. But Zach sorely needed the money and the idea of working on a quantum server was incredibly appealing to him. It had a lot more potential than his silly social media game app. He started wondering.

"Well Brad, I've been working on a project of my own, a social media game I truly believe in. Your project is still super early stage, which means a lot of uncertainty for all involved... Would you be open to partnering so I'm a consultant or something? This way I can keep working on my project but I could also support you part-time for now. What do you think?"

Brad actually seemed excited.

"Hey man, I think the world of you, I just want to work together! Yes, of course this will work. Just don't kill me on the fees. We can draft an SOW, this will be work-for-hire, but yes we can make it work."

Brad looked at him tentatively. Zach could tell this would be a win for him. The SOW, or scope-of-work document, would outline the terms of their collaboration. It would be on a work-for-hire basis, which meant Brad would own *all* of the work Zach would perform and the latter would retain no rights. This would make it easier for Brad to discard Zach later, yet develop a quick product demo now he could show investors. Zach liked that he would work on his own and not tie himself to this project too closely.

Brad's concept was actually a smart idea. So smart in fact that Zach was starting to wonder whether he would be able to use this project to work on his own quantum demo. Brad would never have to know. The technical details were way beyond him anyway. Yet he would pay Zach to do it. He smiled at the chance to turn the tables on Brad.

"Okay, then I think we have a deal. Let me think about the fees, I'll email you something by tomorrow and once we agree we can get started whenever you want me to," said Zach, trying to act nonchalant.

They parted ways quickly and Zach started to walk back home. Part of him knew this wasn't right. His mom would never approve of his idea.

Zach, say what you do and do what you say; always be a man of your word, he could still hear her saying.

Yes, but she had never dealt with people like Brad and Ashley. She had tried to live a life of integrity, but what did it do to her? Always short of money for rent, for medications, struggling with a back-breaking job at the warehouse. And for what? So the Brads of the world would get rich on her back and do nothing? No way Zach was going to let that happen. This was his chance, and he was determined to take it.

5

"You can't do that, Zach," said the voice on the phone. Zach was in a large office, all brick walls, sliding steel and glass door and modern art on the walls. He was in a discussion with one of his board members and clearly the board member wasn't happy.

Zach paused, looked outside for a few seconds, his mind drifting. How amazing the journey of the last few years! The pivotal moment had been this consulting project with Brad. Brad never had a chance, he was like a puppy in the woods, thought Zach. The project had started out all right, with Zach building a simple quantum encryption demo with the NIST account Brad had provided. While building what was asked of him, Zach had in fact spent a majority of his time developing and prototyping the concept Brad should have asked but never did. Brad's concept had failed when Zach bailed on him to focus on his own quantum-grade network security startup. And two years later, as the developer and owner of one of the few working quantum-grade encryption algorithms out there, Zach had embedded his technology as payment infrastructure in many of the largest e-commerce platforms as customers and investors had flocked to him. The momentum had turned, sales were brisk, and he knew it. After all these years of struggling, of scraping by, he could see the change happening. Zach had raised ten million dollars after his first year, helped and guided by his mentors at the Coding Academy. Now that his sales were picking up he was on the verge of raising a massive Series A round.

"You can't sell rights to the Q-box name back to the company, we *are* Q-box," said Otto, the board member.

"Of course I can," said Zach, surprised by his own poise. "The company is named 'Quantum Technologies'. My personal LLC is called `Q-box` and owns the brand. Now that QT wants to use the brand it's actually valuable, I just want to be paid fair market value for it. I'd be foolish not to."

Otto was flabbergasted. Zach's apparent sense of entitlement left him speechless.

"Where do I begin Zach? You founded this company. We backed you. And now, you want to get more for something you should contribute as your own investment? Really?" said Otto, exasperated.

"Well, we can always put it up for consideration by the board and see how the vote goes," Zach replied.

Otto paused and took a deep breath. *He's learning the game*, he thought. *Maybe even getting greedy*. But Zach's technology was unique and had the potential to make them so much money, it would pay for all those crappy investments of the past year and still make them look good with the fund's limited partners when the time would come to exit.

Otto was also keenly aware that Zach had managed to keep super-voting shares, which meant he controlled a majority of the company anyway. The vote would be a perfunctory exercise and the motion would be approved.

"Fine. Have the attorneys draft the document, and we'll sign it," said Otto finally, gritting his teeth.

"Thank *you* Otto, always a pleasure to talk to you!"

"No problem Zach... see you later."

Zach was enjoying this moment. For the first time in his life he was starting to feel like he was rising in status, he had a bit of leverage over his world. He had talked to so many venture capital firms in the early days when he had started his company. Straight refusals from the first fifty or so firms. He was so new at the game, and his software demo wasn't that impressive either. No one would talk to this kid from the hood who clearly didn't understand the social rules of the game. Then he had started crafting his pitch. A giant security breach at Bank of America had helped too, spurring financial services firms to pursue credible encryption alternatives outside their walls. Zach had been ready for that moment with his quantum encryption algorithm. Then he got a first venture capital firm to return his calls, then a second and a third. The bidding started and gave him the opportunity to set conditions on his terms: ten million dollars and super-voting shares that kept him in control. If only his mom could see this he thought, she would be proud. She would be alive too, because he could have afforded her treatment. The thought made him both thrilled and sad at the same time.

Dave, Zach's office manager, walked into the office.

"Hey Zach, I have someone named Ashley in the reception area. She doesn't have an appointment, but she says she knows you from your days at the Coding Academy?" said Dave with a quizzical expression.

Zach smiled.

"Oh. Ashley. Yes, I remember her, it's been so long! Do we have any customers or partners calling us in the next thirty minutes? No? Sure, I'll see her!"

Zach was trying not to show his excitement but his heart had skipped a beat when Dave had first brought up Ashley. Of course, he still remembered her, how would he not? A minute later Ashley appeared in the office, hesitant and smiling.

"Hey Zach! Remember me?"

"Of course, Ash, it's so good to see you! How did you find me? How have you been?"

"Well, you know after we finished the program at the Academy I finished my gap year and went to college. I'm a senior now, can you believe it?"

Zach realized how quickly time had gone. What a difference three years had made! Ashley finished her gap year and went to college, supported by her parents and without the slightest worry about how to pay for it all. Zach had supported himself by working customer service calls at the call center, and trying to get his startup off the ground.

"No way, has it been three years already? Where did it all go?"

"I know... well I was in the area and saw you guys have an office here, so I figured I would drop by and say hi. I miss our days together at the Academy you know," said Ashley, with a smile and looking straight into Zach's eyes.

Zach was trying to figure her out. Ashley's pretext felt contrived, and after seeming hesitant she was now clearly hitting on him. It was slightly disorienting given their dynamic back three years prior. Did she genuinely like him? Zach remembered their last interaction, when he had tried to engage with her, and she had refused to help him. Why would she come by now?

"Really..." said Zach, pensive. He gave her a probing stare, Ashley got to the point without batting an eye.

"Well, there's also the fact that I'm available for an internship this summer. I'm talking to other startups but yours is the best and I know I can truly contribute to make it a success."

Zach's old feelings of disappointment surfaced again, bringing back painful memories, but he was no longer the same person and disappointment quickly turned to cold anger. He was not going to let her see it, though. He would be his controlled self.

"Okay, let me think about it. Do you have a resume? We have a lot of people applying right now, we'll take a look at you with the team."

"Awesome, thank you so much Zach!" said Ashley as she was getting closer and trying to hug him. Zach stepped back coldly.

"No worries. Sorry, I have to get on a call now, Dave will take you back. It was great to see you."

Zach motioned to Dave to take Ashley back, which he did promptly. She had clearly not expected him to ignore her hug and left the room as she had come, hesitant and smiling.

When Dave came back, he found Zach lost in thought. *That was Ashley, wealthy whitey Ashley groveling for my support while she blatantly refused to help when I actually needed it, back when I was a nobody who had just lost his mother. The irony...*

"If she comes back please don't let her in again. No calls either, Dave," said Zach as he crushed the resume in his fist and fiddled with it.

"Okay boss, got it," replied Dave.

He stood there a moment after Dave left, the balled-up resume still in his hand, her scent lingering.

6

Things were going well with Zach's startup. Quantum had gone public with an IPO after only two years of operations. Investors were happy with the company, Zach and his team were growing the business. People were actually interested in them, *and not just Ashley* as Zach liked to remind himself. Customers wanted to work with the quantum encryption technology they had developed, and the truth is it would make their transactions a whole lot safer.

Potential employees, realizing Quantum was turning into the proverbial rocket ship, wanted to come work for them too. Investors had pushed Zach to open an office in San Mateo in Silicon Valley, so they would have access to better talent, and so they did. Zach realized it was simply a matter of time until he'd move there, but he was still dragging his feet. He had lived in Baltimore his whole life, and part of him wanted to leave and never come back, but part of him felt that leaving would be turning his back on his mother, and he would never do that. As Quantum grew, he had become something of a local success story, a big fish in a small pond, and he found he was enjoying it.

Yet he understood it was only a matter of time if he wanted to remain at the helm and grow the business to its full potential. As a compromise Zach had agreed to move to Tyson's Corner in Northern Virginia, a technology cluster on the outskirts of Washington, DC. Tyson was only about an hour away from Baltimore. He had ambition, he wanted to prove to the world how wrong they had been about him, so he would definitely move to be closer to his investors and technology talent.

He was also enjoying having decent healthcare for the first time in his life. He had never had time to go to the doctor and had always pushed it off, but at the same time he had always been puzzled by his mother's death. What did she die of, and was he at risk of dying the same way? She had mentioned the doctor said Hodgkin's Lymphoma and it was related to LFS. Zach had googled LFS, only to find out it meant Li-Fraumeni Syndrome, but that didn't make much sense. He finally grabbed the bull by the horns, got over his procrastination and made an appointment to go see Dr. Cunningham. He called his office and made a wellness appointment for a few weeks later. He had driven up from Tyson's Corner specifically for this, not to some new doctor in Virginia, but back to Mercy, back to Cunningham. If anyone was going to tell him hard news, he wanted it to be him.

As Zach walked into Mercy Medical Center, a flood of memories came back. The lobby, completely renovated after a corporate take-over, now looked like a five-star hotel with a large fireplace and piano in the back. As he crossed the lobby, he caught a fragment of conversation between two administrators near the piano, something about a pilot program, music therapy, evidence-based outcomes. He almost laughed. They hadn't been able to keep his mother alive, but they'd found money for a Steinway. How could they have let his mother die, yet pay for a piano, he thought to himself? He got on the elevator, up to the fourth floor. The waiting area for Dr. Cunningham hadn't changed one bit since the last time he had been there. Coming back to the hospital felt like putting back on some old clothes which belonged to a different version of himself, a smaller, more fearful version of himself. His throat was tightening, a lump forming and making his breathing harder. Anxiety was welling up. He checked in, sat down and waited for his name to be called. A few minutes later he saw Dr. Cunningham come out in the hallway.

"Zach, so glad to see you! It's been too long!"

"I know! Things have been super busy but I thought I'd come by and say hi."

Zach was glad to see him, yet apprehensive at the same time, though he couldn't tell why. Hospitals had a way of making him uncomfortable, he guessed.

"Well, go down the hall and into the third room on the right, I'll be right with you. A nurse is going to see you first."

It had been unusual for him to come out and bring Zach in, a nurse would normally have done that. But the doctor seemed genuinely happy, and that made Zach happy too. He seemed to be one of the few people Zach knew who cared about him and his patients. Zach went into the patient's room. A nurse came in a few minutes later and took his medical history. A few minutes later Dr. Cunningham was back. He sat down and looked at Zach.

"Forgive me for saying this, but you look like a man now! The last time I saw you, you were still a teenager," he said, with a welcoming smile on his face. Zach wasn't sure what to say.

"What can I do for you?" he added.

"Well, everything is fine now, I have a job and I actually have health insurance, so I figured I'd come and see you"

"Great, how do you feel? Are you healthy or have you had any symptoms you want to discuss?"

"I'm fine, it's simply that... We never got to discuss mom's case much and I wanted to understand her illness better. What is LFS? Would it affect me too? Should I be worried? I feel fine though."

"Ah, LFS, yes..." said Dr. Cunningham, pensively. Zach tried not to stare at him.

"Well, I remember your mom's case. We did a lot for her even though she didn't have much of an insurance policy and our administrator thought she was a lost case. Your mom had a type of cancer called Hodgkin's Lymphoma. That, in and of itself, is highly manageable. Hodgkin's Lymphoma affects your lymph nodes and your blood cells, the condition is treatable with decent odds. In your mom's case she was getting older and, because of her job and her lack of insurance, she didn't follow the proper treatment protocol. She never thought she would be able to afford the full treatment. We did what we could, and the truth is we could have helped her if she had agreed to it, but she never wanted to take on more than what she could pay for. That was silly because we would have written the bill off..."

His voice trailed off as he remembered the case. He went on:

"Well what we have to worry about is you, sir. The thing that was unusual about her case was that she tested positive for something called Li-Fraumeni Syndrome. What is it? LFS is a mutation of the TP53 gene, and more importantly LFS is generally inherited, which means you likely have this mutation too."

Zach's eyes were getting wider.

"What does that mean, doctor?"

"It means you're at risk of developing some form of cancer too. It might be Hodgkin's Lymphoma, it might be something else. TP53 is involved in suppressing the growth of tumors, and with the mutated version your body won't be able to turn off tumors as they start happening. And you will probably start having some of these tumors in the next few years."

Zach was speechless.

"The good news is, you seem healthy today, and we can start monitoring you right away. At least we'll be one step ahead," he added.

"Well, does that mean we can cure whatever I end up developing?" Zach asked, hesitantly.

"It depends," said Dr. Cunningham. "It depends on the type of condition you develop, its pathology, etc. We know you're at high risk of developing some form of cancer. We'll still be bound by the same limitations we have today on all forms of treatment."

Zach's mind was racing. He still had so much to do! Growing the company was going to take a few years, and he wanted so badly to show the world what he was capable of, he wanted so badly to build the kind of life he had always wanted. He was so close! His quantum encryption technology was going to change the world, and now there was a decent chance he wouldn't be around to reap the benefits of that and enjoy his moment in the sun? No way!

"This can't be doctor, we have to find a way around it," Zach said in disbelief.

"Zach, as long as you have this TP53 mutation your body is going to respond in a certain way which puts you at risk. Having this mutation is kind of like walking down the middle of a highway during rush hour. You might avoid a few cars and trucks for a while but eventually you will get hit, and it will probably kill you."

Zach mentally pictured his body being shattered to smithereens and shuddered. His mind kicked into hyper focus as it always did when he had to solve a truly hard problem.

"What if I get rid of this TP53 mutation, then what?"

"Well, if it were possible, then yes your body would regain its ability to control cell proliferation and suppress tumor growth, so the chances of you ever developing cancer would drop dramatically."

"Okay, that's a start, so how do I do that?"

"I said if it were possible, because in practice getting rid of this mutation is impossible, Zach. There is no therapy today, and developing such a therapy would take first a lot of money and second it would take years before you could get it approved for human trials."

"What about CRISPR? I've heard people can change their genes using CRISPR."

"Ah, yes CRISPR. Looks like you've been doing some reading on your own. CRISPR is a gene editing technology which was developed decades ago, we use it commonly now to insert various genes in the lab. Gene editing is dangerous to use in human because we can't anticipate the ramifications of a gene edit on the human body. We're getting very close though."

"What do you mean by very close?"

"Well, we've mapped the full human genome. The whole thing. And we do have gene editing techniques such as CRISPR. And we now understand the linkage between these genes. This last part was the hardest step of all, and the genetic research community just recently finished establishing these linkages. The problem is, gene editing is like having a giant bowl of spaghetti in front of you and knowing how every strand of spaghetti in the bowl is configured and understanding how one would push on another. Imagine wanting to pull a strand and figuring out how this strand is going to affect every other strand. Even though you know how to do it in theory, in practice pulling the strand is really hard because there are so many things that can happen and our computer models can't track all of these interactions. This leads to a problem called combinatorial explosion, because there are way too many combinations that need to be figured out."

Zach's heart started racing.

"So this is a big optimization exercise, then? Like a giant computational modeling problem where we need to map out the full repercussions of a single edit across the genome, and its expected impact on gene expression?" he asked.

Cunningham was baffled by how far Zach had come, but did not bring it up. Years of software engineering practice had taught Zach much about problem solving.

"Yes, but it's impossible with today's resources, Zach. First of all you can't do that with conventional computers, you need quantum computers to be able to handle this level of computational complexity, and those are highly regulated. Second of all, this takes a lot of money, as in a lot of time and money. We did a feasibility study on this and estimated we'd need a whole year and about ninety million dollar just to get to the answer. Then we still had to test it at my lab back at Innova General, first on animals then on humans. It was deemed too risky, we never got the grant approved."

Screw animal testing first, my alternative is dying and I need an answer fast. I'll be a guinea pig, thought Zach.

"You know I have access to quantum computing resources, right? The startup I founded is all about quantum encryption. Our machines aren't as fast or powerful as those of NIST, but it's a start. And if you tell me what you need, I can go find those resources."

Cunningham perked up. His interest was clearly piqued.

"What about money Zach, it's not just computing power, this actually takes money. Money to pay for the quantum computing resources primarily, as well as for the staff that will do this. This is a major project you know?"

He was right. Quantum computing had quickly been deemed a national security resource because of its ability to break traditional encryption. Access was highly regulated and prices were still incredibly high as a result, much like mainframe systems in the 1960s. But Zach thought he would figure it out. He did have access to quantum computers through his startup and, as far as money, well, he had access to that too as he talked to investors all the time. Zach just needed to find an angle. He smiled.

"I think I can help you doctor. I can help you help me," he said with a beaming smile.

"Really? Zach, I always thought you were a resourceful kid, please surprise me," said Dr. Cunningham, obviously skeptical.

All Zach had to do was show him. He knew exactly what to do.

7

One hundred million. Zach was going to need close to one hundred million cash. So he would fund Cunningham's research effort, and have a shot at making it to thirty. Quantum Technologies' market capitalization had quickly shot to over two billions, making them a unicorn, one of those technology startups with a valuation of over a billion dollars. So... what was the problem? Zach's stock holdings were worth two hundred million still, he could simply sell half and be done. Yes, he was going to have to finesse that with the board and investors, but he simply did not care. He was by now twenty-five, and really intended to make it to thirty and beat the odds. It was literally a matter of life or death for him.

As he walked back into his office he received a text from Masha, his head of marketing:

"We need to talk. Wanna take you through our latest numbers," her text said, rather tersely.

"OK, give me a minute and I'll drop by," he responded.

People buying QT's products was in fact the outcome of a long sales process that would typically take three to six months. As with many enterprise products the average buyer would first become aware of the product through chance or happenstance, maybe a colleague bragging about it or casually name-dropping. That buyer might then take a few more weeks to learn about it and feel like it was a service worth considering, and decide to meet with the company building the product. The process would then take another few months to play out as people from the purchasing, engineering and other departments would get involved. That original act of curiosity would turn into consideration, consideration into intent. This intent to buy would eventually materialize as a sale and show up on QT's books as additional revenue.

Masha's job was to shepherd this process. The DoD called it PsyOps. Mid-century regimes had called it propaganda. Silicon Valley called it growth marketing. Different words for the same thing: shaping what people believe before they know they're being shaped. Masha was very good at it.

The truth was, marketing worked. Sales funnel indicators for a company's products, like pipeline size or velocity, could be relied on to understand whether the market was embracing a product or turning away from it. Therein laid Masha's dilemma. As Zach entered her office, she gave him a worried stare.

"Hey Zach, glad you're back! We need to talk."

"Okay, what's up?" he responded, a quizzical look in his eyes.

"I need to show you these numbers," added Masha. He could see on her laptop a large chart in the shape of a funnel. It reminded him of these demographic charts showing an age pyramid.

"Here is our pipeline. It's a view of all the conversations and meetings we're having with customers and prospects. Near the bottom you can see the volume of deals that just closed"

Zach nodded. He knew his numbers, or so he thought. QT's valuation was about two billion with about a hundred million in annual recurring revenue growing at about a hundred percent. To maintain its valuation the company needed to add every month about one to two million in new monthly revenue. This past quarter they had added about one and a half. They were on track.

"I know," Zach said. "For this past month we added $1.8 million in revenue."

"Yes, but look at our leading indicators. See, our sales qualified leads and average opportunity size?" retorted Masha. "They've dropped significantly. And the top of the funnel is not looking good either."

She was right. He frowned and looked at the numbers more closely. Their sales numbers looked worse than Zach had expected. Yes, they had just posted a big quarter with the highest sales numbers ever, but QT's sales prospects were drying up.

"Why is that? What drove this change," he asked, turning anxious.

"I don't know yet. It looks like our leads are starting to take much longer to convert and when they do, they convert at a lower rate. I don't know yet whether it's pricing or it's product," Masha responded, matter-of-factly.

Zach was starting to process the facts.

"What does this mean for our revenue forecast?"

"Well, I still need to crunch the numbers but it's cause for concern. Given our sales cycles are now six to twelve months, it means we won't make our number for this year. We're going to have to revise our guidance to capital markets," said Masha.

"What do you mean?"

"There is no way we will deliver the kind of revenue we told our investors we would. This is a material change, Zach. We need to tell our board, and we probably need to reset expectations with our shareholders."

Zach's mind was racing again. Missing his revenue estimates was going to crater the stock. His ownership stake had been diluted enough already by several rounds of funding prior to QT's initial public offering. It was worth currently two hundred million but it was all based on expectations that the company's revenue would keep growing at an incredible rate. QT's valuation was definitely not based on cash flow as they had been losing money from the start. Zach did some quick math in his head. The company would easily lose thirty to forty percent of its value if the word got out. Perhaps fifty percent or more, if markets were to overreact. The consequences were obvious to him. His stake would be reduced to a hundred million or less. Turning that into cash would be near impossible, and he had promised Cunningham he would fund their TP53 project, and that project was key to figuring out the ticking time bomb in his genes.

"Zach, we really need to disclose this, this is a material change," repeated Masha, staring insistently.

He felt as if she could read through him. She understood as well as he did the consequences for everybody's stock-options. A lot of employees would be wiped out. She had no sympathy for him, as she expected his stock would still be worth what amounted to a fortune to most people. Zach couldn't care less. What good would it be if he was going to die within a few years? He'd rather spend it now with Cunningham and get a shot at getting cured. It was only money, he could always go make some more.

There was one problem though, Zach needed to sell now, before the word got out and before the stock would tank. The Securities and Exchange Commission would likely consider it insider trading if they found out. They would try to charge him; he might be put in jail for five years. That would be a death sentence given the circumstances. The point was, they would never find out, thought Zach. Masha owed him her job, her stock options. QT's investors owed him. He had overcome odds before, they would simply figure out a way to right the ship in time, as he always did. Zach had come such a long way, he was not about to let a stupid forecast get in the way.

"I disagree, Masha," he said after a while, looking straight back into her eyes. "All you've shown me are highly questionable projections. I totally disagree with your judgement. It ignores our latest product release and assumes we do nothing. Of course, we will deliver on our revenue commitments. There is nothing to disclose."

"How can you..."

Masha looked stunned. She understood exactly what he was doing. And she knew that he knew. Zach turned around and left her office quickly. He grabbed his phone and pulled up the Meridian app. In a few clicks he sold thirty million. He could see from the trading volume on the stock he wasn't going to be able to sell more without affecting QT's stock price. This was a lot less than he had promised Cunningham, but they were going to have to make do with this for now. Also, once the word got out that a founder had sold this much stock, crap would hit the fan with investors and regulators. Calls would come in fast and furious. This wasn't much of a choice in his mind, as the ends ultimately justified the means. Zach was ready. He'd figure it out.

8

The phone rang, echoing through the Georgetown brownstone. Otto put down his glass of Chassagne-Montrachet carefully on the Queen Anne chest by the fireplace, and picked up his cell phone. Zach Hayes's name was flashing across the display. Otto frowned for a second and said:

"Honey, I have to take this call. Keep going. Hopefully it won't last long." He exhaled slowly and answered the phone.

"Hey Zach, great to hear from you! How have you been?" said Otto.

"Not good man, not good. Things have changed a lot since you and I last talked," replied Zach.

His voice was low, not the cocky alpha male Otto was used to. Zach and Otto had met a few years earlier when Zach was a fledgling entrepreneur peddling his quantum security startup to local investors. Back at the time, the information security industry was still reeling from the discovery that quantum computing algorithms could break the encryption of any online commerce transaction. And Zach had come around, this kid from Baltimore who didn't know his way out of a paper bag, who claimed he could encrypt and monitor transactions for fraud and security issues. Any government agency or large corporation could buy time on an expensive quantum server to perform quantum encryption, but monitoring was the hard part. There were simply too many transactions, too many loopholes, too many opportunities for competent hackers backed by enough money and quantum resources. They could still hack away at a sizable chunk of online business. Zach's algorithm, combining deep learning and a massive self-generated graph of online transactions, had harnessed the power of quantum computing and graph neural networks to make transactions reliably secure on a massive scale. Who knew a kid like him would come up with that? And Otto had been the first to truly see Zach's brilliance and his potential to generate extraordinary profits.

Over the last few years, Otto had become a critically important member of the Board at Quantum Technologies, and somewhat of a mentor to Zach. Together they had brought in almost $500 million in funding and Otto had been the true mastermind behind Quantum Technologies' quick initial public offering, allowing him to cash out his highly illiquid initial investment into the company.

Otto looked straight ahead of him through the window, trying to focus and keep his composure.

"What's up Zach? You're making me worried now. What happened?"

"I had to sell stock, a lot of it, I needed to. Just don't ask me why. So, I did. Only problem is, we may have some issues with our sales projections for the rest of the year... if that comes out, and it might soon, it will look bad for you, for me, for everybody on the senior team."

Zach felt relieved he could at least share with someone what had been weighing him down. Deep down he knew the sale was wrong. It was insider selling. Better executives and entrepreneurs had gone to jail for that. But he had no choice, and Otto would help him, as he always did.

Otto paused for a second. He wasn't sure how to respond. Should he focus on the business issue at hand? Should he blast Zach for acting again in an amazingly stupid way? Zach was usually not that open about topics that would make him come across as weak. Pride...

"Zach, I'm sorry you did this. You're right, this is going to create quite a problem. We should get together in person so we can really talk."

Otto's temples were throbbing. He sat up, pushed back Eva, a tall and lanky Danish model who had been inspecting his lap while he had answered the phone, and readjusted his bathrobe.

"Now, this being said, there are probably a few things I can get my team started on to clean this mess," said Otto. He was now back in full business mode, walking around the room with nothing but an expensive piece of silk on his back, yet always the polished communicator.

"What do you have in mind?" responded Zach.

"Let's think this through, Zach. You selling stock like that, first of all, looks like a lack of faith in the company. It's going to spook investors and tank our stock. Then when the bad news about our revenue guidance comes out, I'm assuming that's what you meant with your euphemism regarding sales projections issues, it will really come across as insider trading and the SEC will be forced to investigate. Not only is it bad for you, it's bad for all of us who hold stock in the company." Otto paused, waiting for Zach to react. No reaction. "Unless I can bring the Russians in. Remember, I was working on getting some Russian hedge funds into our stock as institutional investors? I think I can speed that up and make it look like a secondary transaction for our benefit. We'll tell the markets we are expanding our shareholder base and allowing you, our founder, to diversify out of the stock. I also need you to genuinely do something about this sales issue. Then we should be able to work this out."

Otto was mentally mapping the engagement letter he was going to send Zach and the board. He wasn't going to find investors for the company for free. He would make five percent on the funds raised as always. Otto looked at Eva and smiled. This was going to pay for the addition he wanted to build on his cottage in Nantucket.

As soon as Otto had hung up the phone with Zach, he called Igor Dubinsky. He and Igor were going way back to their days at the University of Chicago Booth School of Business. Later on, as young MBAs, they had both worked on technology equity deals in the investment banking group at Deutsche Bank. Otto had gone on to become a venture capitalist while Igor had gone back to Moscow to start a hedge fund.

"Hey Igor, this is Otto, how are you?"

"Otto! So glad to hear from you my friend, what's going on?"

"Igor, you know this company I invested in, Quantum Technologies, right?"

"Yes, of course. You're on their board, you guys just did your IPO, right? Congratulations by the way, I heard it went well."

"Yes, yes, it went very well. Customers love the product, just love it, and with the company's IP in quantum encryption, the sky is the limit" said Otto, using the acronym for intellectual property. "Actually, I thought you might be interested in coming in. There's plenty of juice left to squeeze, and we're looking for a few smart money folks."

Like most of his peers Otto was always trying to be somewhat folksy, especially when pitching an important opportunity. Igor smiled.

"Ah, Otto, you should have called me three months ago! Our second fund is fully committed now, and we are raising a third fund, but we won't be able to make capital calls until about six months from now."

"Bummer. I understand, though. Well, you know me, always impatient. I need to bring in money now, but I can't go through the usual institutional due diligence. It needs to be investors with an appetite for risk. We've done this for a long time, Igor. This is a great opportunity, your investors will be well compensated for the risk."

"I get it Otto, I get it... I'm assuming you've already talked to the usual suspects in New York?"

Otto did not want to go through traditional investment funds in New York, they would ask all sorts of questions he did not want to answer, they would drag things out. No, he needed dumb money, money from a wealthy family office willing to make a bet first and ask questions later.

"No, I need to get this done quickly, and they would have too many governance restrictions... I need someone with the appetite to make a bet on our technology and be along for the ride."

"How much do you need?"

"Well, I need thirty million," Otto paused, waiting for Igor's reaction.

"Mmhh, there are only so many people who would make this kind of bet, Otto... You could go to the Saudis, but they won't move fast, and they are becoming a lot more like your typical institutional investor these days, you'll still have to go through a lot of due diligence. A lot of Russian funds would invest of course but most of them will create more issues than they will solve for you, trust me"

"I understand... I figured you might have an idea, some advice," said Otto tentatively.

"Well, I can think of one group you might want to talk to. It's the largest investor you've never heard of. A Portuguese foundation in Lisbon. They take a lot of Russian money by the way. They've historically invested a lot in Asia, not sure about how they feel about US technology equities. But they're risk takers, and they act fast..."

"It doesn't hurt to talk, do you think you might introduce me?"

Igor hesitated. Otto could tell right away what was going through his mind.

"You know we'll give you fair compensation if a deal gets done, Igor, I would not expect anything less," said Otto.

"Sure, no worries I was just looking at my address book," replied Igor, pretending the finder's fee had never crossed his mind. "Let me set this up, and we might go meet with them together. Can you fly to Lisbon next week?"

"Yes, whatever works for you and them, I'll adjust my schedule around you guys."

A pause on the line. Longer than Otto expected.

"Igor? You still there?"

"Yes. Sorry. One thing, Otto, when you're in Lisbon, pay attention to the young man. Not just the deal. The young man."

Otto frowned.

"Zach? What about him?"

"Keep an eyc on him."

Otto wasn't sure what to make of that. He put it down to Igor being Igor, always slightly oblique, always performing. He'd been like that since Booth.

9

To Zach's surprise, Dr. Cunningham had been thrilled when Zach called to let him know he was wiring money.

"Oh, that's wonderful Zach, I didn't think you'd come through so fast" he had said. "My grant applications usually take much longer!"

"Well, I'm sorry it's only thirty million. It's less than what we had discussed, but you should be able to get going, right?"

"Are you kidding? Of course, this is fantastic! And yes, I'll be able to get a lot done already."

Zach was relieved. He had hardened quite a bit since his mother's death, and had learned to focus on the only things which mattered to him. Namely achieving power and status, and above all never being poor again, even if it meant breaking the law, which was for suckers anyway. But he still had a bit of the pleaser in him, and had known Dr. Cunningham since his teenage years. Zach was happy he made Cunningham happy; he'd have the means to figure out his TP53 mutation, that ticking time bomb was never far away from his thoughts. And yes, Otto had been mad, but as expected he had figured a way to make things work, hadn't he?

Cunningham called back a few days later.

"Zach, I think I have some preliminary results. First of all, I can confirm you do have the TP53 mutation, just like your mother. Not a surprise, we thought this would be the case in the first place. The other thing is, since we were mapping your genome, we scanned your telomeres too and they were shorter than expected. We're now set up on the NIST quantum servers and scanning through the rest of the genome data we fed them. This is going to take a while but at least it's doable. We're looking at every gene combination and how it impacts gene expression and pathways for developing cancerous tumors. Given the speed at which we're scanning all the combinations, I think we'll have candidate markers ready for tests in a few weeks."

"What does this mean Dr Cunningham?" said Zach, his eyes narrowing as he was frowning.

"Markers are specific genes that are associated with developing cancer, or Li-Fraumeni syndrome in your case. The quantum algorithm we repurposed from the code you gave us allowed us to speed up the search dramatically, so we'll get a theoretical answer as to which specific genes might be dangerous for you in a few weeks. This is wonderful news, Zach, you know? Not only for you, but this can affect a lot of other patients, we have to publish these results as soon as we can confirm them, this could save a lot of lives."

"Um, I don't know about that, let me think about it... I'm very grateful, of course doctor, but remember the funds were provided with a clause of confidentiality."

Zach purposely held back the fact that the funds had also been provided subject to him retaining all rights to commercial applications.

"Well yes, I understand Zach, but surely eventually we should let the world know, don't you think?"

"Sure, when the time comes... Tell me more though. What does this mean, what are we doing next?"

"First of all, we need to confirm these results, so we're finishing the quantum optimization job, then we'll rerun it one more time. If it looks good, as I expect it will, we'll start animal testing right away."

"Okay, and how long is that going to take?"

"Typically takes about five years, in this case I realize we don't have much time, I'm hoping we can compress the timeline to two to three years maybe? We're going as fast as we can Zach."

"What about telomeres? You said you mapped my telomeres? What does it mean, what did you find out?"

"Telomeres are the tail end of your genes. They are a lot like a fuse. The longer they are, the longer your life expectancy. Shorter telomeres are associated with aging and shorter life spans."

"So my life expectancy is shrinking?"

"Well we don't know, we're still re-running tests and checking our numbers. The initial pass doesn't look right, your telomeres came back really short, but I don't believe the results, so we are re-running it."

"What do you mean? What was the result?"

"Keep in mind this is highly preliminary Zach..."

"Just tell me doctor, I can handle it," said Zach, growing impatient.

He wasn't a child anymore he thought to himself. He had grown so much in the last few years since his mother died. In some ways it had hardened him. He was a survivor and cared about one thing only: survive and thrive.

"Well, the very first look seems to indicate that, at the rate at which your telomeres are shrinking, you would expect to be dead within two years. But this is faster than anything I've seen, so we're verifying the results."

"Two years? And did you say the animal testing will take two to three years? That doesn't work!"

"Calm down, Zach, let me confirm results first. I gotta run, I promised I'll call you back by the end of the week!"

They hung up. Zach sat down, dizzy. Time was running short. He did not want to die like his mother. He was too young, he still had too much to do!

Cunningham called back a few days later as promised.

"Well, Zach, I can't believe it, but our initial results were correct," said the physician with a somber tone.

Zach's heart was racing.

"Okay we sort of knew that, so what are my options now?"

"We need to get started on animal testing anyway, the therapy will never get anywhere with the FDA otherwise"

"Screw the FDA, that's irrelevant to me. Yes, you'll get the treatment out to the public but I'll be long dead! What do we do now?" replied Zach, shaking with the rush of dread and anger.

Dr. Cunningham paused. He truly wanted to help Zach. He had never forgiven himself for the loss of Zach's mother. The system had failed her, it should have never happened in the first place. He had felt morally indebted to Zach ever since. An idea emerged in his mind. It was a gray area, but the project was privately funded after all. And, as Zach had reminded him, the research was still confidential. They could put the project on a dual track he thought. Keep animal testing going and follow the long FDA process, that's what the public would see. But also have a fast track, focused on Zach and kept confidential. He would do right by Zach, and advance medical research at the same time.

"There is no way we can do human testing now Zach, this is simply far too dangerous. However, we should be able to start testing right away on human organs. That would allow us to fast track the project and develop a therapy for you much faster," said Dr. Cunningham at last.

"How long would that take?"

"Once I have the organs, we would have test results within a few months. We still would not know about long-term viability, but we could figure out what's working and what's not."

"Great, let's get started!"

"There's one catch Zach, we need human organs, those are hard to find. And we really need to keep this confidential. I'll run animal testing in parallel," said Dr. Cunningham with a heavy heart.

Zach's mind was racing again.

"What type of organs do you need?"

"Well, Li-Fraumeni Syndrome affects a wide range of organs including the brain, your bones, lung, thyroid and kidneys among other things. We need an organ that would be affected so any one of these would work. Getting an organ from a live donor is a non-starter, you would have to deal with UNOS, the national organ bank that manages organ donation in the US. The first thing they will ask you is... "

"Leave it up to me, doctor," interrupted Zach.

"No, seriously Zach, this is no joke. I don't believe we need a live organ, we could generate a synthetic organ in the lab in a matter of months. I've been thinking we should be able to grow human lung tissue, and that then would be enough to test toxicity and viability of the TP53 editing therapy."

"You keep going doctor, and I'll get back to you about these organs," interrupted Zach.

"Please don't do anything stupid Zach..."

Zach had already hung up. Dr. Cunningham looked at the preliminary results on his computer screen. Part of him felt apprehensive. Zach was a good kid, but he scared him sometimes, he seemed ready to do anything to reach his goals. Yet

Cunningham wasn't that different. Medical research was every bit as competitive as the tech startup world, he thought. Figuring out these TP53 pathways would save millions of lives and make him a medical pioneer. He smiled and left to go get his lunch.

10

All Zach had to do was find a lung. Or a kidney. Zach thought of the urban legend, about poor students waking up in a bathtub full of ice in a cheap motel bathroom with a massive scar on their back and a missing kidney. He forced a smile as he walked out of the elevator into the lobby of his condo building. A neighbor, a woman in her twenties, smiled back at him.

Easy enough, at least I know what to do, and I know just where to go to find the right people! The truth is Zach had never been more apprehensive but he tried to steel himself and smile as he approached his car, a Porsche 911 parked in the garage.

How far he had come since his days growing up poor and attending the Coding Academy! He had gone from being a poor kid with no healthcare, to hanging out with affluent entrepreneur wannabes like Ashley and Brad at the Academy, to being the poster child of success he craved to be, and his car was the perfect embodiment of that feeling. How proud he had been when he had first driven it off the lot!

Thank goodness for that pre-IPO bonus. He hopped in, turned on the ignition and zipped away.

An hour later Zach stopped by the Baltimore Urban Clinic building on Saint Paul Place. Housed in a drab brick building that had long ago been painted in white, the Clinic had been their go-to clinic for medical care when they had no insurance and no money left to finish the month. As he walked into the building, a flood of memories came back to Zach. He remembered the days before they had found Dr. Cunningham. A godsend to his mother, the helping hand that got them out of this, almost. The musty smell of mold and dust, mixed in body odors. Smells of hard work, and stress, and no showers, and sadness. Smells of hope, and disappointment, and making it another day, another week, to finish the month. The lobby hadn't changed in at least thirty years, with a mix of tacky wallpaper and faded beige paint. A large waiting room on the left was full. Zach nodded at the receptionist, who wasn't paying attention, and walked into the waiting room.

He sat down, leaned over the side table to grab a three-year-old copy of People magazine and looked around. What a sight. What struck him first was the sheer diversity of the crowd. When he and his mom had been here they had stuck out like a sore thumb, or so he thought, and he had always felt self-conscious about it. Today he could see patients who were obviously homeless, that was expected. But there were also construction workers, young single moms with infants, retirees. All had a mask of boredom and resignation on. Bored by the endless wait in a medical clinic that was clearly understaffed. Resigned to get through with it as this was their only option to receive some form of healthcare.

Across the room Zach saw a man in his twenties, about his age, who was coughing. His eyes appeared a bit red. He sneezed into his sleeve, paused and glanced around with a look of embarrassment. The man seemed like a hipster, a hipster with no health insurance. His clothes were worn out, an old pair of jeans, faded and with a number of rips. He was wearing a gray t-shirt that was dirty and worn off at the edges of the sleeves. On the chest of his shirt, two dark hands facing each other with two index fingers pointed at each other as if in a duel to the death. His shoes, while dirty and worn too, seemed like a solid pair of steel toe boots. The man readjusted his wool cap, pulled out a smartphone and stared at it with rapt attention. On his arm, Zach noticed a biohazard symbol, with an acronym under it: CRISPR.

Luck is what happens when preparation meets opportunity, thought Zach. He was looking at a biohacker. Biohacking had come of age in the last decade or so. It usually involved smart, loner types, prone to risk-taking and willing to experiment on themselves to extend their lifespan or otherwise augment their body's capabilities by genetic means. They would develop inexpensive, risky genetic therapies using a technique known as CRISPR Cas9, a gene editing technique focused on editing clustered regularly interspaced short palindromic repeat sequences, or CRISPR. Cas9 was a particular protein involved in the process. Biohackers had been able to change their skin color and hair color using CRISPR. In fact doing so had become a rite of passage to prove your ability to successfully biohack yourself. Some of the more fringe hackers claimed they could increase their muscle strength or their vision. It all came at a risk, and the press had had a field day reporting on biohacking experiments gone wrong, generally ending with the death of the unfortunate hacker who was uninsurable and uninsured.

Just a benign form of addiction, perfect for an unofficial human trial, thought Zach, smiling.

He saw an empty seat across from the man; he crossed over and sat down. The man did not appear to notice him. After about ten minutes of listening to the din of conversations in the room, the man sneezed again and Zach decided to say something.

"Bless you! Wow, that's quite a cold you have, man."

"Tell me about it... I hate it."

"You been here long?"

"Just about an hour, it's not too bad. I think my turn will be up soon."

The man stared back at his smartphone, apparently engrossed in it unless he was simply trying to avoid Zach.

"This isn't right, simply because you don't have a job doesn't mean you shouldn't have health insurance either," said Zach, trying to grab the man's attention.

"Yeah, but that's the way it is..." said the man in a noncommittal manner.

"You know, you actually look healthy. Well you might have the flu, but you look healthy, man. I used to participate in medical trials to make a bit of money, you should check it out," added Zach, looking for any sign of interest in the hipster's eyes.

The hipster paused and stared at Zach. The wheels were turning.

"What do you mean? I wouldn't even know where to start anyway... isn't it a corporate scam, really?"

"No, you just have to knock on the right door," replied Zach. Other patients around them were starting to listen as well.

"In fact, you'll make a decent amount of money if you can spare a week for a trial," added Zach. He now had the hipster's full attention. Zach could smell greed and desperation. He had been there, he knew exactly the feeling and how to play it up.

He leaned over and whispered.

"If you need the money fast, I can get you started next week, but only if you're into it. They pay big bucks"

The hipster's eyes widened. As Zach was leaning over to hand a card to the hipster, he was suddenly interrupted.

"Can I help you?"

Zach looked up and saw an attractive woman in her twenties, dressed in a white coat. Blonde with short hair and full lips, she was staring at him with her pale blue eyes, an inquisitive, almost angry stare. The badge on her chest said "Emily Dixon, Manager".

"Oh, hi! Um... Sure, but I think he was here before me, why don't you go first," said Zach, motioning to the hipster to go ahead. The man gave both of them a quizzical look.

"Actually you don't seem well sir, why don't *you* go first. We'll take care of him in a little bit," responded Emily. Her tone was firm and did not invite disagreement. Zach hesitated, then got up.

"Contact me if you want to know more," he said, pushing a card in the hipster's hands.

"Sir, please come with me," insisted Emily, anger flashing in her eyes.

She took him to an office down the hall and had him sit in a chair.

"What brings you here today? Can we start with your name and date of birth?"

"Um, my name is Zach... I just wasn't feeling well this morning. Wasn't sure whether it was the flu or allergies, my head hurt so bad," said Zach slowly. He felt so lame. He hadn't even prepared a cover story for why he would show up at the clinic! Zach was just making it up on the fly, as best as he could. Emily pretended not to notice.

"Okay, let me check your vitals, then we'll have the doctor see you," she said in a neutral tone.

She left the room quickly after jotting down his pulse and temperature. A physician came in a few minutes later. The interaction was quick. Zach was virtually silent the whole time while the physician examined him. As he left the room, Zach's mind started going in a million directions.

"That was kind of stupid, I should really have thought this through a bit more. I did nothing wrong anyway, why did I even let them examine me?"

A knock on the door, Emily was back. Her cheeks were slightly red, her lips pursed.

"Zach... your name is Zach, right?"

"Yes."

"Zach, we checked your vitals and there's nothing wrong with you."

"Oh great, I'd better get going then," he responded, relieved and anxious at the same time.

"Zach, we see people like you every week, and only it's gotten worse."

Zach looked at her, not sure what she meant.

"Clinical trial folks. You guys try to come recruit in our waiting room virtually every week. You prey on our patients. Yes they need the money, but what you do with them is wrong. You lie to them about the risks they are exposed to. In some cases you don't even pay them a fair wage. Then, they come back to us even sicker than before. This isn't right. Today you dealt with me. Next time it'll be far less pleasant."

Zach knew what she meant. Running a free health clinic for the homeless meant you had to deal with alcohol abuse and all sorts of other substance abuse. More than once, Zach and his mom had seen a homeless patient, drunk and dazed, be escorted and thrown out of the facility by the medical aides.

"This isn't what you think, I don't work for a clinical trial company"

"Leave now. Right now," responded Emily. Anger made her blush and dilated her pupils. Zach paused, stunned by how beautiful she was.

"Go!" she said, pointing to the door.

Not knowing how to respond, Zach got up and left the building.

Tom had sat with the card for a while.

It was a plain white rectangle. A name: Zach Hayes. A phone number. Nothing else.

He had been running figures in his head all evening. His rent was four months behind. His medical bills from last spring were still in collections. He had sold his backup hard drives two weeks ago. The portable centrifuge was next.

The research was good. He knew that. His implementation was solid, the bacterial tests were holding up, and the concept itself was something no one had published yet. But computers don't run on good ideas. They run on electricity, which requires money, which he did not have.

Fifty thousand dollars. The man had said it like it was nothing.

Tom was not naive. He knew what a clinical trial was, and he had a good sense of what they were asking him to agree to. He had done worse to himself. He was twenty-five years old. He had a mutation of his own that would kill him by fifty. He was out of money and soon would be out of time.

He picked up his phone and called the number.

The last patient had left at seven. Emily had stayed until eight, as she always did, updating charts and making sure the supply closet was stocked and locked. The clinic ran on donated supplies, which meant the supply closet also ran on the honor system, which meant it needed a lock.

She was still thinking about the man from earlier. Zach.

She couldn't quite place her anger. She had thrown out half a dozen clinical trial recruiters in the past year, and none of them had stayed with her the way this one had. Maybe it was the way he had looked at her when she told him to leave. Not embarrassed, not apologetic, just surprised. As if it had genuinely not occurred to him that someone might say no.

She heard a knock at the back door. She already knew who it was. Tom came in carrying two coffees from the bodega on the corner.

"You're still here," he said.

"Someone has to be."

He set a coffee on her desk and sat across from her in the patient chair, the one that wobbled if you leaned back too far. He'd been coming by like this for three months now, just to sit and be around other people. She hadn't asked him to explain it, and he hadn't. Some things didn't need explaining.

"Long day?" he asked.

"They're all long days."

He nodded, turning the coffee cup slowly in his hands. There was a new tattoo on his forearm she hadn't noticed before. A double helix, small, just above the wrist.

"Tom."

"What?"

"Your arm."

He glanced down. "Oh. Yeah."

"What is that?"

"It's nothing. Just..." He paused. "I've been reading about some stuff. DNA storage. You can encode data in a genome. Actual files. It's pretty wild."

Emily put down her pen. "In whose genome?"

"Your own, theoretically."

"Tom."

"It's non-toxic, Em. I did the research. I know what I'm doing."

She looked at him for a long moment. She had her father's patience when she needed it, and she needed it now. Reverend Dixon had never raised his voice at anyone in his life. She had learned from him that the loudest thing you could say was silence.

"I know you know what you're doing," she said finally. "That's what worries me."

He smiled a little. "I'm being careful."

"You're always careful. Right up until you're not."

He looked at the floor. She picked up her pen again. They sat like that for a while, the way they always had. Not filling the silence, just occupying it together. Outside on the street she could hear the number 36 bus groaning to a stop.

"Dad used to say something," Tom said eventually. He said it carefully, the way he said anything about their father, like he was testing the weight of it before he set it down.

"I know what Dad used to say."

"He used to say the body is a temple. Remember? Every Sunday."

"I remember."

"I used to hate that. I thought it was so, you know. Primitive. Control the body, control the person." He shrugged. "But lately I've been thinking maybe he wasn't completely wrong. Just maybe for the wrong reasons."

Emily looked up at him.

"There's something in there, Em. In the junk. The parts they say don't do anything." He tapped his forearm. "I think it does something. I just don't know what yet."

She didn't answer. She wanted to tell him to stop, to be careful, that he was the only family she had left and she needed him to stay in one piece. She wanted to tell him that faith and science were not as far apart as he thought, that her father had understood both, had held them together in his two large hands and never let either one go. But she had learned not to say these things. People heard them as arguments. They were not arguments. They were just what she believed.

"Go home, Tom," she said.

He stood, finished his coffee, set the cup on her desk. At the door he turned around.

"You ever think about what it's all for?" he asked.

"All the time."

"And?"

She smiled. "And I still don't know. But I show up anyway."

He thought about that. Then he nodded, like it was a satisfactory answer, and left.

Emily sat alone in the clinic for a while after he was gone. She listened to the building settle around her, the pipes, the loose ceiling tile in the hallway, the refrigerator unit in the medication room cycling on. These were the sounds of the place her father had built. She knew them the way she knew her own heartbeat.

She thought about the man from earlier. Zach Hayes.

She thought: *I hope Tom stays away from him.*

11

A few days after his visit to the homeless clinic Zach received a phone call. At first, he didn't recognize the number and let it go to voicemail. Within seconds, he read the voicemail transcript. It was Tom, the hipster he had tried to recruit. He called him right back.

"Hi Tom, this is Zach Hayes. Sorry I missed your call. How are you?"

"Oh, hey Zach, thanks for calling me back," said Tom, not sure how to begin.

"Have you thought about our conversation?"

"Well, yes, in fact that's why I'm calling you back. Can we talk about this some more? How would it work?"

Zach smiled. As always, his good fortune and sense of opportunity were starting to work out. He thought of Dr. Cunningham and the TP53 trials, and his telomeres shrinking. He felt anxious again.

"Well, why don't we discuss this in person? We should meet with Dr. Cunningham, he's the principal investigator on this project. That means he runs the show, he'll really be able to tell you everything about it. What are you doing this afternoon?"

"Um, wow, that's fast... I guess I'm available, I could meet you guys after 2pm."

"Science doesn't wait, Tom, and you'll be part of an important project," replied Zach, feeling cocky and focused on closing the sale.

"Meet me in the lobby of Mercy Medical Center this afternoon at 2. Can you do that?" he added

"Yes... I think I can, okay see you then," responded Tom hesitantly.

As soon as Tom hung up, Zach called Dr. Cunningham.

"Hello?"

"Hi Dr. Cunningham, this is Zach, how are you?" said Zach in a perfunctory manner. "Can I meet you this afternoon at 2pm?"

"Well, let me see..."

The good doctor was obviously surprised by the abrupt request.

"This is really important, doctor. I think I've figured out our test strategy. I can't wait to talk to you about it in person!"

"OK then, I guess I'll make time... But I only have 20 minutes"

"That's plenty, see you then!"

Zach hung up, feeling energized. A plan was starting to hatch in his mind. He wanted to share it with Dr. Cunningham in person, so he could better convince him. Yes, in person was definitely going to be a better way to sell this.

Zach had been waiting for a few minutes in the lobby of Mercy Medical Center when Tom showed up, mostly on time. His eyes and nose were red from congestion, but Zach thought it would do. He had been looking at the tall stone fireplace in the back of the lobby and the grand piano that was placed next to it. The instrument was one of these self-playing Yamaha pianos and was set to play a Sinatra song. Oddly enough, this place felt much more like a high-end hotel than a hospital. This just seemed odd, and somewhat wrong, to Zach that in the same city and at the same time you would have a homeless clinic where throngs of working people would show up and receive minimal care, mostly reactive and often ineffective. The contrast with the hospital couldn't be more striking. Another lesson for him on the power of status and money. He was determined to get his way.

"Hi Tom, glad you were able to make it. Let's go, we're a few minutes late," said Zach, while motioning to head toward the elevator bank in the back of the lobby. A few minutes later Zach and Tom were sitting in Dr. Cunningham's office.

"Dr. Cunningham, thank you for meeting with us on such short notice," started Zach.

"No worries, Zach. You mentioned you had a plan you wanted to discuss, and this project of ours is really important to me."

Tom had been expecting some on-boarding process into a clinical trial. This was not it, and he was starting to wonder where the discussion was going. Cunningham was picking up on Tom's uncomfortable body language. He turned to Zach.

"Zach, can I speak to you in private? Let's step outside," said Cunningham. He then turned to Tom. "Don't worry, all is well, we'll be right back".

As soon as they were in the hall outside his office the doctor put his hand on Zach's shoulder, looking slightly agitated.

"Zach, what do you think you're doing? And who is this gentleman in my office?" he said in a hushed tone.

"Doctor, I think I have this figured out. You remember how we talked about getting organs, so we can test our different therapies with our TP53 genetic editing approach?"

"Zach, let me stop you right there. You are out of your mind if you think this person is going to be part of this..."

"Give me a minute to explain"

"We had talked about getting organs from the tissue engineering lab, not bringing a live donor in my office!"

"First of all no-one said he's an organ donor, you're jumping to conclusions, and second of all let me explain," responded Zach, going in damage control mode.

Cunningham paused and looked at him.

"Okay, please explain to me what you think you're doing," he said, defiantly.

"Doctor, do you like this hospital? How many patients do you see and help every year? Two thousand maybe? And who are these patients? I can tell you they're mostly wealthy patients, with a big house, two expensive cars. They come to see you and talk to you about their cholesterol before taking off to go spend a week at the beach to relax because they think their job is too stressful."

Cunningham was listening, intrigued.

"Now let me tell you about the world I come from, the world I grew up in. My world is what most people in this city experience but you would never know it because this was never your part of town. Yes, you helped me and my mom, but you had no idea what it was like to walk in our shoes, so let me share this with you now."

Zach paused to gauge his audience.

"Imagine a world where you have no health insurance. It's not that you don't want it, it's that you don't have enough money to pay the rent, put food on the table, and pay your insurance too. So you go without insurance because eating and having a bed is more important. Imagine a world where hospitals (hell, *your* hospital!) will garnish wages of people like my mom, so your fees get paid even if it means we can't buy food anymore, and we have to go to a soup kitchen. These people still need healthcare, they still need food and shelter. What are *you* doing about it? How does this align with your Hippocratic oath?"

"Well..." Said the doctor, surprised by Zach's diatribe. Zach went on.

"Now, imagine a world where your genetic therapies can help millions of these people, not just the two thousand wealthy patients you see. Imagine helping millions of people getting over the havoc wreaked by TP53 mutations. Now *that*'s impact. *That*'s meaning. So are you going to tell this guy in your office that you can't do anything to help him? Do you understand how desperate he is to get some money? Are you going to walk away from the opportunity to help millions of patients? Oh, I know what you're thinking... We'll help them anyway, we just need to follow process. Well, fuck the process! You know what happens when you follow process? Nothing. That's what happens in the real world. Because they wait for you and while they wait for you, they die. And if you don't believe me, just think about how my mom died. We had no money and no time left. So don't tell them what's better for them while they're dying doctor, because that's just lying to yourself. If you want to make a difference, fuck the process and act now. See the guy in your office? He needs our help *now*."

Zach stopped, emotionally exhausted. His pitch had turned into a passionate plea, and he hadn't expected that. It had brought up feelings and memories he would rather have kept buried, unseen and unfelt. Visibly moved, Cunningham looked at Zach.

"Zach, I don't know, I had not exactly thought it through from that perspective... I suppose he won't be adversely affected if he doesn't have the TP53 marker, so his odds should be decent if that's the case... What do you want to do?"

"Well. First I wanted to talk to you in person. I also wanted you to meet Tom to make it real, otherwise it's always so abstract. I have to talk to him about the trial part. He's a biohacker, I'm sure he's done far worse to himself on his own."

Cunningham turned pale.

"Wait, don't freak out! He needs it, he needs the money, he needs the care, and remember this *is* for a good cause. *You* will be the pioneer that made TP53 genetic editing a reality. Let me handle it and you get the glory."

Cunningham paused, then finally spoke.

"Fine, you talk to him. If you can convince him, we'll all get what we need. But if he refuses, I don't want you to force his hand and I don't want to talk about this ever again."

"Leave it up to me doctor, I'll take care of it, as always."

"If you say so..."

The two of them went back to the office.

"Oh, there you are, I was wondering what was going on..." said Tom, looking slightly unsettled.

"Hey Tom, you know how I told you Dr. Cunningham was running a clinical trial? Well it's for a really important cancer therapy called TP53 genetic editing, and the money is very good."

"Oh, okay, this is awesome. What kind of money are we talking about? One of my friends made a thousand dollars in a week once"

"This will be much better, we're talking about fifty thousand dollars and a month's time."

"No way, seriously? Fifty thousand?"

Tom was smiling like a kid who had just found the pirates' treasure chest. His mind was oscillating between elation and confusion. This was going to solve a lot of problems... Rent, credit card bills, doctors bills. Zach was letting him absorb the news. Cunningham was watching him carefully.

"Wait, why is it so much though, what is so special about this trial?" he finally said, starting to think the offer through.

"Well, you'll have to participate in a medical trial, but we'll take care of everything and you'll be in as good a shape or better when we're done," said Zach, going for the kill. Cunningham, looking somewhat distraught, was sitting by his desk, elbows on his knees and staring at the ground.

"Everything will be okay. The reason you'll get so much money is because we'll need to inject genetically edited materials into your body. But you know what? It's a cancer therapy that only affects cancerous cells. It won't affect your cells if they're not cancerous. It is a variant of a known therapy, and you'll get top dollar for it. Think of all the things you can do with the fifty thousand dollars you'll get."

Tom was hesitant. He wasn't sure what to say. Elation and confusion again. Fear and greed. He thought of the struggles of the last few months. He thought of the money he owed for his old medical bills, he thought about how he could get a new start, as well as receive proper care with this trial.

"I'm a biohacker, I know how quickly things can go wrong with gene editing..." said Tom after a while. "The money's definitely a plus, but how do I know this trial is not going to kill me?"

"Tom, look around you," replied Zach. "This is a top-notch hospital, Dr. Cunningham is top in his field, you'll get first class treatment. We'll have to put you under for a live biopsy of your kidneys and lungs but you're in a first class facility, definitely better than your garage, man."

Zach could see Tom absorbing the information, processing the odds.

"You're not publishing this research, are you?" asked Tom

"Well, this is commercial research, we want to reserve all rights..."

"A hundred. I want a hundred thousand dollars and I'll do your trial," interrupted Tom, finally relenting. Zach looked at Dr. Cunningham and did some quick math.

"Deal," said Zach, extending his hand.

"Okay," replied Tom, shaking Zach's hand. "I get paid upfront, right?"

"You'll get ten percent now, and the rest when the trial is over, in about a month," said Zach before the doctor could say anything. Cunningham glanced at the preliminary readout and frowned briefly, as if something had caught his eye. He said nothing, and moved on.

"Well we'll have to make sure you pass some basic tests first..." said Cunningham finally.

Zach smiled. Toughest sales job in a long time! He had pulled it off, as he always did. Luck favors those who act.

The November sun was hitting the white façades of Avenida da Liberdade at a low angle, and the light was hurting his eyes. He had been walking for twenty minutes, barely noticing the city around him.

The Fundação do Leste e Sul was two blocks ahead. He checked his watch: three minutes early. He thought about how far he had come to stand on this sidewalk. Baltimore. The Coding Academy. The IPO. Cunningham's lab. One decision at a time, each one harder than the last, and here he was in Lisbon, about to walk into a room that could determine whether he lived or died.

He was twenty-eight years old. His telomeres were shrinking. And the people behind that door might be his only shot.

He straightened his jacket and pushed through the door.

12

He walked the twelve blocks from Mercy because it was a clear evening and because a cab was twelve dollars he didn't have. The ten thousand was pending, not real yet.

The room on Pratt Street was small. A mattress, a folding table, two laptops, a soldering iron. The floor was a maze of hard drives and reagent bottles and a portable centrifuge he had bought off eBay for forty-two dollars. He had stopped calling it an apartment four months ago. It was the lab, and that was fine.

Tom sat down and opened the older laptop. His Grover implementation was still running, a four-hour test on a forty-base bacterial sequence from GenBank. The algorithm was holding. Not at scale, he didn't have the hardware for that, but the structure was right. It had been right for a while now.

The idea was simple. Simple the way most important ideas are simple when you say them out loud. Junk DNA was not junk. It was storage. And if you could run Grover on the genome fast enough to find specific sequences, you could use those sequences as address pointers. The body as a hard drive. Biological encryption running on hardware no one could confiscate, no one could hack, no one could take from you.

He pulled out his phone and texted Emily. Got into a trial at Mercy. Good money. Wanted you to know.

He set the phone down. She would reply when she replied. His phone pinged three minutes later:

What kind of trial.

TP53 editing. Cunningham's project. Safe.

Pause. Then: You should have told me first.

He thought about that. She was right. She was usually right. But she would have told him not to do it, and he would have done it anyway, so telling her first would have meant a longer argument. He typed: It's fine, Em. and left it at that.

No reply.

He had four weeks in the clinical setting. That meant time. He had not finished encrypting his research files, and this was a problem he had been meaning to solve. He opened a new terminal window.

He got to work.

PART 2

13

Tom had been running a low-grade fever for two weeks. He hadn't told anyone. He'd medicated himself that morning, checked his temperature in the hospital bathroom before check-in, and decided it was close enough. One hundred thousand dollars was close enough to do a lot of things.

Since they were going to put him under, he had asked Emily, the clinic manager, to come along with him.

"I don't really know anybody else here, and I trust you. Do you think you can take me there?"

"I think so Tom, let me check my calendar," had been Emily's response. Her sense of duty and empathy had prevailed, and she had come with the hipster. A mother bear and her fearful cub. She had sensed Tom had fallen prey to an organ donor scheme, but had no proof of it. She didn't want to ask him as she had gotten badly burned the last time she had tried to get involved in the decision of another patient. Time had taught her that her patients needed money badly. And medical care. And hope. And support. Not someone who judged them, and made choices for them. Tom was no different. She had agreed to take him to the hospital, they simply would not discuss what the procedure was about.

Zach stood up as he saw them step off the elevator into the reception area of the general surgery department. This was a big day for him, and Dr. Cunningham was finally going to get the necessary validation he needed with some of the TP53 therapies they had identified. This wasn't necessarily the most orthodox form of research, but it would speed up the therapy development process by years, and give Zach a new lease on life. He became worried when he saw Emily. Hadn't she kicked him out of the clinic? Didn't she suspect something wrong was up?

Emily didn't wince in the least when she noticed Zach. If she was surprised, she didn't let any of it show. One of Dr. Cunningham's nurses took Tom to an examination room. Zach and Emily sat in the waiting area. After about a minute of silence, Emily spoke up.

"How can you do this? At least I hope you're paying him a lot of money!" she said, trying to control her anger.

"Excuse me?" replied Zach, surprised by the outburst.

"I saw you last month at the clinic, talking to Tom and trying to sell him your scheme. I'm not going to stop you, but I hate this. I hope you're giving him a lot of money. He could use it. They could all use it."

Emily felt the burn of anger as she was staring at Zach. He wasn't sure how to react.

"And you are?"

Zach knew exactly who she was. She was the stunning manager who had thrown him out of the clinic. She looked even more attractive today, and Zach wasn't sure why. He was just buying time while trying to come up with a coherent response.

"You know exactly who I am. My name is Emily Dixon, and I am the clinic manager who kicked you out last month. I can't believe you managed to convince Tom, but he is an adult and makes his own decisions."

"One, we are; and two, a lot of good is going to come out of this," said Zach, gradually finding his footing. "Do you realize how many millions of patients die every year of TP53-related mutations? We're going to solve this, and Tom will be part of it. And please spare me your self-righteousness. I've watched people die from this and I promised myself I would do something about it. So please, we all have a cross to carry."

Emily seemed surprised, taken aback.

"Oh, I'm sorry, I had no idea..."

"That's fine you didn't know."

"Well, can we start over? Hi, I'm Emily, and you are?"

"Zach, Zach Hayes. I run a software company, but I also happen to be funding Dr. Cunningham's research on TP53 mutations."

Zach could tell he was starting to catch Emily's interest. Anger had subsided, and she was now occasionally smiling, a genuine and disarming smile.

"What about you? Why would someone like you be running a homeless clinic on the wrong side of town? I mean, someone as smart as you should obviously be able to do so much more..."

Zach had made a point of complimenting her on her smarts, not her looks. She blushed a bit.

"How would you know? I actually grew up there, my dad was a minister. He's the one who started the clinic. When he passed away a few years ago, I decided to keep it going. At first, I did it because it reminded me of him, and it made me feel like I was keeping my world together. But the more I did it, the more I started seeing how much help people need, and how much of a difference I can make with very little, simply by being there. A guy like you wouldn't necessarily understand, but a lot of people don't have proper healthcare, don't have the means for it. Everything is now so expensive. Sometimes they also simply don't have a clue what to do because no one has ever bothered to take the time to listen to them and help them. So the team and I take the time to listen and help. Faith through good deeds. We give our people hope and dignity."

"Actually, we may have more in common than you thought" replied Zach. "I'm from the West side too, and I understand exactly what you're talking about. My mom ended up without health insurance, with the hospital garnishing her wages and not enough money to take care of her cancer. I watched her waste away as Dr. Cunningham helped as best as he could. It's funny you should mention faith. She prayed all right, every night. I don't know if anyone was hearing her prayers, but it sure did nothing. When she died, I promised myself I was never going to be put in this situation again. I would do anything to not be put in this situation again. Turns out I was gifted with coding, I got lucky with my quantum encryption algorithm and here I am, now funding research so this doesn't happen again."

"Well, you could have fooled me, I thought for sure you were one of these kids born with a silver spoon..." said Emily, laughing. Zach paused and looked at her. Emily did not divert her eyes but stared back at him, lingering on and enjoying every second of it.

An hour had passed when they heard brisk footsteps heading their way. Dr. Cunningham, still in scrubs, had just come out of the operating block.

"Zach, why didn't you tell me?"

"What, doctor?"

"He was sick"

"Well, yes he had a cold, maybe the flu, but what's going on? Is there a problem?"

"Definitely not a cold. As soon as we put an IV in him, I had the lab re-run some blood work, just to confirm the baseline because he looked odd. I didn't think it was going to be an issue, so we proceeded with the open biopsy. The resident is finishing him up now. But I was looking at the results that came back and I'm not sure what's going on. The TP53 treatment worked so well on all the animals we tested, including pigs, which are such a reliable predictor of therapeutic success in human patients. According to our tests he doesn't have the flu, it's something else, but we don't understand it yet."

"So, what does that mean doctor?" said Zach.

"I don't know yet. He may be compromised as a patient for our study Zach. Even if we straighten him out, which I expect we will, we may not be able to use the results anyway because it is such an odd case." The doctor paused. "I'm not sure, Zach. This may be a sign it was not a good idea to start with. I'm thinking we should go back to the original research protocol. I think it's going to take more time, but it's really the way to get things done properly..."

A nurse interrupted their conversation.

"Dr. Cunningham, we need you in OR2. Please come with me."

Her tone didn't leave much choice. She looked pale. Cunningham left with her promptly.

"I hope he's okay..." said Emily, speaking softly as if to herself only.

"Of course he will, Dr. Cunningham is the best" retorted Zach, cocky as ever.

"I pray he is..." Emily's voice was trailing off.

They were standing by the central station in the middle of the general surgery department. A group of nurses were updating health records on the computer system and taking phone calls. Suddenly two nurses took off and ran to the operating block. Another fifteen minutes went by before Cunningham eventually came back. He was shaking his head, looking forlorn.

"I don't understand, everything seemed fine... We need to go rerun all the tests and look for something we missed. We've got to get the postmortem right, and understand the root of what happened."

"Postmortem?" asked Zach apprehensively.

"He flatlined on us. We did everything we could. He's gone."

"What do you mean?"

"I gotta go back, we need to understand what just happened. Give me an hour."

14

This turned out to be the longest hour. As soon as she heard the news Emily virtually collapsed, dropping on a sofa in the waiting area nearby. She buried her head in her hands. As Zach turned around after his conversation with Dr. Cunningham he noticed Emily was no longer by his side. He walked to her and sat down on the sofa next to her. He noticed big drippy tears had started rolling down her cheeks.

"I'm sorry Emily, I can't believe what just happened. Tom seemed fine..." said Zach as he put a hand on her shoulder. She shrugged him off. He felt a bit defensive. Wasn't he the one who convinced Tom to enroll in this trial in the first place?

"Tom must have had some sort of preexisting condition we missed. He was a biohacker, you know? God knows what kind of crazy things he might have done to his body before..."

"Don't you dare!" cried Emily, her eyes flashing in anger. "Don't you dare speak about him like that. Tom was a good guy, he cared about his health which is why he got into biohacking in the first place!"

"It's okay Emily, I'm sorry, I didn't realize you cared this much..."

"Care? He's my half-brother! Maybe dad disowned him, but he was a good person! He was smart, and cared about other people, and cared about himself. And now he's gone..."

Zach wasn't sure how to respond to the revelation that had just been dropped on him. It all made a lot more sense now. Why Emily had cared in the first place a month ago in the waiting room at the clinic. Why she had come with Tom to the hospital now. Why she had reacted this way. The two sat silent next to each other for a while, lost in thought.

It was Emily who finally spoke.

"I knew something like this was going to happen. I told him to stop his biohacking, I knew he was going to end up harming himself..."

Zach was relieved to be left at least partially off the hook. He smiled.

"It's your fault too! Yes, he was messing with things he shouldn't have messed with, but you didn't exactly help!" she added, looking at Zach.

Emily was angry, but she couldn't quite bring herself to be fully angry at Zach. Tom had been so excited about the trial. The money alone was going to give him a chance to start over, a clean slate! He had willingly enrolled, she had seen the excitement in his eyes. And now she felt lonely. Her only sibling had died, the only family of sorts she had left were her patients at the clinic.

Zach intrigued her. She had thought he'd be another one of these corporate predators, wealthy sell-outs preying on patients, but once she had realized his background mirrored hers in unexpected ways, she had unconsciously hoped he would be in some fashion redeemable.

He can't be all that bad if he managed to get a scholarship for the Coding Academy, she had thought to herself. Another pregnant pause, another awkward moment interrupted by Dr. Cunningham.

"Guys, you should go home. This is going to take a while. We need to run more tests. He seemed fine on the outside, but on the inside his organs look like those of a seventy-year-old... I don't understand what happened. We're going to do an autopsy, we'll know more in a few days. Go home. I'll call you later this week Zach."

"Okay doctor," replied Zach, nodding his head. He glanced at Emily. She was still processing it all.

"Come on, Emily, let's go, I'll take you to your car".

After taking Emily to her car Zach got into his roadster. He zipped out of the garage and into the street.

"What a day!" he thought. He was still replaying the events of the day in his mind when his phone rang.

"Hello?"

"Hi Zach, this is Otto! Do you have a minute?"

"Sure, what's going on?"

"Not much, I had to fly to Frankfurt after going to Portugal and I just came back stateside. I know you got the money, I hope everything is fine?"

"Oh, yes..." replied Zach.

With the events of the past month he had not had a chance to catch up with Otto other than through occasional texts. Zach trusted Otto. Otto had been his guardian angel, had invested in him when no one else would, then had taken him under his wing and mentored him, fixed his mistakes along the way. When Otto had wired the money from the Fundação deal they were working on, Zach had cared only about turning around his sales at Quantum, and of course his side project with Cunningham.

"Thanks for wiring the money, that was very helpful, thank you as always, Otto," added Zach.

"You're welcome Zach, but we should really talk about the terms of the deal, I had to do a few unusual things to make this happen. I take it you have our sales trajectory under control?"

"Yes of course," lied Zach. "Tell me about your deal though, sorry it's taken so long to catch up, things have been really busy... How is the foundation since we talked to them in Lisbon? Are they really going to invest? I always wondered whether they were an actual investment fund..."

"Well, yes they are. They're a Portuguese foundation that invests a substantial endowment, but we ended up not fitting their investment criteria once the transaction went through their investment committee."

"So?"

"So, they eventually referred me to a Russian investment fund."

A lie for a lie...

"I had to get a deal done quickly and confidentially. We ended up structuring it as convertible debt, at a forty percent discount to market."

"How much did you say, forty percent discount to market?"

"Yes, we needed to get this done quickly and quietly, Zach."

Zach winced.

"I understand, but come on Otto, that's a bit rich. I don't remember seeing any paperwork either... Did you get this done without board approval? I'm not sure I like this, is the deal even valid?"

If there's one thing Otto had taught Zach in the last few years, it was the difference between creating value and claiming value. Plenty of people created value every day, only to end up poor. Only those who *claimed* value, their fair share or preferably more, would end up wealthy.

"Zach, do I need to remind you of the insider trade you recently executed? Do I need to remind you that I am covering your ass big time? I would expect a little more respect, young man..." responded Otto, curtly.

"Okay, fair enough, didn't mean to offend you. I get it, you are right... thank you, Otto."

"No worries, you just take care of our sales and I'll take care of the paperwork. We need to make sure we can maintain our stock price. If our sales tank, so will our stock price, and that will then truly create an issue with this side deal as it would start unraveling. And I would rather not have to unravel an investment from a Russian fund. It will get complicated fast, Zach." said Otto, rather cryptically.

Zach knew not to ask too many questions by now.

"I get it Otto, I'll take care of sales and you take care of this."

"You'd better. I'll send you the agreement so you can sign it, we'll post-date it as needed. No one needs to know. Talk to you later Zach," said Otto before hanging up.

A few days later Zach woke up in his condo in Georgetown. It was 5am and as always he looked at his phone to check if he had any messages. A news notification flashed across the screen:

BREAKING NEWS: BALTIMORE HOSPITAL QUARANTINED AND CLOSED TO PUBLIC. OFFICIALS FEAR ANOTHER FLU EPIDEMIC ON ITS WAY.

Zach felt as if someone had just punched him in the gut. Frantic and still reeling from the adrenaline rush he called Dr. Cunningham right away.

"Hi Zach, I was going to call you, it's been a long night..." said Dr. Cunningham, sounding tired on the phone.

"Dr. Cunningham, what's going on? Is any of this related to Tom and our project?"

"Well... I have to say Zach, it's been quite a week. Turns out, whatever Tom had is contagious. Highly contagious. We're trying to contain it. You may or may not have it. You need to stay home until we can get to you and determine your status. Stay where you are, I'm on my way with a CDC team. Be there in about twenty minutes. Bye."

The doctor hung up before Zach had a chance to say anything. Contagious? Quarantined? What did that mean? Was he going to be sick? No, it couldn't be, he had too much to do. And what about Emily?

Zach had just gotten out of the shower when he heard a knock on the door. It was Dr. Cunningham, flanked by two technicians, presumably from the Centers for Disease Control in Atlanta. The three of them were wearing masks. Zach let them in.

"Hi Zach. Good to see you. You look good, I'm glad. Let us run a few tests on you and I'll tell you what's going on. You can walk and chew gum, can't you?" said Dr. Cunningham as he stepped into the foyer.

"Um..." was the best Zach could come up with. At one of the tech's injunction he sat down on a chair. The techs opened their cases and started prepping their equipment. It looked like they were getting ready to draw blood. Zach could see a portable blood analyzer and a handful of reagents. He felt anxious.

"Zach, a lot has happened in the last 24 hours. We finally got our autopsy results from Tom last night. First of all, there's still a lot we don't know, which is why we are being extra cautious. As best as we can tell, Tom died of old age."

"What? That makes no sense" said Zach.

"Right, he was about twenty-five years old. But all his organs looked like those of a seventy or eighty year old. He died of heart failure. We're still investigating the cause of his death. It is most likely related to the TP53 treatment, the edited genetic materials we injected. I suspect it has to do with some interaction with the biohacking he had been doing on himself. The real problem is, whatever biohacking he did interacted with the genetic materials we gave him and combined with the flu virus he had."

Zach's head was spinning. Flu viruses were notoriously unstable, frequently mutating and constantly adapting to their environment. They were also prone to combine with a broad variety of genetic materials, making them an unpredictable vector for genetic therapies. This did not bode well. Now the quarantine made sense. The last thing you wanted was a highly contagious genetically engineered virus on the loose.

"Are other people..." asked Zach.

"We're not sure, but we don't think other people are affected yet, which is why we're moving fast. The sequencing we did does show one thing: the genetic materials will only bind to your genome if you have a TP53 mutation. About half of the population has that mutation, so that would put about three million people at risk in the DC metro area if we can't contain it. So far we've been able to contain it," replied Cunningham.

While talking to Zach, he was methodically going about the various tests they were running on him. They had drawn blood quickly, gotten some saliva as well and the techs were mixing chemicals, putting samples in the portable equipment they had brought with them.

"Good..." said Zach, partly relieved. One of the analyzers beeped. A tech looked at it and nodded at Cunningham.

"Good news, Zach. You have the mutation, as we knew, but you're clear. The virus doesn't appear to be targeting you."

"What does that mean?"

"It means you're safe, for now. I don't fully understand the mechanism yet. Your TP53 status should theoretically put you at risk, but the tests are clean. We'll figure out why." The doctor paused. "Emily is a different story."

Zach felt the floor shift under him. He had started all of this to save his own life. Now someone else was paying the price.

"How bad?"

"She's Tom's half-sister. Half their genome in common. She's already symptomatic."

Zach gave a quizzical look to Cunningham.

"We're keeping her quarantined at Mercy in Baltimore for now. We've been able to control her external symptoms, but we can't do anything yet about the genetic materials that got into her. We need to map out the different genetic interactions, so we can make the right edits to her genes and not kill her in the process, but we can't do that until we understand what Tom did to himself."

"How much time does she have?"

"Hard to say, probably a few months but could be less, on the order of weeks depending on how fast her organs age. Memory loss will be the first symptom and so far she seems okay"

"Do we know what biohacking Tom did?"

"No we don't, and he obviously can't tell us what he did. In theory, we might be able to reconstruct it from his genome by backing out the impact of the TP53 edit we injected, but simulating and reversing the interactions is a massive computational job. It's never been done before and would require at least a mega qubit quantum computing platform to process. It doesn't exist today, Zach."

"Well, we'd better get started then" replied Zach, focused as ever.

15

Zach was looking out the window, troubled and thoughtful. He was fascinated by the suburban sprawl of Tyson's Corner, a green canopy of foliage interrupted by all sorts of nondescript office buildings, the Ritz Carlton tower in the back. He thought for a brief moment about how far he had come since his Baltimore days. Here he was, the son of a single mom warehouse worker, in a corner office with an executive assistant and a big desk, taking over the tech industry with his crazy hot encryption platform. Yet all he could think about was what happened at the hospital in the last few days. Otto was sitting in a large couch at the other end of the room.

"Zach, this is important, I need you to engage on this topic," insisted Otto with concern as he walked toward Zach. "We had to file a Form 4 with the SEC when you sold your stock, we had no choice but to comply. The sale is now public knowledge. And on top of it investment analysts are running their channel checks... You realize what this means?"

Zach turned around, annoyed at the interruption.

"No, please enlighten me, master," he replied, sarcastically.

"It means they are checking on our distribution channels and interviewing our sales partners to gauge whether our sales are growing, and by how much. They're getting field intel on our sales, Zach."

"And so?"

"And so the word is, our sales suck! Did you not see our stock drop twenty percent this morning in pre-market trading? Bank of America is issuing a report warning investors that they don't believe we can make our revenue guidance for this year!"

"Otto, you are far too focused on the short term... I'm building this company for the long-term. Who cares if we make our guidance this year or not! You know our technology is the best, it's only a matter of time until we prevail..." replied Zach, clearly unfazed by Otto.

"You're missing the point Zach! The issue is the SEC is digging into this. They've opened an MUI with our name on it. That means we are a Matter Under Inquiry. They've started an investigation of your insider trade, Zach. And selling stock right before it tanks when you're the founder and chief executive is never a good idea, in case you hadn't realized. There's criminal liability involved, people have gone to prison for that!"

Zach was starting to pay attention.

"Then of course there's the word on the Street, which is not good either. The smart money is saying we're another flash in the pan, an overindulgent tech startup who can't deliver.

You know what other problem this is creating?" said Otto. His voice was rising as he laid out the full picture, urgency tipping into something closer to panic.

Sensing this was getting serious, Zach said nothing, pursed his lips, and stared at Otto.

"Russians! The stock tanking is screwing up our deal with the Russians! The stock we sold them is now worth far less. The deal also included a decent chunk of warrants. We told them our stock was a rocket ship, and they were going to make a ton of money from these. Do you understand what happens to the warrants if the stock tanks? They will be worth exactly *zero*! These are *not* mom-and-pop investors, Zach. They will get pissed, and this will get back to us..."

Otto dropped back on the sofa, emotionally spent from his outburst.

"If we can't fix this we're screwed..." he added, his voice trailing off as he stared out the window.

A moment passed, both of them silent and processing the myriad implications of Otto's angry tirade. A knock on the door interrupted them; it was Dave, Zach's assistant and office manager.

"Hey boss, we just got this delivered by mail courier, it seemed important, so I thought I'd bring it right away."

"Ok, thanks Dave, I'll take a look at it. Please close the door, thanks," replied Zach.

His hands were unsteady as he opened the package and pulled out a letter. It was embossed with the gold SEC seal, and at the top in bold capital letters Zach could read:

. . .

SUBPOENA TO PRODUCE DOCUMENTS

This subpoena requires you to produce documents or other tangible evidence described in Item 7, at the request of the Party described in Item 4, in the U.S. Securities and Exchange Commission Administrative Proceeding described in Item 6

The form letter went on to describe the information request. They were also going to have access to all records pertaining to the insider sale, to all documents related to the company's sales estimates and projections. They were going to interview Masha, Zach's head of marketing.

Zach didn't think he could trust Masha. She had clearly been disturbed by their conversation about the sales forecast. For all he knew she might be a whistleblower, the source of all this. He was starting to have a bad feeling about it. He now realized Otto was right, this was a clear and present danger with jail time as a potential outcome. This would undo everything he had worked for, and he was not going to let it happen. He turned to Otto.

"We can't let this happen, Otto. We gotta do something, hire the right lawyers. You gotta know someone, right? Let's get them in here this afternoon..."

"Well, yes Zach but it's not that simple either. I do know people at Wahlberg & Hicks, they are very good, and they specialize in this kind of issue. They are the best at this. I trust them."

"See, I knew it!" said Zach with a smile.

"Not so fast cowboy. They are *very* expensive. Very."

"Please, give me a break... How much?"

"Resolving a matter like this will likely cost us ten to twenty million dollars, Zach"

"Great, let's do it, I don't care!"

"You can't just unilaterally spend this kind of money, Zach. This will require board approval. We will effectively have to ask them to spend up to twenty million to defend a thirty-million-dollar trade by the chief executive. The optics are problematic Zach, we'll need to manage this really carefully."

"I couldn't care less, Otto. I control the board with my founder shares," interrupted Zach. "The board will vote to approve this. And if they have an issue with it, they can just talk to me. I won't do anything about it, but I'll listen to them!" said Zach, defiantly.

Otto was about to respond when his phone rang. He looked at the caller ID on the screen, it was Igor Dubinsky. Otto sighed and answered the phone.

"Speak of the devil... Hi Igor," said Otto with a heavy heart.

"Hi Otto, we need to talk."

"Hold on, I have Zach with me, let me put you on speaker," added Otto. Zach looked at him with a questioning stare.

"Well, boys, you've created quite a situation here," intoned Igor. "Otto, when you went to Lisbon to talk to the Fundação, they didn't put up the money themselves..."

"I figured as much when I saw the money was wired from a bank in Cyprus, Igor, but honestly I didn't care all that much where it came from. We just needed the money fast..." responded Otto.

"Otto, I thought you said they referred you to Russian investors?" asked Zach.

"Zach, I did what I had to do. We had to act fast with them."

"That's right, Otto... Turns out the money came directly from one of their lead investors, the FinAlpha fund," said Igor.

"Okay..." said Otto, leaning over the phone.

"Well, you may or may not know them, they are a Moscow-based hedge fund. They've been quite successful, though rather unorthodox in their approach to investing. First of all, they are obviously close to the Kremlin, they wouldn't be in business otherwise. This means they are close to the FSB too, in fact I believe they may be investing on behalf of some of the FSB's senior leaders..."

Otto was turning pale. The fact that Russian security forces would be involved in this deal, even indirectly, was news to him. He needed to get the deal done quickly and had been sloppy against his own advice. He was starting to connect the dots.

"So, that's a fun way to start, boys," added Igor sarcastically. "Then of course since they're not exactly bound by US law and have really talented software engineers working for them, they've been hacking into the Business Wire servers in New York. Turns out it's of course totally illegal in the US, but a particularly convenient way to get hold of press releases before they are released to the public and stock market investors. And you know what they found? An SEC press release investigating Quantum and its founder for alleged insider trading..."

"It's a false allegation! We'll get cleared, we are responding to the SEC as we speak," said Zach, almost ripping the phone out of Otto's hands. Otto, clearly surprised, was giving him a disapproving stare.

"It's a fabrication, some disgruntled employee with a grudge filed a claim with the SEC, we're going to clear it up, they have nothing to worry about. Sales are solid, and we will prevail," added Zach, clearly not bothered by a bald-faced lie. This was bad but he didn't care. He was going to figure it out, he just needed time.

"Well Zach, I'm glad to hear, but you don't need to tell me. Tell the Russians when they call you, as I'm sure they'll be in touch soon. They'll be the ones you'll need to convince... Anyway boys, you'd better clear this up with them fast, because I want no part in this. This is your heads-up, now you go fix this."

16

With all the commotion created by the call from Igor, Zach had almost forgotten he had promised Emily he would come check on her. She had been moved from Mercy to Innova General two days earlier. Cunningham needed her closer to his lab. Zach zipped along I-95 and made it there in record time. Emily lit up when she saw him enter her room. Zach was wearing a mask and a gown. Dr. Cunningham was by her bedside.

"Hey Zach, so glad to see you!"

"Hi Emily, you're okay?"

"Yes, I'm fine... They've been doing all sorts of tests, but I feel just fine."

She looked around the room.

"I know the protocol. I know why it matters, we all learned it the hard way a long time ago. I just never thought I'd be the one inside the room."

"Right..." said Zach, smiling. He was just happy to see her. There had been a lot going on at work recently and Emily was a breath of fresh air to him. She didn't care about technology or investors, didn't know what monetizing a business model would even mean. She didn't have an angle with him, did not pose as someone she was not. All she cared about was taking care of her patients at the clinic, and she was happy doing so. Her smile warmed Zach's heart.

"How have you been? How come you're not in the room next to me in quarantine also? We were exposed to the same germs..." asked Emily.

"Yes, that's right. But your immune systems are different," replied Dr. Cunningham as he moved closer to the bed. "Actually Zach, you are safe, you don't need to wear a mask, just avoid getting too close."

"That doesn't make sense..." said Emily. "First of all, Tom had the flu, Zach and I should both be affected, shouldn't we? And the trial you were doing was related to a TP53 genetic mutation, which you have..." she added, pointing to Zach. "As far as I know I don't have this mutation, so what's going on?"

Zach looked at the doctor, he wanted to find out the answer too. He sat down on the other side of the bed and took his mask off. He wanted to grab Emily's hand but held back. Zach hadn't had a chance to catch up with Cunningham and figured the physician would know more by now. He was dying to find out what was going on too.

"There's a lot you don't know... We don't know that much more either, but here is what we understand so far, Emily.

Tom was exposed to the H3N5 flu. This type of flu is caused by a highly dynamic virus that mutates particularly quickly. We didn't realize this at the time when we injected him with the edited TP53 DNA fragments. We didn't worry about it because the H3N5 virus shouldn't be able to interact at all with this set of genes. The protein markers are fundamentally different, and simply don't interact with each other. In his case however, somehow the DNA fragments interacted with a series of sites adjacent to TP53. They weren't supposed to, but it appears they did. It also appears to have impacted his telomerase levels and as a result his telomeres started shrinking at an accelerated rate. The change actually appears to have been dramatic." Cunningham paused, letting Emily and Zach absorb the information.

"His telomeres were affected? They shrank? So, he aged... faster?" asked Emily.

"Much faster. You couldn't see it from the outside because his skin was unaffected, but his inner organs looked radically different, much older."

"No way... so much so that it killed him?"

"It's hard to tell at this point. We have more questions than answers..."

"How come Zach is not affected? He has the TP53 mutation and I actually don't, so what's going on there?"

"Well, we're still trying to figure it out, but from what we can tell, the telomerase interaction is not linked to the TP53 sites. It appears related to the edited DNA binding to a nearby DNA segment that you likely share with Tom since you are related. We believe this segment was also impacted by Tom's own biohacking, though we can't tell at this time what sort of hacking he might have done."

Emily and Zach were both taking it in. This was all new information to both. Zach's mind was kicking into overdrive.

"Wait, so you think whatever biohacking he did caused his telomeres to shrink? Or rather, it somehow interacted with the materials we injected?" asked Zach.

"You got it," said Cunningham. "The likelihood of the TP53 edits affecting his telomeres is relatively small given what we know. We've done similar edits on animal models before, including pigs and monkeys. These are fairly good proxies for the human body. We did not expect any issues with this. The most likely explanation is that he modified his own DNA with some biohack, and that wreaked havoc with our edit. I wish he'd disclosed what he did to us..."

"Well, it's a little late now, isn't it?" said Emily, her tone turning sharp.

"Emily, the good news is so far you are unaffected. We'll keep monitoring you," replied Cunningham.

"Hold on, isn't there a way for us to figure out what Tom did? Can't we analyze all adjacent gene sequences and reverse engineer what we did? Then we'd be able to see what we're dealing with..." said Zach.

"In theory we could, but the problem is, we can only observe the result of what he did," replied Cunningham. "We'd need a ton of processing power to reconstruct the hack from the resulting gene sequence. We also don't even know which algorithm to apply to reverse engineer his hack. It's a truly complicated inverse problem, Zach. In some ways it's like having to rebuild a CAT scan from MRI data, but without knowing what you're looking for. The data set is also much larger. It's never been done, Zach."

Emily jumped in.

"Tom did mention a few things about his biohacking to me. He was obsessed with junk DNA. He said people think it's junk, but it's not junk at all. He seemed obsessed with the notion that people are walking hard drives, it made no sense to me."

Zach smiled.

"Well, he wasn't actually that wrong..."

Emily shook her head and frowned at Zach in disbelief.

"Think about it," said Zach, looking at her. "We carry twenty-three pairs of chromosomes. Each chromosome includes about a hundred and forty million base pairs, and a base pair consists of an amino acid pairing using adenine, thymine, cytosine, and guanine. There can be four possible pairings of these amino acids, which can therefore be represented using two bits. Now do the math... two bits per base pair times a hundred and forty million base pairs times twenty-three chromosomes times two is about one and a half gigabytes! So yes, from that perspective you can think of human genes as an exotic walking thumb drive, except you can't stick it in your pocket as easily..." said Zach triumphantly.

Dr. Cunningham was smiling, while Emily seemed lost in thought, still processing Zach's math.

"Now think also about the following," he added. "The active coding fraction of our DNA is about eight to fifteen percent, meaning about one eighth of our DNA is used to do useful things like encode protein sequences in our bodies. That means we don't in fact understand what the other seven eighths are for, it doesn't seem to have a role we can figure out. This is why people call it non-coding, or junk, DNA."

"Well, hang on Zach, non-coding DNA is involved in epigenetic activity, it may have a role in evolutionary developmental biology..." countered Dr. Cunningham.

"Doctor, you and I both know this is fancy talk for '*we just don't know what it does*'... and that's why it's called junk DNA," said Zach sharply.

While Zach was talking Emily had propped herself up and locked her eyes on him.

"I didn't realize..." she finally said.

"Really cool, right?" replied Zach, clearly enthusiastic about this convergence of biology and computer science.

"Now I understand why Tom would say that then..." said Emily. "And what's a Grover search? What does it have to do with any of this? Tom kept saying a Grover search is key to unlocking our junk DNA."

"Mmhh, that's interesting. I'm not sure, we'll need to figure that out" replied Zach. "Grover's algorithm is a special kind of quantum computing algorithm. It's used for database searches and also to reverse engineer certain types of encryption..."

Emily fell back on her pillow, wincing as if in pain.

"Ouch, oh, bad headache. I'm not sure why..." she said, holding her forehead.

Dr. Cunningham glanced at Zach with a knowing look.

"Maybe you should rest, Emily," said the doctor. "We should go anyway."

As Zach and Cunningham left Emily's room, a text flashed across Zach's phone. It came from Masha, Zach's head of marketing and trusted analyst:

"*Need to talk re: sales. latest numbers look way off, am putting a plan together to get us back on track. we can discuss when you're back.*"

"Way off? What kind of message is that?" thought Zach, as he jumped into his car to go back to the office.

17

Masha was staring at her computer screen, her mind racing. She still hadn't gotten over her last discussion with Zach.

Yes, he's not unlike a lot of other brash tech founders and CEOs, she thought. Still, she found his ability to blur the boundaries between reality and imagination startling. It wasn't completely unexpected. When you had access to so much in the way of financial and technology resources, reality found a way of conforming to your imagination. All you had to do was will it with enough willpower and tenacity, and it would eventually materialize... Still, what Zach had done, sell stock in the face of bad news which she knew would negatively impact their share price in a very material way, that was just plain wrong.

Maybe she was not truly American. Maybe she was born in Moscow, the daughter of Slovenian-Russian immigrant parents who had sought a better, and more stable, life in the United States, but she did know what was in fact American. And insider trading was not, not the right kind anyway.

As a child, she had often watched American movies and marveled at what seemed like orderly civilization compared to the chaos of Russia. Back there, you simply couldn't find out what was true and what was not. Life appeared to unfold in an uncontrolled way, guided by the conflicting whims of corrupt bureaucrats who thought nothing of taking bribes, embezzling state funds, and funneling it all into private bank accounts in Cyprus. That was just a way of life. The United States, by contrast, seemed like a dream. The rule of law, separation of powers, its Puritan emphasis on saying what you do and doing what you say. A lot of her friends and parents' friends had mocked it as propaganda, more lies, an obviously unrealistic view of life. Hypocrisy and more lies.

But to her, to the little Russian immigrant girl who had attended Woodbridge middle school in Northern Virginia, who had dutifully followed Mrs. McLaughlin's American history class, there was truth and power to this view. Idealistic as she might be, Masha thought following the truth was not only the more ethical path, but also the simpler, more aesthetic path. The path not followed by her CEO, she reminded herself.

She looked at the numbers one more time and frowned. She didn't like what she saw and needed to explain to Zach what was going on, so they could act on it. Masha was still working through her analysis as Zach knocked on her glass door.

"Hey Masha, I saw your text, what's up? What's going on with sales this time?" said Zach, matter-of-factly. Ever since their last discussion, he had been treading somewhat carefully around Masha. He knew that she held information that could get him in trouble with what was now a formal SEC investigation. She didn't know about the investigation yet, but he was careful not to antagonize her. He also thought she had always been a trooper, and had too much to lose if things went south. She would play along, he thought, they all do with me.

"Well, it's not like I didn't tell you... Our latest actual sales numbers are okay for now, but I'm telling you, this is not going to last, and we need to do something. Our total lead volume is down thirty percent, pipeline value is down twenty five percent. On the plus side our conversion rates — MQL to SQL, SQL to SAL, etc — are flat. Our cycle times are extending a bit, up ten percent," said Masha, finding comfort in the conspicuous use of jargon as a way of projecting competence.

"So... what's the net impact of all that?" replied Zach, trying not to get annoyed.

"That means our sales are still holding up but it's not going to last. It only confirms what I had already told you... You can expect our sales to drop at least thirty percent in the next twelve months, Zach. And because our sales cycle with enterprise accounts is so long, between six and twelve months, our ability to affect this trend is limited in the short term. We can ramp up marketing spend, go get more leads, hire more sales people. It'll be a decent investment for next year but it's going to have a fairly limited impact this year Zach," said Masha, droning on.

"What about our international expansion Masha? Have you factored in the new sales team we are fielding in Asia?" countered Zach, growing anxious.

"Yes, I have. Still not going to make a difference this year, Zach."

Surprised, Zach turned around and saw Otto walking into Masha's office. Zach was annoyed to be caught off guard by Otto. Again. Over the years, Otto's status with Quantum had evolved from lead early investor to senior member of the Board to informal chairman of the company. He kept a small office down the hall from Zach's, and came and went as he pleased. He often peppered the staff with suggestions and random questions, and thought of himself as the glue that kept this crazy ship together. Zach harbored mixed feelings about his mentor's meddling, but had come to accept it since he owed much of his wealth to Otto's support and willingness to take risks.

"Hey, Otto, I didn't realize you were here!" said Zach.

"Well, someone's got to mind the store while you're off going after whatever biomedical ventures of yours..." said Otto, in an uncharacteristically passive-aggressive manner. Zach gave him a quizzical stare.

"You may not have noticed Zach, but while you were out our stock dropped another ten percent," added Otto. Of course, Zach knew. He was trying not to roll his eyes. "Well, I called some of my buddies at Deutsche Bank to find out what's really going on. Our last reported sales numbers looked good, and we haven't changed our guidance yet, so it bugged me that the stock would move so much. Keep in mind it's been ten percent today, but it's actually down over thirty percent over the last few weeks."

"Okay..." said Zach, growing impatient with Otto.

"Well the word is some hedge fund kids have been doing channel checks on our sales. They've been calling our sales people directly, hounding our marketing agency, talking to some of our customers and prospects." Otto paused for effect. "And they are definitely starting to figure out what Masha is seeing in her numbers and what she's been trying to explain to you, Zach. We need you focused here, Quantum needs its founder focused on what he's best at: running and developing the business."

Otto had said those last words with a slightly defiant tone. Zach did not appreciate being chided in front of company staff.

"Otto, we should talk in my office," said Zach, trying to re-assert control of the discussion. He then turned to Masha.

"Masha, thanks for the update, I appreciate it. I got it, let me discuss this with Otto for now. Why don't you and I get back together later tomorrow? I want to review your updated marketing plan. Let's make sure we have some measures in there to close the gap."

Zach and Otto then headed for Zach's office. Zach closed the door and turned to Otto.

"Otto, I know you've been instrumental to this company, and I personally owe you a debt of gratitude. But I really don't appreciate when you talk to me like that in front of our team. It accomplishes nothing, and it looks like we undermine each other."

Otto, looking flushed, was about to respond when Zach's phone rang.

"Hello, this is Zach Hayes"

"Hello Zach, this is Vitaliy Kharkov, from FinAlpha Investments..."

"Oh yes, Vitaliy, how are you? How can I help you?" replied Zach. He had never met Vitaliy, but he knew FinAlpha was the investor Otto had brought in to salvage his insider trade.

"You may remember we recently invested thirty million dollars into your company..."

"Yes of course, thank you so much for your trust, Vitaliy. I'm sorry we haven't had a chance to meet yet, but I've heard great things about you from Otto," said Zach, clearly unperturbed by white lies.

Otto glanced at Zach with an inquisitive frown. He didn't like in the least his name being mentioned in close proximity to Vitaliy's given current circumstances.

"So did I Zach, so did I about you. But I'm looking at our stock price now, and I'm starting to have second thoughts."

Zach paused. He didn't like the turn of the conversation with the Russian hedge fund manager.

"Otto and I know the same people at Deutsche Bank, Zach. I talk to them too, and I do not like what I've been hearing recently. It's just not good for business, and it's going to hurt my financial returns if we don't remedy this situation quickly."

"I'm not sure what you mean, Vitaliy. Our last reported financials were excellent, and we've maintained our guidance and outlook for the end of the year. You shouldn't pay attention to hearsay," replied Zach, quickly transitioning into damage control mode.

"Look Zach, I am going to go straight to the point then. I am... how do you Americans say? Pissed, that's right, pissed. I am pissed, Zach. When people hurt my portfolio, I hurt them back. Ten times more. You don't hurt my portfolio, and I don't hurt you. So you're going to find a way to fix your stock price, you're going to get your sales under control and my portfolio will do well, and we'll all be happy."

Zach was stunned, he wasn't sure how to respond.

"How close are you to the homeless clinic manager who got sick with this flu epidemic going around, Zach? I heard the flu is really nasty this year, and she might not make it. It would be a pity, truly, such a smart and attractive woman, to be swept away like that..."

"Don't you..." said Zach, recovering his ability to talk.

"Don't you talk back to me, you little *soplyak*!" said Vitaliy, cutting him off.

"Let me make it really simple for you: you fix this issue, and we're all happy. You don't, and I will be genuinely pissed that you and your partner lied to me. I will come after you and your people, and you and I will both curse the day you took my money. It's really simple. And in case you don't believe me, Zach, I will give you shortly a taste of things to come. Just to make sure you understand how strongly I feel about this. Have a good day, Zach."

Zach hung up, stunned.

18

Otto was staring at Zach.

"So?" inquired Otto.

"Emily! He's going to get to Emily!" replied Zach, almost stuttering. "I have to do something, quick!"

"What do you mean?"

"I'll tell you Otto, I'll call you. But I gotta run, *now*. They're after Emily..."

A few minutes later Zach ran into the lobby of Innova General hospital. As he ran to the elevator, he saw two men by the information desk. Middle-aged, one of them with a tracksuit. *What a dumb idea, who would wear a tracksuit? Oh no, crap...* Careful not to look at them again, Zach jumped into the elevator and pressed the button for the fourth floor.

They're here, I can't believe it, that was fast. Vitaliy is not messing... He was about to blast off the elevator and run to

Emily's room when he had an idea. He turned back and pressed every button from the fifth floor on up.

"At least it'll slow them down some, I need every minute I can get" he muttered.

As Zach barged into Emily's room he found Dr. Cunningham, at her bedside checking her vitals.

"Doctor, so glad I found you guys!" cried Zach. Cunningham turned around, puzzled.

"Emily is in danger, I don't have time to explain. She needs to leave."

"Zach, hi.... She can't. You know she's been quarantined, and she needs medical assistance... What's going on?" asked the doctor.

"Some bad people are after us... Russians... they're in the building. They will take her, maybe kill her. Come on Emily, get up, we need to go, now!"

Both Emily and Cunningham were now staring at Zach, more puzzled than ever.

"They threatened me personally and are coming after Emily to hurt me. Come on guys, no time, we have to go!"

"Zach, I'm a physician, the hospital has rules, I can't let you do this, you realize that..." replied Cunningham, attempting to reason with Zach.

"Doctor, she's very likely going to die if we don't get her out now. She's definitely going to get hurt. Our little TP53 research project? Poof! If it wasn't in trouble after Tom's death, it'll definitely be over then. That means you won't be in a position to help *anybody* and your patients will get hurt."

Zach's urgency was increasing with every exchange.

"Emily, please put on your shoes we gotta go, now," added Zach. Emily got out of bed, still startled, and put on her shoes.

"Zach, she might be contagious, how are you going to deal with this?" asked Cunningham.

"Doctor, we both know most of the population is not susceptible to the mutated virus. She will be wearing a mask when in public. We *can* manage this... The odds certainly beat *her* odds if we stay here."

Cunningham was silent but obviously relenting. He stepped aside, leaving them a clear path out of the room. Both Emily and Zach bolted out of the room. Zach looked toward the elevator and saw the track suit (again!) talking to the nurse at the nurses station. Zach grabbed Emily's hand and ran the opposite way toward the stairs.

"This way, quick Emily. We gotta go to my car... I'm parked on the second level."

Moments later, as they were leaving the hospital garage Emily turned to Zach, and took down her mask.

"Now can you tell me what's going on, Zach? What is this about? Who are these men?"

"I'll tell you but I gotta call Otto first, hold on"

Zach dialed Otto's number.

"Hey Zach, finally! Where are you?" said Otto as he picked up the call.

"Hi Otto. Sorry I had to act fast. I have Emily with me, I just picked her up at the hospital."

"What??"

"We need to get out of dodge Otto, Emily is not safe here, you know that," replied Zach.

"Really? Okay... well I'm on my way to the airport, going to London to see if I can sort our mess with some of Vitaliy's better friends. What are *you* going to do now, how is any of this helping us?"

Zach had an idea.

"Are you on your way to Reagan National? Are you flying your private jet?"

"I know what you're thinking Zach. Yes, I am. Why don't you guys meet me at the FBO there?"

"FBO?"

"The private VIP terminal, where we'll board the jet. We can catch up there," replied Otto.

Zach smiled. A break finally... He loved Otto.

"Fantastic, we have a spot on Otto's jet, we'll be there in a few minutes," he said with a sigh of relief. Emily was growing alarmed.

"A jet? Zach, you'd better tell me what's going on or I'm calling 911!"

"Here is the deal, Emily. Otto and I took money, investor money, from some truly bad people. Russians affiliated with the FSB. We had no choice, we needed the money, and we thought we could manage it."

Emily was staring at Zach.

"We needed the money to fund research for this project that's affecting you. This virus that's in you, you know? It's an experimental virus, it was supposed to contain edited genes for therapeutic purposes, but somehow it got combined with Tom's genes. We didn't expect the virus to recombine and become this bad but it did. So we need time to reverse engineer the recombined DNA, and we need to dodge these angry Russians in the process."

"What does any of this have to do with me? Other than I somehow got affected by your stupid virus?"

"Well, they think you and I are somehow involved..." said Zach sheepishly.

"Involved? You mean romantically involved? Oh, please!" cried Emily. Zach cringed.

"Well, it doesn't matter. They think we are, and they've threatened to hurt you to get to me. These are bad people, Emily. They just have no respect for human life."

"Great! So, what do we do now? Shouldn't we call the police, the FBI, someone who can protect us?"

"We'll be dead by the time we get any help, Emily," replied Zach. He failed to mention he really did not want to explain to the authorities a bunch of Russian investors were after him because of an illegal insider trade gone wrong. He had created this mess, and his self-reliant self was confident he would solve the mess.

"I hate you, you know? I hate the day I met you... Because of you Tom is dead, and now this? When this is over I never want to talk to you again!" said Emily, in an outburst of passionate anger.

Passionate as she was, she was also practical. She sighed.

"Well, let's fix this. It's what I do, fix people's problems. We'll deal with the rest later," she said, leaning back in her chair. She was calming down. Zach smiled. He liked her passion, he liked her mindset. In some ways she was a lot like him.

As they approached the terminal Zach could see a sign above the entrance: *Crestline General Aviation*. They found Otto in the lobby waiting for them.

"You're here, good! Let's go, the plane is ready..." said Otto as he rose. Emily pointed to the bathroom, nodded at Zach and disappeared for a few minutes. Zach sat down next to Otto in one of the lounge chairs, and smiled again. He might be in the midst of a life-threatening chase, but had never felt more alive, and enjoying the trappings of power was just the cherry on the cake for this kid from Baltimore.

"I see she's wearing a mask... is she contagious?" inquired Otto, sitting back down next to Zach.

"Not to worry, she's been cleared, she's not contagious. And most of the population is not susceptible anyway... but her immune system is weakened, and she doesn't need to be exposed to other people's germs," replied Zach.

Another lie, but he couldn't care less. The ends always justified the means in his mind. All they had to do was get on the plane and away from the Russian's henchmen.

Emily came back a few minutes later.

"All right, the flight manifest is updated, let's get on the plane and go. We are wheels up in five minutes!" said Otto cheerfully. The three of them boarded the Falcon 3000LXS and sat down in plush leather chairs. Zach saw the catered tray in the kitchen galley and realized he hadn't eaten in the last twelve hours. He felt ravenous. He grabbed a platter and sat back down next to Emily who, exhausted by the chase and practical as ever, was attempting to nap.

Emily woke up a few hours later. Across the rosewood table Zach and Otto were in the middle of a heated discussion.

"Zach, I didn't realize... at least we're getting you out of harm's way now, but London is not much safer. It's only a matter of time until Vitaliy's guys find you and Emily there."

"It's a big city, Otto, definitely safer than Washington. They won't know where to look for us there, whereas finding us where we live was obvious."

"Yes, you bought yourself some time Zach, but you'd better figure out a plan."

"I think we'll lay low for a few days, and we'll think through our next steps. Maybe I can find us some short-term rental there."

"Don't go for Airbnb, Zach. They have very good hackers and will know to look there... "

"I understand, I figured if I booked a corporate rental through Quantum's account it'd be less obvious? I won't go through a public site, I'll go through our private operator... You have Wi-Fi on this plane, right?" replied Zach.

He pulled out his laptop and booted it up. Zach was careful to use his Quantum VPN connection. Using the company's virtual private network would ensure his interaction would be encrypted and out of the reach of unauthorized users. Zach's company had just rolled out a quantum-encryption-based VPN service that he knew to be unbreakable, now was a perfect time to use it.

You gotta eat your own dog food... he thought to himself, as he watched the VPN client software establish a private connection to the network. Within minutes Zach had booked a one-bedroom short-term corporate rental on Longridge Road in Earl's Court. It was small but, hey, everything was small in London. Best of all, it was inconspicuous. He could always sleep on the sofa; Emily could have the bedroom. He had used a fake name and a corporate credit card number for the booking. He thought it would make it harder to trace the rental back to him. Zach looked back up to Emily, who had taken her mask off.

"There! I got us a place to stay in London for a few days..."

19

The sun was setting on the London skyline as the Falcon 3000LXS landed at Farnborough airport a few miles south of the city.

"Wow, that was faster than I thought," mused Zach, looking at the patchwork of farming plots during their descent.

"Well, we flew at forty-one thousand feet, above the international airliners, at a cruise speed of six hundred miles per hour, so yes, we're fast," replied Otto, flashing a big grin. "The perks of owning your own jet."

They zipped through the VIP terminal and into the car service Otto had booked. About an hour later they stopped in Earl's Court at 72 Longridge Road.

"Thanks for the ride, Otto, I appreciate it," said Zach as he was exiting the car. "Come on, Emily, this is our stop. I got us a furnished rental here for a few days."

The limousine departed and seemed to float away, the engine barely purring as it disappeared into the London traffic. Zach and Emily looked up. They were standing in front of a typical Victorian brownstone, three-story high. Zach felt transported into an old James Bond movie and was expecting to bump into Sean Connery any minute. He smiled as he walked up the steps to the front door. He pulled out the keys they had just picked up at the rental agency (he couldn't believe they had still been open!) and opened the creaky old door. A musty smell came gushing out of the small lobby. To their right were a row of mail-boxes. The staircase was right in front of them, barely a few feet away, while an apartment door was visible in the back to the right of the stairs.

"I think we're on the second floor," said Zach as he climbed up the stairs. Emily was following closely behind him. Virtually every step of the staircase was creaking as they went up.

So much for being discreet, thought Zach. *At least everybody knows if you're coming or going.* It wasn't lost either on him that, as far as he could tell, there was only one way out of the apartment, through this narrow hallway down to the main door.

Zach winced as they walked into the apartment and through the two rooms. It was clean, furnished with mostly new, IKEA-type furniture. It was also small and noisy. From the window they could see Longridge Road on the right and the heavily trafficked Warwick road on the left. They could hear virtually every car and truck passing by below them. Occasionally, they would feel a rumble as a subway train would whiz by a few hundred feet below. It reminded Zach of a cleaner, slightly dressier version of the small house in which he had grown up in Baltimore. He thought about his mother.

"Well, there is one bed and one sofa," said Emily, standing in the doorway between the bedroom and the living room. "I can take the sofa but I will need to use the bathroom!" she said, smiling. She was starting to feel the fatigue of a day spent running.

"No, don't worry, I should take the sofa. It's easier that way," replied Zach, feeling chivalrous. "Man, I just remembered we don't really have a change of clothes... at least we grabbed disposable toothbrushes on the plane!" he added, half-sarcastically and half-triumphantly.

The following morning, Emily decided to go explore the neighborhood and buy a few supplies. Zach opened his laptop and started digging into the DNA data Cunningham had sent him after he completed the gene sequencing of Tom's biopsies. Zach had gotten online using his secure, quantum-encrypted VPN and was careful not to leave virtual tracks behind him before logging into the NIST computing platform he had access to. Zach was staring at twenty-three data files, one for each chromosome pair, taking up about 1.6 gigabytes.

"Funny, I can put a whole human being on an old USB stick," he thought to himself, smiling. The task of decrypting and somehow identifying an arbitrary sequence of DNA adjacent to the TP53 marker in Tom's DNA was overwhelming. There was no way a conventional computer would ever be up to the task, not in a reasonable amount of time anyway. Zach's only chance was to use quantum computing. Because of their reliance on qubits, or quantum bits, units of information that could take on many different values as opposed to the binary bits of traditional chips, quantum computers could accomplish in a few minutes a task that would take thousands of years to complete with a traditional computer.

Zach loaded the data file with Tom's DNA data into the remote quantum server, and started his first genetic search algorithm. He figured he would let it run for the day and see where it goes. In the meantime, he was curious to look at the files Emily had dug up too. Tom had left her a handful of files for safekeeping. Emily had access to them through her phone's cloud storage application, and she had transferred them to Zach's account.

As Zach was going through Tom's files, he couldn't quite make out the meaning of what he was seeing. Clearly these were notes Tom had taken for himself as he was working on his biohacking experiment. It kept referring to an organization Tom was researching, the Young Humans World Hierarchy, or simply the Hierarchy. Tom also kept bringing up his own junk DNA in the notes.

Why would Tom focus on his junk DNA? It's inactive, whatever biohack he was working on wouldn't have an effect on him, thought Zach, puzzled. And then, how would it even interact with the edited materials they had injected in him? And who was behind this Hierarchy? Or did he misunderstand Tom's notes? Was the Hierarchy a shorthand for a theory he was developing? It made no sense to Zach.

At least not yet, he thought to himself as he was interrupted by Emily. As soon as he saw her carefully closing the apartment door, he knew something was going on.

"I think one of your Russian guys might have found us," she said, with an oddly calm voice. "I'm not sure, maybe I'm paranoid but this weird guy was following me. I was stupid, I thought I was just being paranoid. I think I lost him but I'm not sure."

"No way," replied Zach. "There's no way they would know we're here! I didn't even know I was going to be here twenty-four hours ago, and I used our quantum-encrypted VPN when I made the reservation..."

They both rushed to the window to look and see if anybody suspicious was down below in the street. No one. As they stepped away from the window, they heard a muffled sound: the front door creaking below them in the lobby. They glanced at each other.

"A neighbor?" said Emily, trying to channel fear into hope.

"Let me check..." whispered Zach back.

He carefully opened the apartment door and ventured in the stairwell, stepping carefully to avoid making the floor creak. He leaned over the banister and saw a man in his forties with blue overalls apparently doing some work on the mailboxes. Zach sighed with relief. It looked like the building manager had sent the super to perform some maintenance on the mailboxes.

Wow, we were really paranoid! Zach felt sheepish but relieved. Something was off though, but he couldn't put his finger on it. Zach stepped down a few steps and took a second look at the super to better figure out what he was working on, when the man looked up and nodded to him. Zach hesitated, he wasn't sure what to do. Run back to the apartment? But if the man was a bad guy that would be a sure signal. Zach decided instead to play along and kept going downstairs, acting as any neighbor would on a morning run to the convenience store.

"Hi, how are you?" said Zach, aware that his accent would immediately give him away as an American in London. The man nodded back with a smile, but said nothing.

As Zach was walking by, he noticed the super seemed to be cleaning the mailboxes. By chance, he appeared to be cleaning *their* mailbox, number 3, which seemed especially polished. The man was wearing thick gloves, which was a bit incongruous. What forty-something, tall, and rugged man would wear gloves polishing a mailbox? As the man looked back at the wall and kept cleaning with a rag, Zach gave a furtive glance to the bottle of polish he was holding. The bottle was relatively small, made of brown glass. It actually looked more like a medicine bottle than a cleaning product. He could only partially make out the inscription: *ИМЕК*...

Puzzled, Zach kept the charade and left the building then made a left into Longridge Road. What was the man doing holding a bottle of some Russian cleaning product? Luckily, Zach had a photographic memory and had memorized the Cyrillic alphabet back in school, out of boredom. Intrigued, he pulled out his phone and plugged the five letter acronym into a Google search. The first result that came back was about Jarek Dymek, a Polish athlete. That didn't seem right. Zach then had an idea. Since this was a Russian word, why not do the search on a Russian search engine? He then went straight to Yandex's site and typed in the acronym one more time. ... И... М... E...K.

There! he thought, his heart racing as he pressed the enter key. The search engine brought back pictures of the bottle he had seen with the name Димексид next to it, it clearly looked like a medication. Getting impatient, Zach then searched for a translation and quickly found one. His heart sank when he saw the results.

Dimethyl Sulfoxide is reported as an ingredient of Dimexid in the following countries: Georgia, Russian Federation.

DMSO! The man was applying DMSO to the mailboxes! Russian security services had been known to poison former agents using the solvent. Zach then glanced back around to make sure the man hadn't followed him. He quickly jumped into the opening of a building a hundred or so feet down the street, anxious not to be seen while he was thinking through how he was going to get back into the building. The super came out after a few minutes, looked right and left then disappeared into Warwick Road to the right. Zach ran back to the building.

Emily! I hope she didn't come down and touch anything! As he approached the door Zach took out his sweater, and wrapped his hand in it before opening the door. He was careful not to establish direct contact with his skin. He then raced upstairs to the apartment.

"Where were you? I was terrified but didn't want to go out until you came back," said Emily obviously relieved. "What's going on Zach, what took you so long?"

Without saying a word Zach dumped his sweater in the kitchen trash then turned to Emily.

"I think you were followed Emily. The man downstairs in the lobby was applying DMSO to our mailbox"

"DMSO! No way..." she replied, frowning.

"Yes way," said Zach cutting her off. "Russian DMSO no less. A good way to kill without being seen. You can easily dissolve any toxic substance in it. The solvent then will go right through your skin and kill you before you even understand you've been poisoned."

"Russians? You guys *had* to take money from sketchy Russian guys? So, what do we do now?" asked Emily with a sarcasm that was slowing growing into anger and frustration.

"That doesn't matter anymore Emily. We need to get out of here before they come back," replied Zach. "We need to get out of here, now."

Zach and Emily needed a place to hide, preferably out of the city, definitely out of England. In their rush to leave Washington, DC Zach hadn't thought through the fact that a large contingent of Russian financiers and mobsters had made London their second home. In fact, Russians felt so much at home in London that on multiple occasions FSB agents had had no compunction about killing former agents and friends of the Kremlin who had naively taken refuge there, thinking the British police would protect them.

No, they needed some place out of the city, preferably remote and out of England, where they could lose the Russians. Zach looked around the apartment, lost in thought as he was trying to figure a way out of this mess, when his eyes landed on the coffee table. A glossy travel magazine caught his attention. The cover showed a beautiful island in the Mediterranean with the following headline: *Bonifacio, a haven between earth and sea in Corsica.* Zach smiled as an idea formed in his head.

"Hey Emily, have you ever been to Corsica?" he asked playfully.

"What are you talking about?" she replied, puzzled.

"Corsica. It's far yet not too far from here, out of the city, in a country that is hopefully not as friendly to Russian nationals. And it's beautiful. Looks like a great place to go hide for a few days, don't you think?"

Speechless, Emily was starting to smile.

"We can book something online, I think we're still safe doing so since I use our quantum-encrypted network. I want to avoid planes this time, since they must have had access to our passenger manifest somehow, and followed us after we landed. How else would they have known where we were going? We can take a train and get on a boat without using our names, it'll be hopefully more discreet this time. I'm pretty sure the guy is gone for now and I didn't see anybody in the street. Let's leave now before they come back."

"Corsica... well Zach, you are a man full of surprises!"

20

The forty-five-foot ketch was gliding smoothly over the surface of the ocean. The day before, Zach and Emily had arrived in Nice in the South of France after an uneventful train ride from London. Zach had promptly found a skipper at the Port-de-Nice marina willing to take them on a chartered sailboat to Corsica for a week. Sure, the request had seemed odd to Paul, the skipper, but the fact that he was going to bill full rate to Zach with half upfront had taken care of any question he might bring up. They had left immediately, anxious not to waste time.

With dark stormy clouds drifting to the north, the rising sun was now casting a bright orange light over Mount Balagne. The mountain, visible from twenty miles at sea, was the first tangible sign to sailors from times immemorial that the journey from the continent to Corsica was about to be safely completed. Paul, the boat's skipper, stood at the helm on the deck while the rest of the crew, Zach and Emily, were sound asleep inside the cabin after a long shift. The night had been tough with an unexpected storm blowing forty knots, forcing them to change course and keep a floating anchor behind the boat, a much slower speed being the price of safety. The Mediterranean was a treacherous sea, calm and easy to navigate in appearance, when in fact the unpredictable weather had claimed countless ships and lives.

"Nothing an old sailor can't deal with," muttered Paul.

Sailing's emphasis on preparedness and teamwork, the fact that real lives were always at stake, turned what could have been a hobby into a real game with real outcomes, and Paul liked that. He was enjoying this fleeting moment of calm, the triumph of human endurance, when he heard some noise inside the cabin.

"Are you guys waking up? I sure could use a little coffee up here!"

"Yeah, I'll put some water on the stove," grunted Zach.

Minutes later Zach climbed back on the deck with two warm mugs, looking as disheveled as a frat boy after a night of binge drinking. Last night's storm had been his first ever on a sailboat, and although its bodily impact was similar to that extra tequila shot he shouldn't have taken back in earlier days, the storm just hadn't been quite as fun.

"Man, I thought this was going to be the end of us last night. I can't believe we made it through," said Zach.

"Come on Zach, it wasn't so bad. I love rough weather. It focuses your mind, forces you to concentrate on essentials. Plus it's not like we're on a dinghy. This ship could take us across the Atlantic!" said Paul, obviously happy to have inflicted a small dose of fear and pain on an unsuspecting soul.

They noticed the loud sputter of a powerboat in the distance.

"Look," said Paul. "I wonder what an offshore is doing out at sea. You generally don't see these guys until the afternoon, when the babes are out on the pier."

Emily emerged on the deck. Even after what had been a difficult night for the three of them, the twenty-eight-year-old looked stunning. Somehow the coarse wool sweater, the lack of make-up, the slight wind-induced redness of her cheeks, made her seem even more attractive.

"Good morning guys! I feel so much better now that the storm is over. I heard you talking. What were you looking at?"

Zach found himself dumbstruck, for the first time in a while. Paul turned around and smiled.

"Hi Emily. I'm glad you're feeling better. We were just wondering what a powerboat is doing out here this early. They usually come out in the afternoon and stay much closer to the shore," said Zach.

"They must have gotten lost..." muttered Paul. "Well, either way it looks like they are going back to shore, see?" he added as the boat disappeared in the distance.

They kept on sailing for another couple of hours until they finally came within a quarter mile of Calvi and its harbor. Zach went inside the cabin to grab a pair of binoculars. He started scanning the coast line stretching right in front of them.

"Mmhh, is this Calvi? I can't believe it, I didn't expect it to be so crowded," he said with a slight grimace. He could see tourists on the pier, restaurants by the old harbor bustling with activity. "Can we find a place that's a bit more quiet?"

"Well, let me think about it..." replied the skipper. "We can keep going due south-by-southwest and in another thirty minutes we will be at the Bay of Girolata. This time of the year I doubt there'll be anybody other than us. We just won't get access to any port facilities while we're there."

Zach studied the marine map. Girolata was about forty miles south of Calvi surrounded by wilderness and with only one small road for rural access. Paul was right, it really was out of the way. They would still have access to the rest of the world with the boat's satellite link. This was a perfect place to lie low for a week, so they could figure out how to deal with the Russians and what had happened to Tom.

"Perfect," said Zach. "Let's go for it!"

Thirty minutes later, as planned, Paul was dropping anchor in the Bay of Girolata. All they could see around them was a wall of cliffs and steep hills, covered in dry brush. Just ahead of them was a small sand beach, making for an easy landing with a dinghy if they needed to go to shore. The water sloshed gently, clear as a crystal. Zach could see the anchor all the way down on the ocean floor, fifteen feet below them.

Once they eventually settled Emily, exhausted, went inside the boat's front cabin to catch some sleep. Zach felt restless. He wanted to go back to Tom's DNA files and dig deeper into what was or wasn't going on. Zach grabbed his laptop, made himself comfortable in the cockpit and logged back online into the quantum computing platform where he kept Tom's DNA files. He was careful as always to use fully encrypted communications while using the boat's satellite connection, so he wouldn't leave any mark of his presence online.

Zach didn't understand why Tom would keep mentioning junk DNA in his notes and to Emily. That made no sense for biohacking purposes since junk DNA was believed to be inactive and exhibited no known effect on the human body.

"Why?" thought Zach. His laptop's fan started purring loudly, as it posted a software update notice. It looked like a big update that might clog his Internet connection and clutter his drive. Zach thought of an idea. He remembered his conversation with Cunningham and Emily a few days earlier about human DNA being like a thumb drive with about one-and-a-half gigabytes of storage capacity.

"Unless... unless you use it to store information. Information that's not related to your genome. Data that is not biological!"

Zach was getting excited. This sounded crazy though. Zach started looking at the DNA data files. He honed in on the junk portion and realized it just appeared to be a set of encrypted files. There was clearly structure to the base-4 data contained in them, but without an encryption key, assuming that's what he was looking at, the data would be useless.

He fired up his decryption utility software and started scanning the files to identify file structure and format, encryption type, anything else he could find out. With a conventional computer he would not stand the slightest chance to decrypt Tom's data within a human lifetime, but he was logged into a high-end quantum computing server and thought it would be worth trying to break the encryption. After a few tries, Zach figured out Tom's files were all AES-256 encrypted, and decided to focus his efforts on the first file of the set. After about five minutes, the quantum decryption algorithm managed to break the file's encryption. Zach could barely contain himself. He glanced around and saw that Emily was still sleeping inside the front cabin, while Paul the skipper was enjoying a beer on the front deck, his legs hanging overboard. Zach looked back at his computer. The file's decrypted content appeared on the screen. It read like a log with notes from Tom.

"5/05. *Am making progress with Fano but the Hierarchy is tracking me. Need to use stronger encryption.*

5/07. *Bad day, couldn't figure out how to boost storage capacity but I think I can improve the upload speed. Initial tests are encouraging with speeds exceeding 50 kbps. I need to finish this before the Hierarchy catches up*"

After a few minutes scanning the decrypted file Zach turned his attention to the other files, hoping he could quickly glean more information. Unfortunately the files appeared to be encrypted with a separate key. He would have to break the encryption key one file at a time. Zach's phone rang, it was Otto calling.

"Hello Zach, where are you? I thought you were still in London, but from the ring of your line I can tell you've left the country," asked Otto.

"Hey Otto, we needed to leave in a hurry. Turns out the Russians found us incredibly fast in London. Am still not sure how, and I'm a bit freaked out to be honest. We're in a safe place now," replied Zach, careful not to disclose his actual location. He wondered whether he could still trust Otto.

"Okay, well in the meantime I have been reaching out to the Fundação people to try to mediate this whole Russian debacle. I think with a bit of luck I can buy us some time Zach, but we really need to figure out how to get our sales back up, frankly. That's the easiest, cleanest way to move our stock back up and get these damn Russians to back off. And with you away and on the run you're not making this any easier you know? You need to get your team on this. Because if we can't solve this soon...."

"Otto, I know, thanks for pointing out the obvious. I've stayed in touch with Masha back home, she's got our close-the-gap plan together, she's solid and I trust her," replied Zach.

"Great," said Otto, with visible relief. "I have seen her work Zach, but please tell me you're personally on this?"

"Yes, I am," said Zach. He just wanted to get rid of Otto at this point. All he could think of was going back to Tom's files. "Look, I gotta go Otto, let's talk again later. Bye."

He hung up and immersed himself back in his laptop. Tom's second file was proving much harder to crack. It had taken only a few minutes to crack the encryption key of the first file. Zach expected the next file would be easy as well, but that was not the case. Somehow the encryption method appeared to be utterly different. Pausing to ponder why the two files would be encrypted so differently, Zach's mind started to wander. Of course if Tom was paranoid, encrypting all thirty-two files with different technology would be more secure. But why do so? Was he genuinely that paranoid? And how did that relate to the edited DNA materials Dr. Cunningham had inserted in Tom's genome during the TP53 trial?

The TP53 edits were unencrypted so Zach could in theory search for the gene sequence and find where it ultimately landed, that would be a good start if they were going to understand what had happened to Tom and figure out an antidote. If not... Zach shuddered at the thought of what would happen to Emily. She seemed so fit right now, yet soon her telomeres would shrink at an accelerated rate, her organs would age rapidly, and she would likely be dead of some organ failure in the next month or so. No, Zach needed to figure this out and fast.

21

Zach emerged from the cabin into the cockpit the following morning feeling groggy. He hadn't slept well the night before. Too much going on. It was now shortly after sunrise, and he was hoping the early morning breeze was going to clear his mind once and for all. He settled in the back of the cockpit with a cup of coffee and looked around. The Gulf of Girolata around him was coming alive. He smiled as he heard the gentle slosh of a pod of dolphins playing in the water. The findings of the prior night were still swirling in his mind. He had called Cunningham and left a voicemail. He knew the doctor was busy, yet he couldn't help feeling frustration. Zach was the investor after all, the donor. Shouldn't Cunningham get back to him ASAP?

The cabin cover creaked as it pulled open. Zach looked up and saw Emily come out. Her eyes were puffy with sleep, and she had simply thrown on a sweater and a pair of jeans, yet he was mesmerized by her. Her nose was slightly red, her eyes a clear green blueish hue. She stretched her long legs and sat next to Zach.

"Hey stranger, what are you working on?"

"Oh, same old stuff, still looking into Tom's files and trying to figure out what he did to himself."

Emily chuckled.

"You know, if you had told me a week ago what was about to happen, I would have thought you were crazy... yet, I can't believe it *did* happen."

She smiled and went on.

"A week later Tom is dead, and I somehow followed some cocky dude to the other end of the world. At least you had the good taste to take me to Corsica. It could have been worse I suppose...."

Zach wasn't sure how to react. Emily was finally warming up to him, and he really hadn't expected that.

"Right... see, I'm not such a bad guy?"

"Joke aside though, you'd better figure this out and soon. I need to go back home, we can't just be camping out here forever on this sailboat, you know?"

Zach looked into her eyes as she was talking. She clearly didn't fully grasp the gravity of the situation. How would she? The episode with the Russians had prodded her into following Zach, but she didn't comprehend the risk to her health, having been exposed to the virus that had killed Tom. Well, it was technically not a virus that killed him but the genetically edited materials the virus had carried. It truly made no difference; she would be dead soon either way if Zach didn't figure it out.

"Yeah, I know. Let me figure it out, I think I have a shot at cracking the code," said Zach before immersing himself back into his laptop.

"All right, well, I'll go take a dip before breakfast then. Might as well enjoy our forced vacation!"

Emily disappeared into the cabin to go change herself, while Zach dialed Cunningham's number one more time. He really needed to talk to him. A voice finally came on the other end of the line.

"Alleluia! Doctor, you're alive!"

Cunningham ignored Zach's sarcasm.

"Hey Zach, I have a day job too, you know? First of all, how is Emily? Please tell me you've been avoiding crowded areas..."

"Yes sir. We flew private to Europe, we're now on a boat in an isolated area. Emily's been fine so far." He didn't want to disclose his location in case the line was tapped somehow. He also failed to mention the train ride from London to Nice as he simply didn't want to deal with the inevitable lecture that would follow if he did.

"Good."

"So, here is what I want to chat with you about. I think we may have a path to reverse engineering Tom's biohack. If I can do that, then we can come up with an antidote and reverse the damage we did."

"Okay?"

Zach spent the next few minutes updating Cunningham on his findings with Tom's junk DNA, the encrypted materials. He was careful to stay focused on genetic findings only, and left out Tom's log. There was no need to bring up the Hierarchy, Zach wanted to figure that out first. He simply needed Cunningham's help to reverse the impact of the biohack onto their therapy.

"Well," said Cunningham after a while, "it sounds like you've definitely made some progress, Zach."

"Yes, I know!"

"I think I can send you the TP53 sequence we edited in the viral materials we injected Tom with. If what you say is right, you'll be able to identify which sites they attached to. We'll still need to simulate and reverse the potential chemical interactions that occurred at these sites, but your approach makes sense to me, the quantum platform is the way to go. No way this would ever work using a traditional computer."

"Great, can't wait to have these files from you doctor! Talk to you later," replied Zach before hanging up. Looking around he saw Emily who had by now changed into a bathing suit and was ready to take a dip in the ocean. The water was bright turquoise, and the sun was gently warming their skin.

"I'm going swimming," said Emily. "We can't be here and not enjoy it at least a little bit. See you on the beach!"

"I really gotta finish this. Give me thirty minutes and I'll join you," replied Zach. Emily didn't wait. She jumped straight in the water from the back of the boat and started swimming toward the beach a few hundred feet away. Zach sighed and focused back on his work. Paul had gone below to nap, the front cabin hatch clicking shut behind him.

A few minutes later a link to the files showed up in his email. He uploaded the files to his online file system and got his DNA site matching software started. Within a few minutes he got an answer. The software had matched precisely the location of the viral strands that had gotten attached to Tom's DNA. As expected, the materials were unencrypted and comparatively easy to locate, virtual graffiti on Tom's genome. Next was the hard part, unraveling through a computational simulation the chemical interactions that had taken place in these sites, so Zach could recover the original encrypted materials in Tom's DNA before the viral materials had been injected. Anxious, Zach started a diagnosis script on the data to assess the size of the job at hand. The results came back unambiguous and worrisome. Even using his leading-edge quantum computing platform, there wasn't enough power to simulate and reverse engineer Tom's biohack. The system would either run out of memory or take several lifetimes to complete the task. Zach was frustrated. To have come all this way to run into this! There had to be a way, otherwise the viral infection would turn into an epidemic. Its impact would be catastrophic. Most important of all, it would likely kill Emily.

He was still deep in thought when he heard water sloshing. Looking behind him, down in the water he could hear Emily.

"Zach, help! I don't know what happened, I can't get back on the boat!"

"You ok?"

"I don't know, I was swimming back from the beach when I

got really tired all of a sudden. I'm exhausted, I don't know why..."

He helped her up the swim ladder. She sat on the stern, breathing harder than a short swim should have warranted.

"You okay?"

"Fine. Just tired."

She pulled her knees up and wrapped her arms around them, looking out at the water.

"I used to swim a mile every morning. Back home."

Zach sat down across from her. He closed the laptop.

"Back home meaning Baltimore?"

"Back home meaning the pool at the Y on North Avenue. Six a.m., before the clinic opened."

She paused.

"My dad used to say that was vanity. Swimming for the sake of it, not going anywhere. I told him going somewhere was overrated."

"He sounds like he had opinions."

"He had opinions about everything."

She almost smiled.

"He would have had opinions about you."

"Good ones or bad ones?"

She thought about it seriously, the way she approached most things.

"He would have seen you coming from a mile away. The hunger. He'd have recognized it. He grew up hungry too, different kind of hungry, but still. He would have understood that part. The other parts..." She shrugged. "He was a patient man. He would have waited to see which way you went."

Zach looked at the water. The surface of the bay was completely still now, the afternoon light turning it the color of old glass.

"Which way do you think I'm going?" he asked.

Emily didn't answer right away. A tern landed on the bow and sat there, improbably still.

"I think you're smarter than you are wise," she said finally. "And I think you know it. And I think that gap is where most of your problems live."

He laughed, a short, genuine laugh, the kind that surprised him.

"That's the most accurate thing anyone's ever said about me."

"Tom was the same way."

Her voice changed slightly when she said his name. Not breaking, just changing register.

"He was the smartest person I knew, honestly. The things he understood, the connections he made. But he always thought if he just knew enough, he could outrun the consequences. Like the rules were for people who hadn't done the math."

"Maybe they are."

"No." She said it simply, without argument. "They're not. That's just what smart people tell themselves."

The tern took off. They watched it go.

"What do you believe in?" he asked. He wasn't sure why he asked it. It came out before he could calculate whether it was the right question.

She tilted her head slightly. "You mean God."

"I mean anything. You have this... " He gestured vaguely. "This thing. Where the world is clearly terrible and you still seem to think it means something. I've never been able to do that. I've always just tried to fix the terrible parts."

"Maybe that's the same thing."

"It's not."

"No," she admitted. "It's not." She looked at her hands. "I believe that showing up matters. Even when you can't fix it. Especially when you can't fix it. My dad sat with dying people his whole life. People who had nothing, who were sick, who were scared. He couldn't fix any of it. But he stayed. He stayed until the end every time." She paused. "That changed people. Not fixed. Changed."

Zach was quiet for a moment. The light was dropping now, the mountains above Girolata going from green to shadow.

"My mother died alone," he said. "I was at school. By the time I got home..." He stopped. "I've been fixing things ever since. I don't know how to just stay."

Emily looked at him. Not with pity, he would have hated pity. With something more careful than that.

"You're here," she said. "Aren't you?"

He didn't answer. But he didn't go back inside either.

They sat on the stern as the bay went dark around them, the anchor chain ticking softly against the hull, and for the first time since Baltimore, Zach Hayes was not thinking about the next move.

22

The following morning Emily found Zach, as had now become his daily routine, nestled in the cockpit and hunched over his laptop. Paul was getting breakfast ready in the kitchen galley. A small camping table was set up in the middle of the cockpit. The sun had risen about an hour ago and the air was still, the dryness comfortable. Emily looked rested, clearly happier and more relaxed than the previous day.

"Hey guys, good morning! I am *famished*! Can't wait to get some breakfast..."

"Here you go Emily, you guys grab breakfast. I've set things up in the cockpit, let me know if you need anything. I need to clean up the cabin," intoned Paul.

Emily sat down at the table. Zach put down his laptop and followed suit. She looked at him, her expression changed.

"Today is Sunday... I would have been in church for our Sunday service."

Zach wasn't sure how to react.

"Okay, well, hopefully you'll be back next week. They may not have noticed you missed today."

"Yes, they will. The good news is they'll probably think I'm still sick. Unless they went to the hospital to check on me..."

"By the way Emily, I've been meaning to ask you. Why do you go to church?"

"What do you mean?"

"Well, what's the deal about it? I mean, you are a saint all week at the clinic, you take care of everybody there. Don't you want to chill on a Sunday and recharge before the week starts all over again?"

"But that's the point Zach, Sundays in church *do* recharge me..."

"What is it about it? I guess it's an introvert/extrovert thing? I'm an introvert, I need time alone to recharge, to me being around so many people would be draining."

"No it's not an introvert/extrovert thing, as you say. It's about doing good, about community, about love, Zach."

Zach's heart skipped a beat. He couldn't tell where the conversation was going and wasn't sure whether Emily was trying to signal something. He stared at her with a quizzical look on his face.

"Christian love, Zach. Remember, *turn the other cheek*?" added Emily, quoting the New Testament.

"I've always wondered about that. Where I come from, *an*

eye for an eye works fine. Anything less and you come across as weak. And weak gets you in trouble."

Now it was Emily's turn to give Zach a funny look.

"My mother was like you, you know. She took care of everybody. Took care of me at home. Took care of her co-workers at the warehouse. Went to church, occasionally. You know what it got her? Nothing. When she needed help the most, she got none. She died because she couldn't afford her treatment and no one would help. She died alone because I wasn't even there when it happened."

Zach's voice was strengthening. He was trying to contain the rising anger he thought long gone.

"I'm sorry Zach, I had no idea."

"No worries, this was a long time ago. But in my world, there's no such thing as turning the other cheek. You're either strong and do what it takes, take what you need. Or you're weak and die alone. Well, I guess we all die alone eventually, but you might as well live a better, longer life."

"How sad... I'm sorry it's caused so much pain for you."

"It's okay, you didn't know. So, what's *your* lesson, what guides you then?"

"As I said Zach, it's all about love. That's the only lesson there is. The only thing that matters after we're long gone, Zach. That's my lesson, that's why I do what I do."

Both paused to eat a bite. A moment passed. Emily eventually broke up the silence.

"Well, I hope you change your mind some day."

Zach smiled.

"Maybe, who knows? I'd better get back to work, we really need to figure out what biohack Tom did, or we'll run out of time and none of this will really matter."

Zach went back to his laptop. He needed to figure out a way to rig together a more powerful computing platform, so he could reverse engineer the biohack. He had learned one thing during his early years as an engineer. Always go back to first principles and build from there. Everything that surrounds us was built by people who at one point or another went back to first principles and figured out a better way. He trusted his instinct, he trusted his abilities, he knew he would figure this out.

He pulled up the schematics for the quantum server from the online knowledge base and stared at them for a while. The quantum chipset was state of the art. It consisted of 128 octagon lattices, each lattice itself an arrangement of eight units supporting a quantum bit. This was a 1024-qubit design, the latest commercially available design. Because its computational power grew exponentially with the number of qubits, it was exponentially faster than a conventional computer, which explained how it would break encryption algorithms previously thought unbreakable. Yet for all its power it was still unable to decrypt Tom's DNA. Zach came up with an ingenious way to jury-rig four chipsets together into a virtual quad core to make a virtual 4096-qubit system. It was worth trying he thought. The problem though was going to be maintaining quantum coherence between all four chipsets so all 4096 qubits would operate in sync. Zach realized he could try to use the error correction code they had developed at Quantum to maintain coherence and operate the virtual quad core. He didn't have a copy of it, but he thought he would be able to access the production code. That code was loaded on the quantum encryption gateway he was using online when accessing his VPN. Zach quickly logged into the gateway using his root user credentials. Being the founder he had access to the entire computing infrastructure of the company.

Within minutes, he was able to locate the source code and download it to his machine. Out of curiosity he decided to check the logs of the encryption gateway. He was still puzzled by the fact that the Russians had known where to find them in London. He knew his quantum encryption to be unbreakable, in theory, but wondered about it. Quantum encryption relied on strange quantum properties, in particular on the fact that only the recipient could inspect the encrypted bits. Should someone intercept the message, the encrypted bits would be in a different quantum state, and the recipient would realize right away the transmission was compromised.

As he pored over the logs comparing different gateways across the network Zach realized with horror that some of the bits transmitted had collapsed into different states at different points of the network. This meant someone had intercepted his transmissions, which would only be possible in one of two cases. Either the eavesdropper had far more advanced technology, or the transmissions were somehow reflecting different realities. The latter was impossible. *There is only one reality*, thought Zach. Although there had been that paper out of Edinburgh a few years back. Two physicists demonstrating that separate observers could measure incompatible quantum states, both results valid within their own reference frame. The mainstream had dismissed it as a fluke. Zach had filed it under interesting but irrelevant. He filed it there again now. It had to be a more advanced technology. *How on earth had someone developed more advanced quantum technology?* None of this made sense.

Zach paused and looked around. Paul had come back from the front deck after lounging in the sun. He was going down the ladder into the main cabin when he slipped and tumbled down. Clearly hurt, he couldn't help but yelp a brief cry.

"Vot der'mo!"

Zach froze. That didn't sound English or French at all. In fact, it sounded distinctly Russian. Paul stood up, his head in the cabin opening. Zach's eyes locked onto his. A million thoughts rushed through his mind, as his body was working through its fight-or-flight response. Before he had a chance to do anything Paul jumped on him in the cockpit and attempted to put him into a headlock.

Zach was thrashing and frantically trying to loosen Paul's grip but to no avail. Paul kept Zach in a headlock with one arm and reached for the main sheet. He started wrapping the rope around Zach's neck. Zach felt blood throbbing in his head. In a moment of desperation, he extended his arm on the side, reaching for something, anything. He sensed cold, hard steel under his fingers. The winch handle! He grabbed it and hit Paul in the head as hard as he could. Paul loosened his grip. Zach extricated himself and was now facing his attacker. Paul, recovering from the blow, lunged at Zach. Zach hit him again in the face with the winch handle. Paul stopped. His skin had broken and his cheek was now bleeding. Feeling the rush of aggression coursing through his veins, Zach did not stop. He hit Paul's head again, and again, and again. He slammed and slammed until Paul lay at the bottom of the cockpit, his face a bloody lifeless mess.

Zach sat on the side for a few minutes in a state of shock, processing what had just happened. The fight had happened so fast that Emily was still sleeping in the front cabin. He spotted his smart phone at the bottom of the cockpit, smeared in Paul's blood. Zach leaned over and started cleaning it, wiping it on his pants. The phone vibrated. It was Otto calling.

"Zach, this is Otto. I think the Russians have figured out where you are. I just spoke with Igor...."

"I know"

"You know?"

"Yes, I think one of them just tried attacking us. We're okay... for now."

"Crap. Well I'm glad you're okay but you should probably get going. I was catching up with Igor trying to see if there was another way of unwinding their investment, and he made it clear to me they're after you and they're tracking you."

"Well we'd better get moving then. I gotta go, Otto. talk to you later."

23

Emily emerged through the main cabin hatch.

"Hi Zach! I feel so much better now. I heard you guys making a ruckus, what's going on?"

Zach was dumbstruck. Emily couldn't see Paul's body at the bottom of the cockpit. *Where do I even start?* He turned around and smiled.

"Hey, glad you're feeling better... "

Please don't come out on the deck, not until I've had a chance to explain it to you...

"Stay in the cabin and chill, I'll be down there with you in a minute..."

Before Zach could finish his sentence Emily was climbing the main cabin ladder out and into the cockpit. She froze when she noticed the limp bloody mass on the floor.

"Oh my god! Zach! What happened?" she cried.

"Don't freak out Emily! Everything is fine now. Paul tried to attack me. I figured out he was Russian, and he jumped on me. I had to defend myself, he was going to strangle me... I didn't mean to do this but it was him or me. I can't believe I'm still alive... I think the Russians have figured out a way to track us somehow. Otto just called me to warn us about it."

Emily was stunned, speechless. She came out and sat down next to Zach. A moment passed. She was about to speak when they heard the loud sputter of a powerboat in the distance. *Why would an offshore be out cruising at 8am?* thought Zach. *Is that the same boat we saw the other day?*

"Check this out," said Emily "is it me or are they coming toward us?"

Zach grabbed a pair of binoculars.

"Mmmh. I guess you're right. Well, they can go eighty knots when our top speed is eight knots, I guess we'll have to see what they're up to."

The powerboat, a 2,000-III Scarab S-502, was rapidly approaching. Two men were visible on the deck. Zach was tracking the powerboat through his binoculars. His senses were telling him something was wrong. Growing up in the streets of Baltimore, he had quickly learned to develop an acute sense of situational awareness. The powerboat seemed too powerful to be a customs boat. The time also was wrong. No, this was not a patrol or a leisure outing. This was a boat on a mission, a mission that appeared to involve their forty-five-foot ketch, much to Zach's dismay. Suddenly he realized the powerboat crew was holding semi-automatic rifles. Alarmed, he turned to Emily.

"Emily, go call these guys on channel 16 and ask them what they want. You've seen Paul do it, just switch the top dial to 16. They seem armed and I don't like it. Meanwhile, I'll get the anchor up and start the engine. I'll set course full speed on Bonifato Bay, due south. That'll give us more time to figure out what's going on."

The ketch started rocking slowly as it picked up speed. Zach knew this was a futile attempt to gain more time and could feel the adrenaline rushing through his veins. They would not be able to escape the powerboat if it was in fact trying to catch up with them. He could only hope to figure out a plan by the time the mysterious patrol would reach the sailboat.

"Hey Zach, they're not answering," said Emily, popping her head through the escape hatch. "No way we're having a customs inspection..."

Emily never finished her sentence. The powerboat was now less than a hundred feet away. Zach heard a series of loud cracks. He turned around and spotted a splatter of blood on the white epoxy deck as Emily dropped back in the cabin. He put the engine in neutral and jumped into the cabin. Emily was groaning in pain. Luckily the bullet had grazed her ear. She was okay. Zach turned white and felt a cold sweat starting to drip down his spine. He couldn't move. Emily was right next to him, shaking with fear and pain. A thousand thoughts raced through Zach's mind. *Shit! These guys are going to shoot us like rabbits, and we don't even know who they are.*

As the powerboat was approaching Zach could hear the crew, now more than two men, shout orders in a foreign language. It didn't sound French or Italian, the two most common languages in this part of the Mediterranean. No, it sounded clearly Russian. For a brief moment his eyes locked on Emily's. He could almost smell her fear, that visceral fear he had experienced when he found his mother dead one Sunday afternoon.

Something caught his attention on the floor. Right next to Emily he noticed the scuba equipment they had brought along for their diving excursion in Bonifato Bay.

"Emily, grab the containers and the masks! Quick!" snapped Zach.

Emily was fumbling around, still recovering from the shock of her near death experience. Zach could hear the Russian crew getting closer. The powerboat was preparing to board. Zach's reflexes kicked in. He grabbed Emily and pushed her out into the cockpit. He grabbed two containers and two masks, and threw them at Emily.

"Grab that and jump over the starboard side! Go!"

Emily seemed to have snapped out of her initial shock. She quickly reached for the equipment, looked at Zach for a brief second and jumped overboard. She disappeared underwater immediately.

Zach heard footsteps coming from the stern. Their pursuers had just boarded the ketch and were firing shots in the water. He was stuck! Zach turned around, desperately looking for an escape. He raced to the front cabin, jumped right through the hatch and into the blue water. The last thing he heard was the crack of live rounds hitting the aluminum mast.

Zach looked around, hoping to see Emily. He felt a hand on his shoulder and before he could react a compressor mouthpiece had been thrust into his mouth. He turned around and saw her. Emily gave him the OK sign and handed him a mask. She quickly swam further down and dragged Zach while he was adjusting his scuba gear. They stopped at approximately fifty feet below the surface. They couldn't hear anything anymore. The silence and apparent peace surrounding them was in eerie contrast with the sudden chaos they had just been through.

Zach knew they were a few miles from shore. They didn't have fins, and only about one hour of air to go. No way they could reach the shore if they stayed underwater all the way. Emily had mustered a great deal of strength but Zach knew she wasn't going to last, not with her condition. He thought they could at least start swimming in the right direction and hope their pursuers would lose track of them. They swam for twenty minutes without stopping, trying to save air by making slow but determined strokes. Zach would look up from time to time. The water was dark and murky. He could barely tell the sun was out, and thought he might see the shadow of a boat at the surface. The engine sound was unmistakable though. The attackers' boat was standing right on top of them and seemed to magically follow the divers even though Zach knew they couldn't see them.

They have a fishfinder! The scuba containers would show as two bright spots on the sonar screen if they indeed had a fishfinder. Zach realized they were trapped. With only about thirty minutes of air to go including decompression time and pursuers they could not hope to lose, they needed to start going back up.

Just as the two of them hit the surface they heard the same familiar shouts and saw a small inflatable dinghy dart toward them. Before long they were onboard the powerboat, tired, cold and apprehensive. A man in his early thirties wearing a short beard and military fatigues approached them. He had the demeanor of a group leader. He barked orders, two of his men pushed Zach and Emily into the cabin.

"So here you are Mr. Hayes. You gave us quite a bit of trouble, you know," said the leader. The accent was thick but the man was clearly articulate.

"The investment into Quantum Technologies, your company, did not work out as expected. You can imagine my partners were upset to see their equity wiped out by commercial issues you never discussed during due diligence. So many questions, so few answers! I believe you owe us a conversation, Mr. Hayes."

24

Zach's heart sank. He pursed his lips, signaling without realizing it he wasn't ready to talk. The man hit him in the face. Zach's face was burning from the blow. His eyes turned cold and hard as he stared straight back at his aggressor. The Russian paused. Then, smiling he turned toward Emily and raised his arm to hit her.

"Don't touch her!" cried Zach.

"Then you'd better talk to me..."

"What do you want to know?"

"My partners trusted you with their money. What happened to it?"

"They invested in our stock, our stock went down. Shit happens."

"Bullshit! The stock went down right after they invested... What happened?"

"Our sales went down, we didn't meet expectations"

"And you knew of course, which is why you're now in trouble... Tell me why, why did it actually go down?"

"Technology changes fast and so does our competition. Our commercial encryption product was getting obsolete faster than we thought. We started losing deals to competitors."

"So what are you going to do about it? We need the money back. Either repay us or get the stock back up."

"I can't repay the money, it's already been put to work and it's secured by our treasury team anyway."

"So?"

"I have a plan to get the stock back up. We will launch a new form of encryption soon, it's totally unprecedented and will blow our competition out of the water."

"Mr. Hayes, this sounds fantastic, really..." said the Russian, before suddenly landing a hard blow on Emily. She whimpered. She was too exhausted by the swim and her body was starting to feel the impact of the virus. "But somehow I don't believe you. Give me one reason — one reason! — not to kill you both right now..."

Zach's mind was racing. Emily looked really pale.

"She is sick, she is very sick and contagious. You've all been exposed to it by now."

The Russian paused and stared at Zach.

"When you guys came after us at the hospital? We were with her brother. He died of this illness. We realized you were after us, we had no choice but to leave. But the fact is, she's sick, and she will die if we do nothing. And the same thing will happen to you too, you will die just like her brother did."

The wheels were clearly turning in the Russian's mind as he glanced at Emily then back at Zach.

"I know where to find the antidote that will treat her, and you guys. I just need a bit of time to fly back to the US and get it prepared."

Zach could see the Russian gradually relenting.

"Come on! Give me a chance and we all get to live. And your bosses' stock will recover too. Come on, I just need a chance to take care of it..."

The Russian thought for a few seconds then turned to Zach.

"Okay, you have one chance and one week! We keep your friend with us. If you are not back in a week with the antidote we kill her then we'll come after you too. No second chance Mr. Hayes. Make good use of your time."

None of you guys will get a second chance if I don't get the antidote, thought Zach trying to repress a smile. He had just managed to earn himself a chance to get out of this mess. Time to get to work.

Zach was zipping along the Reston parkway at ninety miles per hour in his Porsche 911. Dulles airport was behind him, he was on his way to meet Dr. Cunningham. The trip back from Europe, unlike his actual stay there, had been uneventful. The stopover at the London Heathrow Marriott had been a relief after days at sea. Amazing what a hot shower and familiar food could do. An hour later he found himself in Cunningham's office.

"Zach, so good to see you! Am glad you're fine, is Emily okay too?"

"She's hanging in there. For now. She definitely needs our help, doctor."

Zach quickly brought Cunningham up to speed. Being chased by the Russians, digging into Tom's DNA, needing more computing power, rigging a virtual quantum quad core together.

"Zach, I'm no quantum engineer, or whatever else it is you guys call yourselves these days, but I don't see how this approach will work... Four mega qubits are an awesome amount of computing power to behold; frankly I can't even fathom it. But I don't think you'll ever get past decoherence issues with the four cores, which means your rig is effectively useless. What am I missing?"

Zach paused.

"You're not missing anything doc. That's the brick wall I've run into. Look, we need to figure this out. If we don't, not only does Emily die, but the virus will likely spiral out of control, we won't be able to control the epidemic..."

"Well let's think this through... Why was Tom saving content to his DNA in the first place? Why not simply use a computer?"

"Well, I'd argue he thought of his DNA as a computer."

Cunningham gave Zach a funny look. Zach went on.

"So, if he was using his DNA, his junk DNA as a computer, he must have thought this was a better way, a more efficient way to process information, somehow?"

"Well, didn't Emily mention Tom was obsessed with the Grover search algorithm? Is that related in any way?"

"A Grover search is a form of database search. It can be a much more efficient way of searching and retrieving complex information out of large databases. The algorithm wasn't used much until quantum computing came along because it's simply not practical with traditional computing systems."

"Wait, Zach. I remember seeing some research about how the human genome is an example of a Grover search happening in nature. Yes it's coming back to me, the paper was all about how DNA is naturally performing Grover searches, as if it was designed for it."

"Okay, so what would it mean in our case? Imagine Tom was trying to store and retrieve massive amounts of information. The information needed to be processed, encrypted using quantum means. He would have easily run out of computing power unless he was using the right algorithm. Then he figured out the Grover search was the way to go and all he needed was a suitable computing platform to perform the job... So what would you do if you needed to crunch through a big Grover search job and had run out of option with traditional and quantum computing?"

Cunningham smiled as he realized the answer was now obvious.

"You would try a DNA-based computer."

"No way!"

"You would try to use DNA to perform the computations. Why you would try this on yourself is beyond me, this seems incredibly dangerous."

"Well we'll figure out why later, but I think this is worth trying, doc! Where do we even start? How can we start rigging together a DNA-based computer? "

"I can help with the biochemistry part, we can use some space in my lab but you'll need to handle the computing part, Zach."

"That's fine doc, it will take me back to high school, when I used to build my own souped-up deep-learning GPU rig because I couldn't afford a high-end computer..."

25

"Zach?" inquired Dave, his assistant. No response.

"Zach, some people are here for you..."

He turned around, swiveling the oversized leather chair away from his window overlooking Tyson's Corner. He was tired. Exhausted by jet lag and his discussion with Cunningham the evening before, he hadn't been able to get a good night's sleep. He couldn't stop thinking about Emily and the Russians either. He had come back to the office this morning to check on business matters while the parts they had ordered for the DNA computer were being shipped. Zach was still after all the founder and chief executive of Quantum Technologies Inc. His team hadn't seen him much this past week, but they were too professional to bring it up. They had focused on keeping the business going while the boss was away.

"Who is it Dave, who?"

"Um, the SEC, boss. Rebecca Jones from the SEC. She's here with a few colleagues."

"Fine, bring them in."

Moments later a woman in her late thirties entered the room. The two men who were with her headed the other way and appeared to be leaving. Dressed in a gray pantsuit, her auburn hair pulled back in a bun, she was wearing horn-rimmed glasses, and little to no make-up. *She'd be hot if she wasn't an accountant,* thought Zach. He caught himself and focused on her face.

"Hi, Rebecca Jones, from the Securities and Exchange Commission."

"Hi Rebecca, Zach Hayes. What can I do for you?"

"Thanks for meeting me today, sir," she replied with cold formality. "We are investigating a stock sale you completed a few weeks ago. May I sit down?"

Moments later, while Rebecca Jones was in Zach's office, her two colleagues stepped out of the elevator and onto the second floor, right next to Masha's office. Masha, as Zach's head of Marketing, kept all sorts of files in a fire-proof file cabinet outside her office. It was mostly legal agreements, business partnerships etc, since they needed to keep executed copies on hand. Most of her files were digital and stored on her computer or in the cloud. The two men walked straight to the file cabinet, opened the top drawer and started making copies on a nearby copier. Masha was intrigued by their behavior.

"Hey, hi, can I help you?"

"Hi, Dennis Bell with the Securities and Exchange Commission. We are collecting some files and making a few copies, we'll put everything back in place. Do you mind my asking your role here at the company?"

"Um, sure. Masha Torre, I run the Marketing department here."

"Nice to meet you, Masha. You should also know we notified your legal department. If my memory is correct, you are on the list we sent them of individuals who are under legal hold. That means you shouldn't delete any files on your computer, particularly any file that pertains to analysis and forecasting of sales results, as well as any email or chat you might have had on the topic."

Masha felt a huge jolt coursing through her body. The SEC! The SEC was investigating them. This was bad. She had warned Zach about their sales going soft, she had briefed him. She had warned him not to do anything stupid. Yet he had sold his stock, he had done it right in front of her!

"Don't you guys need a warrant or something?" she asked, tentatively. The SEC agents stopped. Dennis stared at her.

"Do you guys have anything to hide? Do you mind if we take a look?"

The twinkle in Dennis' eyes was a mix of provocation and hesitation. *No way, they don't have a warrant! I almost fell for it, I can't believe it,* thought Masha.

"Actually, I do. You should not be without an escort. Please put these files back. I will take you back to the reception area."

"Very well Ma'am. You know we'll be back, right?"

Masha didn't answer. She motioned the agents to walk back to the elevators.

"I'm not sure, which stock sale are you talking about?" asked Zach.

"You sold about seven hundred thousand shares for thirty million on June 6th, sir."

"Oh that may be, I am on a 10b5-1 trading plan. The company sells stock on my behalf periodically."

"I'm aware, sir. If you had stuck to your executive trading plan and continued with predictable arms length stock sales you would be on the right side of the law, and we wouldn't be talking. I'm here to investigate a large and unusual sale you completed recently, right before disclosing a material adverse change in your revenue outlook."

"Okay, that may be, I'd have to go back to our records. There's a lot going on here every day you know..."

"I'm sure there is, which is why we sent your legal team a notice to put all records pertinent to this investigation on hold. You are not to delete or otherwise destroy any of the records listed in the legal hold notice."

"Let me call our in-house counsel then, so he can join us."

"No need to get lawyers involved at this stage, Mr. Hayes. I came here without our own counsel to see if we could start a conversation on business terms, and bring it to a friendly resolution for everyone's sake."

Zach was about to respond when he saw Masha pop her head through the door. She raised her eyebrows and puckered her lips, in a frenzied way that indicated she needed to talk.

"Excuse me, Ms. Jones, I have to step out for a minute. I apologize, I'll be right back."

Zach stepped out and pulled Masha aside. He suspected something was going on. Masha was fairly business-savvy and would not have pulled him out of a meeting without a valid reason.

"Masha, what's going on? Can we talk later? I am in a meeting with the SEC."

"I know, sorry. Her colleagues were on my floor, going through our paper records without a warrant."

"What?"

"Yes, they were going through contracts and other fairly innocuous records, but without a warrant. I stopped them and took them back to the reception. I thought you should know. They didn't seem to care, said they would come back with a warrant."

"Mmmh... Thanks for doing this Masha, that was definitely a good catch. I'd better get back in. We'll definitely catch up when I'm done."

"They're here for your stock trade, aren't they?" asked Masha. She had a hard time masking her apprehension.

"Too early to tell," lied Zach. "Let me wrap up with her then we'll catch up."

Zach went back into his office.

"Hi Ms. Jones. Sorry for the interruption. Looks like you have some very proactive colleagues! One of my collaborators escorted them back to our reception area where they are waiting for you."

The SEC agent gave Zach a quizzical look.

"I'm not sure there's much to talk about. Sounds like you know what you're doing. If you need documents, please come back with a warrant. We are a publicly traded company, we need to follow process. You have your stakeholders and I have mine."

"Very well sir, I'll be back then. With a warrant, and with our legal team."

"You do what you gotta do, have a great day."

As soon as his assistant led Rebecca Jones out of his office, Zach closed the door and called Otto.

"Otto, the SEC was just here. We should talk in person, not on the phone. Can we meet today?"

"Sure, I'm working from home today. You can come any time."

"Your brownstone in Georgetown?"

"Same as always, Zach..."

"Okay, I'll be there in thirty minutes."

Zach sat down in Otto's office and glanced around. What Otto described as a home office seemed more like an old school British club. With mahogany wood paneling, a sizable antique desk by the window and a green leather couch in the back, it exuded wealth and power. The rows of built-in bookshelves, loaded with various legal and business books, gave it a somewhat intellectual touch that Otto relished.

"So, Zach, what's going on? Are you in trouble again?"

Zach related to Otto the SEC's visit to the company's headquarters.

"That's not good, Zach, not good at all," said Otto when Zach was done.

"I know, that's what I came for. I need your help Otto"

"Well, we're dealing with the United States government here. We'll be quickly outmatched if we're not careful. Seems to me like we need to buy time. We need to resolve our issue with the Russians first. We can't fight on all fronts at the same time, and they have Emily. Of course, they're also threatening to kill us all..." added Otto with a smile. Otto continued.

"It's also in their interest to see this SEC matter resolved positively since our stock will get pummeled if the word gets out or if we can't come to some kind of agreement with them. It's all about money, Zach. We're lucky in that I think the Russians' interests are aligned with ours at the moment. So... I think, in an odd way and although they're holding a figurative gun to our head, I think they'd be willing to help us for now."

Zach was confused. They seemed screwed, yet Otto was still smiling. Did he understand the gravity of the situation?

"What do you mean Otto?"

"The Russians can't do that much for us, but the one thing they can do should really help us stay a step ahead of the SEC..."

"And what would that be?"

"They can hack into the SEC's servers and keep track of the investigation, Zach. They've been doing it for years. How do you think their M&A arbitrage hedge funds do so well? They get hold of draft press releases before they become public and trade on the information! I'll talk to Igor and buy us more time. The Russians will keep tabs on your Rebecca Jones, so we can stay a step ahead and resolve our issues with them first. They'll even modify records and digital evidence if they have to."

"If you say so, Otto..." said Zach.

He looked at his watch. He had promised Cunningham he'd be back at the hospital before the end of the day. The riddle of Tom's DNA was not going to solve itself and it was the key to saving Emily and resolving their issues with the Russians.

Rebecca Jones' words were still echoing in Zach's mind. He had to save Emily before the SEC would complete their investigation, before the mutation would get to her. Time was running out. Zach left in a hurry.

26

It was late in the day when Zach made it to Innova General Hospital. He found Cunningham in his office next to the genetics research lab. The doctor was engrossed in a laboratory supplies catalog.

"Hey doc, I'm back"

"Oh, hi Zach. I was just looking at what kind of supplies we'd need to procure for our DNA computer. I started assembling the basics in the lab, but I'm not sure we have everything. You want to see it?"

"You bet, I can't wait to see it. Show me!"

The two stepped out of Cunningham's office and into the laboratory next door. Zach wasn't sure what to look for. Cunningham pointed at a lab bench to the left.

"Here"

"Where?"

All Zach could see was a bunch of bottles of reagent on the table. A few test tubes with liquid in them were standing next to the bottles. To the right was a cellular microarray and a large array assay machine, which itself was hooked to a computer.

"I know it doesn't look like much Zach, but this is the setup for our DNA computer."

Zach gave Cunningham a funny look. The doctor ignored him and continued.

"I experimented with some of these tubes earlier today. We can mix DNA strands into these tubes. We use nucleotides as bits. The DNA strands behave as an artificial neural network, very much like a deep learning algorithm would. I've always thought it is odd, because this is a case of life imitating science imitating life!"

Cunningham paused to contemplate the irony of their setup.

"We vary chemical concentrations to adjust the weight of each pattern, then we mix the strands. The strands act as a massively parallel neural network."

"So... We're simply going to mix chemicals and somehow get our answer?"

"Yes! But not any chemicals, Zach. First of all from a computing standpoint we can store a couple of terabytes of data using genetic materials in each spot of the microarray, and each microarray holds a hundred spots. This microarray effectively becomes a massively parallel computing system, which we can access using the assay machine."

"But how fast is it, really? Won't the chemical reactions take time to complete?"

"Yes Zach, it will take a few hours, maybe overnight, to complete. But all combinations will be processed in parallel, so the full job should be done by tomorrow. Think about it... This decryption is too massive a job for a traditional computer. It was too large even for your quantum server! We tried rigging together a quad core, but we couldn't overcome decoherence issues. This should work, Zach. It will take overnight, but by using DNA as a deep learning neural network we can do this... The key is combining the three technologies for what they do best. DNA computing is a natural fit for your Grover search algorithm, quantum computing for all other encryption tasks, and traditional computing for data management and input/output."

"All right then, let's get started on Tom's DNA," replied Zach.

In spite of Cunningham's best hopes it took a few days to get to the first result. The DNA computations would indeed complete in a few hours but integrating the three systems together, so they could use the same data formats took more coding effort on Zach's part. Finally, on the third day, Zach was able to decode the encryption of the second file. He quickly scanned through the content of the file and saw more references to the Hierarchy he had read about in Tom's log the first time. It seemed to describe an organization called the Young Humans World Hierarchy. Zach thought Tom was describing a cult of some sort. Like many cults it appeared to have a set of laws, or principles, that Zach couldn't quite understand.

Do not destroy a genetic drive.

Do not expose a drive to destructive chemicals.

Do not deplete the supplies of a drive.

Use proper protocol when recombining drives.

Do not transmit false or incorrect information.

What did this even mean? It almost sounded to him like instructions for handling factory equipment. Zach snapped out of his reverie. He was going to have to wait to go through Tom's encrypted research notes, what he had started calling the hierarchy files. The important part is he now had the means to reverse engineer the changes Tom had made to his junk DNA when encrypting the hierarchy files. Armed with the actual content of the encrypted file, Zach could start the next job to figure out the portion of Tom's DNA that had been impacted by their TP53 treatment. This in turn would lead to the antidote for Emily and anybody affected by the epidemic. Zach feverishly moved on to this next task, decrypting the TP53 sequence which got scrambled by Tom's biohack. He set up the microarray one more time into the assay machine, sat down at the computer next to the equipment and typed: *grover_search --input micro_array_31 --verbose*, then pressed the enter key. The assay machine started purring as it handled the command.

Zach looked around, barely able to contain his excitement. It was late again. Cunningham had gone home a few hours earlier. Zach started dialing his number to share the news when he looked at the time on his smartphone. Eleven o'clock. He stopped. It was way past Cunningham's bedtime... He decided to call Otto instead.

"Hey Otto, I think I have something..."

"Hi Zach, what do you mean?"

"Well, I've been digging into Tom's files. Remember, he was the guy who died on us at the hospital?"

"Okay?"

"Well, somehow both he and the Russians mentioned an organization called the Hierarchy. I don't know yet how they're connected but that seemed like too much of a coincidence to me. Then the other thing is Tom was using some really strong encryption with his files. In fact, the strongest encryption I've ever seen Otto."

"Okay Zach, and that's going to help with the SEC investigation and the Russians because..."

"Forget about that Otto. We are on the verge of an epidemic caused by a virus we don't understand. Emily's life is at stake. We need to figure out what happened with Tom's DNA, so we can fix it."

"Zach..."

Zach sensed frustration in Otto's voice.

"And regardless of what we do or don't figure out with Tom's files, Cunningham and I prototyped a computing rig that just cracked the strongest encryption I've ever seen. Encryption that was stronger than our standard quantum server setup, Otto."

Otto was silent, processing the facts as disclosed by Zach. Zach continued.

"We can productize this and make it part of our commercial lineup Otto."

"How long is that going to take, Zach?"

"Well, it's hard to say. It's still very much at the research and development stage, you know?"

Otto paused. He wasn't sure whether to laugh or be mad. He took a deep breath and tried not to be patronizing to Zach.

"Zach, let me be direct with you. The Russians are after us. Well, after you mostly, but they will come after me too if they don't get what they want. These are not nice people. You know what they will do if we can't get out of our mess? They will *kill* you!"

"Otto..."

"And next we have the SEC. They will not kill the company, but if we are not careful they will have you barred from the company for life and in jail! These are not games, Zach. This is not startup land anymore. You need to grow up and focus on the threat right in front of us. Give the Russians what they want, make them go away! Stay focused, no more distractions!"

Zach was taken aback. It was obvious to him his encryption work was the path to figuring out a way to save both Emily and the company. Figuring out the encryption riddle would show the path to curing Emily, and would lead to a new product that would solve sagging sales. That would solve all other problems with the Russians. *How does he not see this? It's so obvious, he just doesn't get it...* thought Zach.

"Otto, I gotta go. We'll talk soon. Bye," said Zach curtly before hanging up. He was mad. For all his technology investing experience, Otto was *not* a technologist and didn't see or trust that Zach was on the right path. Zach felt alone, genuinely alone for the first time in a long time.

27

The array machine beeped unexpectedly. Surprised, Zach turned around and walked to the computer screen. The job was finished, the Grover search algorithm had completed its task. Already! Excited, Zach sat down and started reviewing the decrypted materials. Scanning through the file he started smiling. He had, right in front of him, the decrypted genetic sequence which had gotten scrambled when they had administered the TP53 treatment to Tom. That meant they could now prepare the antidote for the epidemic and edit it out of Emily's DNA. Finally, a break! But he needed to act fast, as he knew Emily was thousands of miles away, overseas, and fading fast.

After a short night Zach came back to the hospital early. It was 7:30am and Dr. Cunningham had just finished his rounds. Zach found him in his office reviewing patient files.

"Hey Dr. Cunningham, good morning! You'll never guess..."

"Good morning, Zach. Did you figure it out?"

"Yes! I was able to reverse engineer and decrypt the TP53 sequence that got corrupted by Tom's biohack. I have the correct sequence now, all we have to do is reverse-edit Emily's genome, and we're home free," said Zach triumphantly.

"And we're home free..."

Cunningham paused to contemplate the task at hand. Zach made it sound much easier than it actually was. The doctor looked back at Zach.

"Well Zach, that's great news! We still have a few things to figure out though."

"What do you mean?"

"Well, CRISPR editing is not that simple. There are many things that can go wrong, but I'm particularly worried about off-target cutting and using the right delivery system."

Zach gave the doctor a funny look.

"Off-target cutting is exactly what it sounds like, it means the antidote we would inject Emily would edit the wrong gene site. We'd be right back to our starting position if we edit the wrong genes. Remember? That's basically similar to what happened with Tom's biohack. The editing got all scrambled and totally messed up the operation."

"Okay, and we solve this how?"

"Well for this I think I might have a solution. I've been working on a mutant Cas9 system that shows increased specificity and reduced incidence of off-target cutting, so we should use it but keep in mind this is experimental..."

"It's not like we have a better alternative, doctor... What about the second issue you brought up?"

"The delivery system? Yes, that's a tough one. We'll probably need to experiment. Here is the problem. In most instance, the delivery system of choice is a viral vector of some sorts. So we do a lot of work with adenoviruses, they tend to be very efficient. But in Emily's case, since she's sick already and her immune system is distressed, I'm afraid injecting an adenovirus would simply trigger more inflammation and an adverse immune response."

This was starting to sound like gibberish to Zach. All he could really hear was that this was going to be more complicated than he thought, which meant they were going to need more time.

"Doc, we need to figure this out soon. I'm not sure what you want to do, but Emily is sitting thousands of miles away, she's getting sicker by the minute, and we need to figure this out."

"Well, Zach, here is what I propose we do. I didn't wait until today to get started on this. The day Emily got sick I realized we had to figure this out fast and research takes time. I started getting set up with a population of mice I injected with the exact same TP53 mutation we found in Tom, to experiment with toxicity and efficiency of different treatments. I haven't gotten to the treatment part but I have a dozen mice that are ready to go. Now that we know which genetic edits we want to make I can use some of the mice to experiment with different delivery vehicles. Micro-injection is the gold standard but I don't think it's practical in the case of Emily, as we need a method that works outside the lab with very limited medical support. I think we should stick with viral vectors. Let's use an adenovirus as a baseline. We can also test an adeno-associated virus and a lentivirus. That's three separate methods right there. Let's get these set up, we should be able to figure out toxicity fairly quickly. Send me the correct genetic sequence to be edited and I'll set up the test. We'll need a couple of days to see what happens to the mice."

"All right doctor, it's up to you now. Let's hope this works."

Zach left the hospital and hopped in his Porsche 911 to drive back to the office. He was barely a block away when his phone rang. He heard a heavily accented voice on the line.

"Zach, it is Yurij."

"Hi Yurij, what can I do for you?"

"Checking on you... Your friend is not doing so well, you know? I hope you are working on our deal and fast, or we may not even need to kill her."

"Emily! Let me talk to her. Let me make sure she's okay..."

"As you wish... Here she is."

"Zach, I'm okay for now, but the virus is definitely affecting me...."

"Emily, I'm so glad you're okay! I'm working on it, Cunningham and I are preparing the antidote as we speak, it will be ready in another couple of days."

He didn't have the heart to tell her the truth. He wasn't ready to accept the truth. Zach knew they were going to figure it out, he simply wasn't sure how yet. He had full confidence in Cunningham's abilities. Emily sounded exhausted.

"I feel weaker by the day, Zach, I hope you'll get here soon..."

"Enough!" said the Russian, grabbing the phone from Emily's hands. "My friend is sick too, Zach. You'd better bring this antidote as planned and soon. If he dies, I will personally find you and kill you, you understand?"

Zach swallowed hard.

"I understand, Yurij."

Yurij hung up without saying another word.

The wait the next couple of days was unbearable. Zach knew Cunningham's mice needed a few days of exposure until they would have enough data to figure out which treatment was working, but they were really running out of time. He was worried about Emily. No one understood the exact effect and timing of the TP53 mutation. What if it started acting faster in her?

When the time finally came to evaluate which delivery system worked, Zach went back to the hospital. He could have called Cunningham, but he wanted to see the results for himself. He wanted to look into the doctor's eyes, and see how confident he would be about the treatment.

As Zach walked into Cunningham's office, he noticed an empty chair with files scattered all over the desk. A nurse came by.

"Hi, if you're looking for Dr. Cunningham, he's in the lab."

"Oh, thanks for letting me know, I'll go meet him now."

Zach walked across the hallway and into the laboratory. Behind a wall of tubes and pipettes he spotted Cunningham, hunched over a cage containing a handful of mice, and checking his notebook.

"Hey doctor, it's been a few days, I figured I'd check on you... how are the mice doing?"

"Hi Zach! Funny you should ask... I prepared some tissue samples last night and ran some analyses. The results came in the morning, and I was just looking at them."

Zach thought it noteworthy that "preparing tissue samples" would in fact involve killing the mice they had infected with the new genetic materials. Some lives had to be sacrificed so others could be preserved. They were playing God, and Zach hoped it wouldn't backfire on them.

"What does it say? What do you see?"

"Well, I expected some level of inflammation with all three viral vectors but the response is stronger than anything I've seen. By that I mean all three mice we analyzed showed unusually high levels of inflammation, Zach. This is a problem, because these are the most efficient means of delivering our genetic payload in a targeted manner."

"So, you mean the treatment is not working?"

"I'm afraid not Zach, the inflammation is way too strong. Then, on top of it, there's always the risk the viral shell will somehow mutate during the trip overseas. It's not like we're treating Emily in a lab either. We need to come up with something else."

"Well, we don't have time, so we'd better come up with something fast..."

"You know I was just wondering... Let's go a different path and try a non-viral delivery method. I've seen potentially interesting results with DNA nanoclews."

"Nano what?"

"Nanoclews are tiny little spheres of DNA. Imagine bunching together a strand of DNA into a ball of yarn, but with an empty space in the middle, just like a little cocoon. It is totally virus free, which should address the inflammation issue. It should also be much more stable, so we don't run the risk of the genetic materials somehow mutating on your way to Emily in Corsica."

"Great, what are we waiting for? Why didn't we start there?"

"This is a brand-new technique, it simply hasn't been tested as much as viral methods. I didn't want to take a chance on a new untested technique."

"It's not like we have other options, doctor. If you think it'll work, let's go with this. We're running out of time!"

"You're right, Zach. I think I can get a dose of antidote prepared by tomorrow using the nanoclews."

"OK, you do that, and I'll call Otto. I'll need his jet to fly back to Corsica ASAP. Thank you so much for figuring this out, doctor! We're going to save Emily, and we're going to make more of this antidote to prevent an epidemic from getting out of hand. You're a genius!"

Cunningham frowned. He wasn't much of a fan of Zach's bouts of exuberance. He understood all too well the risks they were taking. Yes, if this worked he would be hailed as a hero for spearheading a new treatment method with massive potential. But it was as likely to blow up in their faces in a spectacular way. Only time would tell.

28

The private jet touched down at Calvi-Sainte-Catherine airport in northern Corsica. Zach glanced out the window. It was a small, barely regional airport. He could see to the north the Bay of Calvi, with a majestic blue sea. Around him were rugged mountains and brush that reminded him of southern California. The jet taxied to the general aviation terminal, and eventually came to a stop. Zach stepped out and into the terminal. He immediately recognized Yurij, his Russian handler, in the sitting area. Yurij stood up as soon as he saw him.

"Mr. Hayes, I'm glad you could make it."

"Hi, is she okay?"

"There's no time to waste, let's get going... You have the antidote, right?"

Zach nodded. Yurij led him to a Range Rover. He grabbed plastic zipper-style handcuffs and a bag made of black cloth on the back seat. Zach could feel a lump growing in his throat, he swallowed hard.

"Get in there, please. I won't hurt you, but we need to take precautions."

Zach couldn't tell whether the Russian was messing with him or not. He seemed almost courteous, which seemed almost out-of-place given he could at any time turn around and obliterate Zach out of this world. Zach sat down on the back seat. Yurij put the cuffs on his wrists and the black cloth bag on his head.

"Let's go."

They drove for about an hour through the Corsican brush. As best as Zach could tell they were driving south, most likely back to the Bay of Girolata where they had first stopped during their sailing trip. Or perhaps they were going to the town of Osani, the first populated outpost near Girolata. The road turned out to be a hard one, with many curves and hairpins in the mountains. Zach was starting to feel queasy when the car came to a stop. All he could hear was the wind blowing through the brush.

Yurij grabbed him and led him to what looked like a small farmhouse. Once they were inside, he took Zach's mask and handcuffs off. Zach looked around.

He was in a small living room. On one end a small kitchen galley, with appliances that had seen better days. On the other end a tattered sofa and an old tube television set. He recognized one of Yurij's colleagues on the sofa. He seemed to be resting, his skin looked pale and saggy. The weather was sunny, the temperature mild, yet the man was buried under a blanket. He was sweating profusely, which was confusing to Zach.

"Is he sick too?"

Yurij nodded. Zach peeked through the doorway in the back of the room. It led to a bedroom where he could see Emily. She was on the bed. Zach rushed to the room.

"Emily, I'm here! You okay?"

No response. Maybe she was sleeping? Zach grabbed her hand. It felt limp, but was still warm.

"Emily, can you hear me?"

Still no response. Zach inspected her face. She was breathing calmly. He turned on the small lamp on the nightstand. Then he grabbed her head gently, pulled one of her eyelids and turned her face toward the lamp. Still no response, no change in her pupil. He turned toward Yurij.

"How long has she been like this? She looks unconscious, possibly in a coma. She needs medical attention now!"

"Since this morning. And yes, of course she needs medical assistance, that's why you're here. Going to the hospital is not going to do her much good. Remember what happened to her brother?"

Zach nodded. Yurij was right. He put his backpack down and reached for the antidote. He laid out the bottle and the first aid supplies he had brought with him on the nightstand. Zach grabbed a small syringe and started preparing an injection with the antidote. He had never given a shot to anybody before, but Cunningham and the nurse had shown him back at the hospital. Put the arm into some kind of tourniquet, grab a vein that pops out and carefully insert the needle into the vein. *Every heroin addict does it,* or so thought Zach. *I should be able to do it too.* He administered the antidote to Emily.

Yurij put his hand on Zach's shoulder and motioned toward his colleague on the sofa.

"Him too..."

Zach nodded and paused. Luckily, Cunningham had given him two spare doses, but he wanted to keep them for Emily in case she needed more. The Russian wasn't very patient and gave him a shove. Zach had seen their work when they ran out of patience and decided now would not be a good time to test the Russian's limits. He obliged and prepared a second dose. After he gave the shot to the Russian on the sofa, Zach went back to the bedroom and sat next to Emily.

"Now we wait, we'll know in a few hours whether it's working or not."

Yurij nodded and sat in the living room, next to the sofa. Zach was exhausted, he had been running on constant adrenaline for the last few days and hadn't slept on the plane. He felt jet-lagged. He closed his eyes for a brief moment and fell asleep.

Zach woke up a few hours later. As soon as he woke up, he turned to Emily. He put his hand on her shoulder. She was still unresponsive. Her breathing felt fainter to him, or was his mind playing tricks on him? He tried measuring her heart rate. He could barely get any pulse from her wrist. Zach looked around, saw Yurij in the other room, staring at him. Zach ignored the creepy feeling that descended on him and grabbed his cell phone. He called Cunningham.

"Hey doctor, it's Zach."

"Oh, hi Zach, is everything okay?"

"Fine. I'm with Emily. I injected the antidote about three hours ago..."

"Zach we need to talk..."

"No, me first. I gave her the antidote but I don't see any change so far. Actually her pulse seems fainter, her breathing slower. I'm not sure it's working, doctor..."

"Zach, I've been testing the nanoclews while you were gone and, how do I say this? I don't think this is going to work, at least not with the current batch."

"What??"

"Well we rushed this, remember? I've been testing the same batch on the mice, and it seems ineffective. In some of them it actually makes things worse, but I'm still checking the results."

Zach stood up, he felt anger rising through his body.

"You are still checking the results? You are still checking the fucking results while I'm here at the other end of the world trying to save Emily? When were you going to call me, doctor?"

"Zach, I know, calm down. I need to establish facts first before we have anything to act on. This is all happening real time. As best as I can tell something is missing from the payload. At first, I thought maybe the nanoclews were not going to be stable enough to make it through the trip and the inevitable changes in temperature, but that doesn't seem to be the case. The compound is stable enough. So I'm now looking into the payload, and whether we inserted the right genetic materials in there."

Zach shook his head. He hadn't meant to get mad at Cunningham. He was right, they had done everything so fast, and they were dealing with a newly mutated virus of some kind. Proper protocol would take months to establish a treatment, and they had long ago abandoned any semblance of proper protocol.

He turned around and looked at Emily. She looked different.

"I'll call you right back, doctor. I need to go."

Emily was a shell of herself, a vessel emptied. He moved closer to her face, close enough to feel her breath. Nothing. Not a single breath, not a single heave of the chest. He grabbed her wrist. No pulse. Just dead flesh. Zach knew what it meant, and felt as if someone had slammed him with a sledgehammer in the gut. This brought back memories of Baltimore. Memories of finding his mother dead in their sordid childhood home, dead because of lack of medical care, dead because of poverty, with police officers roaming the apartment and no one to turn to. He had sworn he would never, ever put himself in this situation again, and yet here he was, in a sordid home surrounded by Russian hitmen staring at the lifeless body of a woman he was just realizing he had come to fall in love with.

Zach didn't know how to handle the sadness, the anger, the despair. He let out a barely human wail.

"No!"

Yurij quickly came to the room as soon as he heard Zach. He glanced at him, then at Emily's limp body on the bed, then back at him and understood right away what was going on.

"She's gone."

Zach dropped into the chair by the bed. He had been in this room before. Not this room, a different one, smaller, in West Baltimore, on a Sunday afternoon when he was sixteen. Same quality of stillness. Same terrible finality in the air. The way a room changes when it goes from containing a person to containing the memory of one.

He had sworn, standing in that Baltimore room, that he would never be here again. He had spent a decade making sure of it. The startup, the money, the quantum encryption, the lawyers, the jet, all of it had been, at some level, a way of ensuring he would never again be a seventeen-year-old kid with no power, standing in a room where someone had just stopped being alive.

He looked at Emily's face. It was calm. That was the worst part, somehow, the calm. As if she had just decided to sleep, as if she might turn over any moment and tell him something true about himself.

You're smarter than you are wise. That's what she had said. On the stern of the boat, with the bay going dark around them.

You're here. Aren't you?

He had been. For once in his life, he had been exactly where he was supposed to be. And it hadn't been enough. The antidote he'd carried halfway across the world, the deal he'd negotiated, the Russians he'd try to outmaneuver, none of it had been enough. He had been so certain he could fix it. He had always been able to fix it.

He reached over and took her hand. Still warm. He held it anyway.

He didn't know how long he sat there. Long enough that the light in the room shifted. Long enough that he heard Yurij move in the other room, heard the creak of a floorboard, heard the man settle back down.

He thought about Tom, Tom who had died on a table at Mercy, Tom whose junk DNA had set all of this in motion, Tom who had knocked on his sister's door with two coffees from the corner bodega. He thought about Emily's father, the minister who had sat with dying people his whole life and never once looked away.

He stayed, she had told him. He stayed until the end every time.

Zach stayed.

When he finally stood up it wasn't because he was ready. It was because staying had become the same thing as leaving, and the only thing he had left to give Emily Dixon was the promise that her death was going to mean something.

He set her hand down carefully on the blanket. He stood there for one more moment.

Then Yurij appeared in the doorway.

"I know you have another dose of antidote," the Russian said quietly. "Give it to me."

Something broke open in Zach's chest. Not grief this time, something harder and colder than grief. In a fit of rage, Zach ran after him and shoved him against the wall.

"No way! You guys killed her! You killed her and now you want me to help? Go fuck yourself and give me my backpack!"

The Russian immediately went for the gun on his hip. Zach, blinded by anger, tried to wrestle his gun away from Yurij. It was a fairly stupid move since Zach had no combat training, but rage was stronger than reason. The two fumbled for a minute until Zach somehow managed to grab the gun. In a split-second, without thinking, he stepped away from Yurij, pointed the gun at the sick Russian and pulled the trigger.

Yurij stopped dead in his tracks, stunned by the bang of the gun still ringing in his ears, and stunned the young engineer would shoot his colleague. He stared at Zach.

"You... You just shot him!"

Blood was starting to ooze out and spread on the sofa. The sick Russian was staring at the ceiling, motionless, clearly dead now. Zach was shaking. It had all happened so fast. He hadn't meant to kill the man. He was just so angry. Angry that Emily died, angry that he let it happen, angry that the Russians got in the way.

"You have no idea what you're dealing with, Zach. The Hierarch will get us both for this, he will get us both!"

Zach stared at Yurij. This was the second time he heard of the Hierarch. The first time had been going through Tom's files. How did Yurij know about this? Before he could process it all, Yurij lunged toward Zach.

"Give me this gun, you idiot!"

Zach jumped back, and in a moment of fear pulled the trigger again. Yurij dropped on the floor, writhing in pain.

"You idiot, you just shot me in the leg!" swore the Russian.

Zach was numb. He looked around and saw across the room the entrance door, crooked and slightly ajar. *The car! The Range Rover is outside, all I need are the keys!* He turned back to the Russian.

"Give me the keys, Yurij..."

"What are you talking about?"

Zach cocked the gun and pointed it at Yurij's head.

"The keys to the car, asshole!"

Yurij pulled the keys out of his pocket and handed them to him. Zach grabbed his bag with the last dose of antidote and ran out of the farmhouse.

29

Zach stopped. He was briefly blinded by the Corsican sun. He could barely open his eyes for a few seconds. Zach could make the shape of the Range Rover in the middle of the courtyard. He ran toward it and climbed into the driver seat. He had no idea where he was. Zach knew he was an hour away from the airport in Calvi. It had to be south since that was the only way to go: Calvi was on the north coast of the island. He put the key in the ignition and started the car. He remembered he had his smartphone in his backpack. Zach pulled it out feverishly.

"Hey, give me directions to Calvi airport!"

His phone, as reliably and monotonously as ever, started guiding him toward Calvi-Sainte-Catherine airport, general aviation terminal. Zach floored the gas pedal and left in a cloud of smoke. As soon as he was on the road he called Otto.

"Otto, so good to hear your voice!"

"Hey Zach, is everything okay?"

"I don't have time Otto... I'm on my way back to Calvi airport. Can you tell your guys I'll be there in less than an hour? Can we be wheels up as soon as possible?"

"Sure... I guess you'll explain it to me later. Where are you going? Back to London? They will need to file a flight plan with air traffic control."

"Whatever, yes that works. I'll contact you from the plane once we're airborne. Thanks!"

He hung up and almost missed his turn on the windy road. The ride was impossibly scenic, surrounded by the mountains of northern Corsica. Had it been any other day, with Emily still alive and at his side, this would have been an idyllic time, the drive of a lifetime. But not today. *The drive of a lifetime alright...* He thought.

About an hour later he stepped out of the car by the terminal at the airport. He ran through the VIP lounge and onto the tarmac. The Falcon was parked to the right about a hundred feet away. Zach could hear the gentle whir of the turbines. The pilot was in the cockpit completing his checklist. The plane appeared ready to go. Zach climbed up the stairs and into the cabin as fast as he could, almost crashing into the precious mahogany kitchen galley. He looked to the pilot on the left.

"We're ready?"

The pilot gave him a thumbs up.

"Welcome back, sir!"

"Let's go, now!"

The pilot nodded and shut the airplane door. A few minutes later the plane was jetting off the runway and climbing above the Bay of Calvi. Zach looked through the window. He could see the harbor to the West, with the beach full of people next to it. Vacationers sunbathing, splashing in the warm seawater, eating, running, enjoying life. The contrast with Zach's last twenty-four hours of madness was striking. He imagined for a minute what it would be like to sit on that beach and not know the first thing about biohacks and Russians chasing you.

He snapped out of it when he remembered he had to call Otto back. Given the uncanniness with which the Russians had tracked him down, he was becoming paranoid about proper communication protocol. He didn't think they would trace his call back on the ground. He had used the local national carrier mobile network and didn't believe they could have hacked into it. But from the plane it was a different matter. All passenger communications were effectively over the Internet using the plane's WiFi service and were simply not as secure. He decided against a live call with Otto, and fired up the messaging app on his laptop instead. He was careful to go through his most secure VPN using quantum encryption. There was no more secure method of communication. It was simply unbreakable.

Hi Otto. You there?

Hi Zach, you ok?

Yes, made it back to the plane, currently airborne on way to London. Things went really awry here. Antidote didn't work.

Emily ok?

No, she's gone.

What???

Yes, she's gone. Antidote didn't work, was not able to save her. I had to run.

OMG

I bought some time but the Russians will be back after me. I want to fly back to DC to work with Cunningham on antidote. We must have overlooked something. It was really supposed to work. Don't understand why it didn't.

You can't. You shouldn't

Why? What?

The Russians will know to expect you back in DC, they will track you down right away.

So???

*So you should stay in London. Keep your head down while we figure this out. Make sure you always use quantum encryption for all communications. You can contact Cunningham to work on the antidote but do not reveal your location to *anyone*, not even me.*

OK, I'll stay in London then. We're on our way there, the pilot is taking me to Farnborough.

Be careful Zach.

You too Otto.

Bye.

Zach pushed away his laptop and closed his eyes. He had about an hour before the plane would be arriving in Farnborough airport, a few miles west of London. For the first time in a while he felt like he could let his guard down. He sighed and reclined back to take a nap.

As expected, the Falcon landed an hour later. Zach looked outside the window while the plane was taxiing on the tarmac. Sure enough, it was raining. Not the rain showers he was used to on the East coast, but instead an unending drizzle, trickling from a depressingly low cloud cover down to the concrete ground. What a contrast from sunny Corsica!

The plane was approaching the terminal. Unlike a commercial terminal, the general aviation terminal was designed for VIPs with their own jet. It looked like a single story building, basically a high end lobby with a shell around it. Passengers could easily come and go through it with minimal security. They were boarding their own plane after all. Zach enjoyed the feeling of exclusivity and ease he got from being dropped off by a private jet a few feet away from the plush terminal.

As the plane was about to come to a halt, Zach noticed two men standing by the entrance door to the lobby. They were staring at his plane. They didn't look like staff. The men didn't look like passengers either. Zach kept staring back at them. One of them seemed familiar to him. Zach felt beads of cold sweat running down his spine. *Crap! This is the guy who tried spreading DMSO on our mailbox the last time we were in London! They found us, but that's impossible, how did they?*

He turned to the pilot.

"Don't stop! We need to turn around and leave, fast!"

"I'm sorry?"

"Trust me, I'll explain later. Let's turn around and leave, now!"

"Okay, turning around sir. Where are we going? I need to file a flight plan with air traffic control. We can finish the paperwork when we're airborne, but the sooner we tell them the better it is."

"Fine, tell them we have an emergency. We need to leave now, it's a matter of life or death!"

The pilot stiffened up and frowned.

"Oh, okay sir, I hadn't realized. On it right away."

Zach was racking his brains. The Russians had somehow figured out where he would be next. That was impossible! He had been careful in his communications with Otto. He had used full quantum encryption. The latest, most secure kind. That meant the Russians had somehow found a way to break his unbreakable encryption. Impossible. Maybe they just had a lucky guess? A coincidence? Where else was he going to go back to but London? Still, the fact that they knew exactly where and when to find him was unsettling. Or did this mean Otto betrayed him? Betrayed him to save his own hide? After all the years they had spent together, Otto, his mentor, would betray him? That didn't make sense either yet this seemed like the only possibility.

He needed a place to go to where he wouldn't be tracked down. A place where he could hide yet have easy access to his computer network. A place where most people would speak English, so he wouldn't struggle with day-to-day transactions. A place that wasn't in England. He remembered something Emily had mentioned to him once... *Amsterdam!* That was the perfect hideaway. He was about to tell the pilot to set course to Amsterdam when he stopped. He couldn't fly to Amsterdam, or the pilot would know. The pilot would tell Otto, who might or might not betray him. He decided he would fly to Brussels then make his way to Amsterdam on his own. He still had cash in his backpack, so he could pay cash for a cab ride to Amsterdam. It'd be a long cab ride, a few hours, but the cabbie would be glad to make the cash and there would be no online record of the transaction. Zach turned to the pilot.

"Brussels, let's go to Brussels. But wait as long as you can to file the flight plan."

"Yes sir, Brussels Zaventem it is. I'll notify air traffic control once we're at altitude."

30

The flight from Farnborough to Zaventem was short, and less than an hour later Zach was on the ground. Mindful of being tracked by his assailants, he made sure he stayed off-line this time. As soon as he made it to the general aviation lobby, he hailed a car service. The driver, a burly Kurdish immigrant who spoke a mixture of French and English, seemed all too happy to find a long-haul customer. The fare to Amsterdam was going to be a few hundred euros, a week's wage for a day's work!

His ride turned out to be longer than Zach expected and particularly boring. The car was zipping along the A-27 across Flanders. The sky was gray, the clouds low and dark. On both sides, the plains of Flanders, cycling from wheat fields to wooded areas, with occasional windmills. Zach was surprised not to see any tulips. *So much for the chamber of commerce pitch,* he thought.

He finally made it to Amsterdam after dark. He wasn't sure where to go. Zach wanted to preserve the little bit of cash he had, three hundred dollars was only going to last so long.

Staying at a high-end hotel was out of question. He didn't want to ask his driver in case the Russians would somehow get hold of him. He thought of the red light district, at least it would be easy to get lost there, and hopefully he could find a cheap hostel, a bed and breakfast, something. Fuck, he would even stay at a brothel if he had to, anything as long as it would keep the Russians from finding him.

The driver looked in the rear view mirror and asked Zach in a mixture of broken English and French.

"*Monsieur*, in Amsterdam in about thirty minutes... drop-off where?"

"Red light district?"

"Sorry?"

"Um, red... light... district... ?" Zach repeated slowly, hoping his driver would understand better the second time.

"Oh, *le quartier des putes...* yes, okay, okay," replied the Kurd with a big grin. He clearly wanted to say more but his English was lacking. This was going to be a difficult conversation. Zach didn't want to engage either, the less his driver knew the better.

"Great, thank you," replied Zach as he put on his earbuds and pretended to listen to music on his phone. The Kurd got the cue and focused back on the road.

Thirty minutes later as expected, Zach stepped out of his ride, an old beat-up Peugeot 408, and looked around him. He was on the edge of the red light district in Amsterdam. Behind him was the Kloveniersburgwal canal with the Zuiderkerk building in the back. The church struck him as majestic, lit up at night. In front of him was a crowded street. It was getting late but you wouldn't know from the crowd, an odd mix of tourists, johns, prostitutes and small-time dealers. Some were there for sightseeing, most were there for some sort of transaction.

Zach put on his backpack and started walking through the district. The streets were narrower than he had expected. He felt very much like an American tourist and couldn't believe his eyes. As he made his way through the district, an odd mix of people would accost him.

"Hey, coke? Want some coke?" said a man in his thirties, handing him a small bag of white powder.

"No, thanks," replied Zach, walking past the man without stopping. The street was lined up with shops, most with a large window. Zach almost expected to see a variety of goods such as a bakery, a bookstore, a butcher's shop, as he had in many European cities and undoubtedly would in other parts of town. He was surprised to find the same oddly familiar pattern. A light, outside the front door, would indicate whether the shop was open or not. Through the window of an open shop he could see what appeared to be a dark-lit bedroom, with its owner standing on the doorstep.

The woman, pudgy and scantily clad, stared at Zach languorously.

"Hey honey, let me show you a good time," she said in almost unaccented English.

He did not respond. *Do I really stick out that much? How did she know?* thought Zach. He kept walking, she moved on to the next john. He needed a place to stay and started to wonder whether he had miscalculated with his plan to stay in the red light district. Staying at a hostel was actually not a good idea. He would be in a common room with bunk beds and half a dozen backpackers. The setup invited conversation and conviviality, and that was the last thing he needed. He simply wanted to be left alone for a few days. Getting on his smartphone to find directions to the nearest hotel was also out of question. The online session would not be secure and the people looking for him were skilled enough to track him. He was not going to get online until after he had had the chance to review his quantum encryption setup. Even that might not be secure enough, as he suspected the Russians might have cracked it when they found him in London and in Corsica. No, he was going to have to slog it old school.

Zach looked around and saw half a block away what appeared to be a small hotel. He decided to go for it and walked into the small lobby. Behind the counter was an ageless brunette, with not a whole lot of clothes on. This was becoming a theme tonight, he thought. He walked up to the counter.

"Um, hi."

"Hi," replied the brunette with a warm smile.

"I need a place to stay, and I was wondering..."

"Do you know who you want?"

"Um, no, not really..." replied Zach, not sure which way the conversation was going

"Let me take you, we can pick someone together."

A light bulb went off.

"Oh, uh, wait, no... that's not necessary. Can I just have a room for the night?"

The brunette smiled.

"Ah, you're one of those... I'm Inge by the way."

Zach flashed a genuine smile back, realizing how ironic the situation was. Inge had an air of European sophistication about her, and Zach was oddly attracted to her. On any other day, at some bar back in Washington, DC, he would have hoped to get lucky with her. This time, getting lucky would mean just the opposite.

"I just need a place to stay..." he repeated, hoping the connection he felt would be mutual. Inge hesitated.

"Well, you're cute, you look honest... how much can you pay per night?"

"Fifty dollars?" said Zach, hoping the amount would suffice. Inge paused one more time.

"There's a room on the third floor, in the back. It's small and I keep my stuff there, but you can stay in that room if you want, I won't need it until the morning. You'll have to pay upfront."

"Can I stay a couple of nights?"

"During the night, yes but I need it during the day."

Zach thought the price was steep for half a room in a brothel and no privacy, but his options were limited. This way he would be off the grid, and hopefully safe from his Russian pursuers. Zach handed her two fifty-dollar bills.

"Thank you so much, here is for tonight and tomorrow."

Inge grabbed the cash without a word. She showed him the narrow staircase in the back and went back to the front desk. He climbed the stairs quickly and found the room on the third floor, just as she had said. It was a small room, a closet really, with a twin bed in the middle and barely a foot of clearance around it. He didn't care, it was good enough for the night and no one knew he was here. He had paid Inge cash and had not told her his name. Zach dropped his backpack on the bed and scanned the room. At one end of the room was a cabinet with built-in shelves. He opened it and found what appeared to be Inge's personal belongings, a mix of clothes and bathroom items. At the other end of the room was a small door, opening into an even smaller closet with a diminutive shower stall and a matching sink. Zach brushed his teeth and laid down on top of the bed. He felt like he had just broken into some-one's tiny home and was not comfortable changing. He could hear all sorts of noises around him, patrons and providers going about their business. Zach was exhausted and fell asleep quickly.

The door, opening with a loud, creaky sound, woke him up the following morning. The rising sun was casting a bright ray of light into the room. Standing in the door opening he could see Inge, her svelte body towering above him. She seemed tired but was smiling at him.

"Hi, I need the room"

"Hi, oh sure, come in I'll be right out."

"I'm done around 7am, I'll be back about the same time tomorrow morning, in case you need to get ready" added Inge. Zach got up promptly and gathered his belongings. He was glad he hadn't changed and was ready to go.

A few minutes later he sat down, a tall caramel macchiato in hand at a Starbucks a couple of blocks down the street on the edge of the red light district. Before he could do anything else, Zach needed to figure out how the Russians had tracked him and whether his quantum encryption was compromised. He booted his laptop up and established a secure VPN link back to his quantum server.

The first thing he needed to do was go through the gateway event logs for something unusual either right before or right after his last connection. He pulled up the log, located the lines around the time of his last connection, and zeroed in on the encryption key exchange between his machine and Otto's computer. Quantum encryption was particularly secure because the quantum gateway would generate a key using qubit entanglement. This meant the key, a series of qubits, would be shared between him and Otto in a state of quantum superposition in which it had no specific value yet. As soon as one of them would look at it, the key would transition to a collapsed state with a specific value that would be shared and unique between the two of them. Because of its quantum properties, if anybody eavesdropped on the key it would collapse into a specific state prior to being read, and Zach would know someone else had seen the key and the communication line was not secure.

What was strange in this case, it looked as if the key was duplicated through a quantum beam splitter at the quantum gateway, and sent to two different destinations, one being Otto's, the other one unknown. Stranger still the key was collapsed into two different states. One duplicate had arrived at Otto's machine still in a state of superposition, as if no one had eavesdropped, while the other duplicate had been collapsed into a specific value and gone to its destination. It was as if the same key was being used by two different connections *in two different realities.*

Zach remembered a series of experiments that had been conducted a decade earlier. Physicists had been able to split photons into two different realities, validating experimentally the paradox known as Wigner's friend. The implication had been either there is no objective reality, or the universe itself violates locality, distant events can instantly influence each other.. The results sounded so crazy the research community had shrugged it off at the time. Yet here it was, Zach was staring at the same result right in front of him. Except this time someone had exploited the Wigner's friend paradox to break his unbreakable quantum encryption!

This still made no sense to Zach. Perhaps this was related to what Tom was after? He had gone to great lengths to encode his files using genetic computing. Was he trying to safeguard his files from quantum hackers? There was only one way for Zach to find out. He was going to have to decrypt the rest of Tom's files. He had only broken through two files so far, there were thirty files left. The DNA computing rig he set up with Cunningham would be able to break through the rest of the files. The only issue was he couldn't be sure his communications would be secure, the Russians might track him down again. He decided he would encrypt his link multiple times and go through multiple servers as best as he could. They might break through it eventually, but it would slow them down and buy him the time he needed.

31

With Zach effectively on the run, Otto had started spending more time at Quantum's headquarters in Tyson's Corner. As a senior board member and mentor of Zach, he had his own office down the hall from Zach's and used it occasionally. The word to the staff was that Zach was on a roadshow to meet with investors and advisors. Otto was manning the store back home, ensuring Masha and everybody else was focused on getting the company's sales back on track.

He looked concerned this morning. He had just received an email from Igor. As promised, some minions of his back in Moscow had hacked into the Wall Street Journal server and found a draft article that appeared relevant. The draft was now showing on Otto's screen. Below the article, were three lines apparently written by Igor:

The article is the least of your concerns. Focus on keeping the company together. Zach is airborne. He'll surface in Brussels within the hour. He is not ready yet, but he is getting there.

Otto stared at the last two lines. He hadn't told Igor where Zach was. He hadn't told anyone. He put his coffee down slowly and started over from the top of the email.

SEC TO OPEN INVESTIGATION INTO INSIDER TRADING AT QUANTUM TECHNOLOGIES INC

WASHINGTON DC. The Securities and Exchange Commission is opening an investigation into alleged insider trading by its founder and chief executive Zach Hayes. According to anonymous sources a subpoena will be issued later this week formalizing the status of the investigation.

Otto frowned. This was truly going to do a number on their stock price.

"Awesome, thanks for letting us know, Rebecca... We appreciate the heads up," he mumbled to himself. Somehow sarcasm seemed to help. He was still reading Igor's email when he heard a knock on the door. It was Dave, Zach's executive assistant.

"Hi Otto. Sorry to bother you. The SEC is on the phone, and they really want to talk to Zach. I've already told them he's not available. It's Rebecca Jones, she seems to remember you. She asked if she could talk to you instead."

Otto paused and thought about it. *Speak of the devil...*

"Okay, I'll take her... Why don't you come in? Close the door, sit down and listen, we can compare notes after the call."

"Will do, sir. Let me transfer her call to this line."

Dave's fingers danced on his tablet, transferring the call

using his mobile interface. Seconds later they heard a familiar voice.

"Hi Mr. Krueger, thank you for taking my call, this is Rebecca Jones from the SEC."

"Hi Ms. Jones, my pleasure as always. How can I help you?"

"Well, my last conversation with Mr. Hayes did not go so well. We are launching an investigation and have a series of legal notifications in the works. I wish we didn't go that route, but Zach left me no choice. I wanted to let you guys know, and give you one more chance to work with us instead of against us."

"Oh, wow," replied Otto, taken aback. "I appreciate the chance Ms. Jones. I'm sorry you felt the need to go down this path... Of course, we'd rather cooperate with you and work constructively. What can we do to get this on the right track?"

"I'm glad you asked. We have a data request I'd like to send you, in lieu of a warrant, that covers seven different areas..." said Jones as she started droning on through her list of demands.

Otto put the phone on mute and stared at Dave. Part of him felt mad Zach had let it get out of control this bad with the government. This investigation was not making his job of keeping their stock afloat any easier. Part of him was mad he even had to deal with this in the first place. He was going to make Dave make it go away.

"Dave, you're a young man. You've met her, right?"

Dave nodded silently.

"I want you to go meet with her, take her out for dinner. A really nice dinner at a really nice place. I want you to wine her, dine her, and fuck her. Like a fucking stud! Make her take this data request back or pare it down, we can't have this going on right now. Do what you gotta do, I don't care."

Dave's jaw dropped, his mouth agape. He didn't know what to say, still shocked by the contrast between Otto's usual statesmanlike demeanor and the vulgarity of his diatribe. He looked at the polycom. The mute indicator was green, not red. Somehow Jones and her team had heard the whole exchange. She had stopped going through her data request. A few seconds passed, the air thick with embarrassment. Jones was the first to break silence.

"Okay... that was our data request, we'll send you an electronic copy after this call."

"Great, thank you for that," replied Otto, pretending nothing happened. Jones was only too happy to play along.

"Then we'll be back in touch later this week regarding the investigation. I appreciate your cooperation. Goodbye."

"Sounds like a plan, goodbye."

Otto hung up and turned to Dave.

"Crap! Well, so much for that... We're fine Dave, just let me know when she comes back. In the meantime, let's engage Wahlberg & Hicks. They're the best law firm for white collar crime situations. They deal with this all the time, they'll know what to do."

"White collar crime?" asked Dave, incredulous.

"Oh Dave, it's an expression... Don't worry about it and get them on the video bridge please."

A few days later, as expected, a gaggle of SEC agents showed up at the Quantum Technologies headquarters. They flashed their badges to the receptionist and proceeded to go to the second floor, where Masha's office was. A minute later they were knocking on Masha's door.

"Ms. Torre? This is Dennis Bell from the SEC again. We're back, as promised, with a warrant..."

"Hi. Oh, really? What do you need?"

"Your documents. All of them. Emails, sales reports, management reports, marketing analyses you might have run, handwritten notes from meetings. Everything."

"No way, this sounds very broad... Can I see your warrant? Do you have the document with you?"

Masha's heart was racing, her hands felt feverish, she could feel her fingers shake ever so slightly. She tried to maintain her composure. She didn't want to let the SEC roam free, but the warrant looked pretty official, and deep down she knew they were right. Masha stared at the warrant handed to her. Its scope was very broad, including everything the agent had mentioned. This did not bode well. A judge had had to agree to this and it meant they had some evidence already to justify this. She handed the document back to Bell.

"Um, okay. Where do you want to start?"

"Why don't you step out of your office and my colleagues can handle it from here? Make sure your computer is unlocked. Then you and I can grab the conference room next door and have a chat, I have a few questions for you."

Masha did not like the sound of it, but she really didn't have a choice.

"Sure, there you go."

They sat down moments later in the meeting room. Masha remembered going hunting once with her father as a little girl. Her father had insisted she come along, but she didn't like killing animals. As a compromise, they had settled on hunting rabbits with a BB gun. She recalled the vivid impression she had had, watching the rabbit pop its head up only to be hit by a pellet. She had run to the poor trembling thing, holding it in her hands before it passed. Masha had never hunted again, but the fear of the animal, the look in its eyes, had stuck with her for a long time. Why did this come back to her? She shook it off and turned toward the SEC agent.

"So, Ms. Torre, if you don't mind, I have a few questions."

"Sure, shoot away."

As the agent began talking Masha could see through the glass door Dave, Zach's assistant. Their stares crossed paths for a brief moment. He seemed alarmed and walked away briskly.

"... so, have you and Zach Hayes ever discussed sales results together?"

"Of course we have, I'm the head of marketing! It's my job to discuss sales results with the CEO."

She hated when government types would do that. He knew the answer, yet he had to ask. She didn't like this game, yet she understood they had to go through it.

"When was your last discussion?"

"I can't actually remember, we talk on a regular basis. You'd have to check my calendar, all my meetings are generally booked there."

"Okay, we will. Do you remember having any discussion with Mr. Hayes about sales dropping, a disappointing sales forecast, anything material regarding an adverse change in sales expectations?"

Masha hesitated. She realized right away where the agent was going with this line of questioning. That meant they had to have flagged Zach's stock trade. She understood the trade was so wrong of him. She had told Zach as much! And now, here she was, being questioned by a government employee.

"Let me think..."

She was trying to get more time. She knew what Zach did was wrong, yet she felt fiercely loyal to him. He had given her this opportunity when no one else would, she had been paid handsomely with generous equity grants. She wasn't going to throw him to the wolves. Yet she knew it was wrong and was struggling with it.

"Ms. Torre, is there something you're not telling me? Insider trading is a crime, it's theft..."

Bell paused for effect.

"And let me remind you, accessory to theft is also a crime."

"Well, there was this one time..."

Otto stepped into the room and interrupted her.

"Masha, you don't have to talk to him. They have a warrant, but they shouldn't talk to anyone in the building without legal counsel."

He then turned to the agent.

"I don't appreciate you guys talking to employees like this. You and I both know we should have attorneys in the room. From now on you'll go through me, and we'll put a proper protocol in place. We'll cooperate, we'll schedule interviews for you guys, but no more roaming the hallways. Clear?"

The agent stood up and moved closer to Otto. He stopped inches from his face.

"Clear. Make sure your people are available, we'll send you a list of employees we want to talk to."

As the SEC agent walked away, Otto sat next to Masha.

"Masha, you okay? You can't do that. I know Zach is not here, you should have called me first. We did nothing wrong, we have nothing to hide, but we need to go through proper channels, okay?"

Masha nodded.

"No more impromptu conversations, you let me and the attorneys handle it from now on."

"Sure."

"All right, I'm glad we talked," said Otto cheerfully. "See you later!"

Masha decided to go home early. She couldn't focus on work. Otto's words were still ringing in her ears. *We did nothing wrong, we have nothing to hide... Really? So why are we in legal lockdown mode then?* She didn't trust Otto, and she didn't trust company attorneys either. They would look after the company's best interests, not hers. She knew, in her heart of hearts, that Zach had done something wrong, and it was only a matter of time until hell would break loose. She needed her own attorney.

She drove without thinking, the way you do when a road is so familiar your hands know it without you. She had three hours before Lana's school let out.

The condo was quiet when she got home. She stood in the kitchen for a moment without taking her coat off, just standing there. On the refrigerator, held up by a magnet shaped like the Slovenian flag her mother had given her, was a drawing Lana had made two weeks ago in art class. A woman with yellow hair, Masha's hair was not remotely yellow but Lana had a limited palette, standing next to a smaller figure. Underneath, in the careful block letters of a seven-year-old: ME AND MOM.

She took her coat off.

She made tea she didn't drink and sat at the kitchen table with her laptop, telling herself she would work, knowing she wouldn't. She had seen Zach trade. She had been standing right there.

He had to have had a reason. That's what she kept telling herself. He always had reasons. She had followed his reasons for four years, had built her career on his reasons, had brought Lana into a one-bedroom apartment on a startup salary because she believed in his reasons. And she wasn't sorry. She wasn't. He had seen something in her that no one else had, and she had spent four years proving him right.

But she had stood right there.

She heard the school bus two floors below. She closed the laptop and went to the window. Sure enough, the yellow bus pulling away from the curb, and Lana on the sidewalk in her red coat, backpack enormous relative to her small frame, looking up at the building with the focused expression she wore when she was counting floors to find their window. Masha waved. Lana broke into a run for the entrance.

Three minutes later she burst through the door.

"Mom! Guess what?"

"What?"

"Mrs. Patterson said my solar system project is the best in the class. She said it's going to go in the hallway!"

"I told you the rings on Saturn were a good idea."

"You said they were too much."

"I said they were a good idea and also too much. Both things can be true."

Lana considered this with the seriousness she applied to most things, then dropped her backpack on the floor, always the floor, never the hook two feet away, and went to the refrigerator.

"We have no good snacks."

"We have apples."

"I said good snacks."

Masha watched her daughter root through the refrigerator with complete unselfconscious focus, her yellow-drawn hair in reality a dark brown ponytail, her red coat still on.

Whatever happens, she thought. Whatever I have to do.

She got up and hung Lana's backpack on the hook. She turned off the foyer light and stood in the dark for a moment, listening to the building settle. Tomorrow was going to be a hard day.

32

Zach took a sip of his macchiato and winced. It was extremely hot, and he had just burnt his tongue. He stared at the login prompt for the quantum computing server he and Cunningham had set up to process DNA data. His heart was racing, his fingers hesitant. He still had thirty files to decrypt to fully understand what Tom was researching. The task seemed impossible. There was no time to waste, he snapped out of it and started typing feverishly. He launched a decryption job on the next file, then, feeling like his time was being better used, went back to the first file he had already decrypted.

That file had mentioned an organization named the Hierarchy. His Russian assailants had also mentioned the Hierarchy and its leader, the Hierarch. That seemed like a good place to start, a good thing to understand if he was going to solve this riddle and get rid of the Russians. He pulled up the contents of the file on the screen and started flipping through it. Within seconds a strange geometrical chart caught his attention.

It showed an equilateral triangle with a circle inscribed inside, the edges of the circle tangentially touching the edges of the triangle. The three bisectors of the triangle were drawn. Seven dots were visible, one for each vertex, one in the middle of each edge, one in the middle of the triangle. Zach was intrigued, he felt like he had seen this figure previously, but he wasn't sure where. He kept on reading.

Only the Fano conjecture can explain the purpose of the Hierarchy, and why it was formed in the first place. The Youth Supreme Hierarch is really not an entity but a communication protocol that combines a daemon and a local agent operating within a distributed operating system. The storage system appears to be partitioned into thirty-one different buckets, the contents of each bucket will be described in separate files for security purposes.

The Fano conjecture? A communication protocol? To communicate what? And with whom? A communication protocol implied a sender and a receiver. Tom had gone to extraordinary lengths to encrypt this. Not just to hide it, but to preserve it. As if the information itself needed to survive something. Zach had the unsettling feeling he was reading instructions written for someone who wasn't here yet.

He paused and stared through the window of the coffee shop for a few minutes. Here he was, in a foreign city, on the run. Russians were after him, and somehow both them and Tom were in some way related through the hierarchy. How was that even possible? He had randomly picked up Tom at a homeless clinic in Baltimore. Otto had brought the Russians on as investors. This had to be a coincidence, but honestly what were the odds? Zach knew it was only a matter of time until he would figure it out. It would also only be a matter of time until the Russians would catch up to him. He dove right back into Tom's files.

33

A few days later Masha found herself in a wood paneled conference room on the fifth floor of a beautiful mid-century building, blocks away from the National Mall. She glanced out the window and saw the top of the US Capitol. She looked around the room and noticed expensive modern art on the wall, a thick Persian rug on the floor. The place oozed with wealth and power.

The exchange with the SEC agent had genuinely spooked her. She knew she needed legal help she could trust, so she wouldn't get crushed as Zach's insider trade was inevitably going to unravel. She also realized it wasn't right and it bothered her. Luckily Beth, her roommate in college, had since become an attorney at Wahlberg & Hicks, and she was the first one Masha had called. She trusted her, she knew Beth had her back.

Masha turned around and saw Beth entering the room. Beth Ramirez was a petite brunette in her mid-thirties with a J.D. from Georgetown law school. The daughter of Guatemalan immigrants, she had gone on to become an

American success story. There she stood in her dark pantsuit, poised and smiling. She gave Masha a warm hug.

"Masha! It's been so long... what brings you here? You said you had some issues with work?"

"Oh Beth, thank you so much for meeting with me. It's been such a crappy week. I didn't know who to turn to, so I decided to reach out. Thank you so much for making time for me."

"Time for you? Come on, we were roommates! Of course, I would make time. Tell me what's going on..."

Masha went on to relate the events of the last few days, describing in a good amount of details the visit the SEC agents had paid to her office and the discussion that had ensued.

"So, what were they looking for, what did they drill you on?"

"Well, they kept asking all sorts of questions about what information I did or did not share with Zach Hayes, the founder and CEO. I'm the head of marketing, I also analyze sales trends and produce a sales forecast every month. They wanted to figure out whether I had discussed the forecast with Zach."

"Okay, so focusing on insider information that could be used for insider trading... Is that what the issue is?"

"I believe so."

"Do you have any sense of whether Zach in fact traded on this information? Did he share anything with you?"

Masha paused. This was a tricky question. She admired Zach for his vision, his relentlessness, his easy manner with people. He came from nothing and had created a company from scratch. He had given her an opportunity to prove herself as an executive when no one else would. And he was cute. She wasn't sure whether he liked her that way, but she had always felt some kind of odd tension between the two of them. And she had hoped at times... Power was a great intoxicant.

"What do you mean?"

"Do you know whether he ever traded on the information?"

Masha wasn't ready to throw him under the bus.

"I don't know... I don't think so. I'm not sure. Yes, I've briefed him many times and I see him occasionally on his computer trading, but who knows what he's up to?"

She couldn't come to terms with the fact that she had witnessed him trading on the information the moment she had told him about sales issues. He hadn't even been discreet about it, his intent was clear as day. But how could she share that? And destroy him? He had to have had a reason, a reason she couldn't understand but would become clear over time. She was struggling with her need to protect him, and the strong sense of right and wrong that had always guided her.

Beth could tell something wasn't right about what her friend was telling her. But she also knew the SEC would produce trading records, and they would ultimately find out whether and when Zach had traded his stock. Then, it would be a matter of establishing intent. And who was to say what his intent was? After all, her job was to protect Masha, the roommate that had always been there for her back in the days. And if Masha had a thing for this guy, she was okay with it. She would make sure Masha would stay out of trouble.

"You're right... Well, no worries, we'll figure it out as we go. In the meantime I need to run a conflict check with the firm before we can establish a client-attorney relationship. I don't expect it to be an issue, I should have an engagement letter out to you in a few days once the check is cleared."

"Thank you so much, Beth! I can't tell you how much better I feel knowing you are helping me with this."

They hugged and parted ways.

A few days after Beth had been formally engaged as Masha's legal counsel the SEC had reached out and requested an interview with Masha. She had insisted on doing it on her terms, with her attorney and without Otto. She was trying to navigate the whole situation carefully. She had wanted all along to support and protect Zach as best she could, but this was now becoming a bridge too far, and she finally had come to terms with this process. *The truth shall set you free.* No more lies, just the truth, plain and simple.

Agent Bell entered the room, followed by Rebecca Jones, and Beth. He walked toward Masha and extended his hand with a warm smile.

"Hi Ms. Torre, it's good to see you again. I appreciate you sitting down with us"

"Hi, my pleasure."

They sat down around the table, Bell jotted down a few notes.

"So, Ms Torre, let's pick it up where we left things off the last time we met. Do you remember having any discussion with Mr. Hayes about sales, anything material regarding an adverse change in sales expectations?"

Masha paused and blinked repeatedly. She did not want to go down that path, she did not want to let go. Yet she realized her options were extraordinarily limited. Masha swallowed hard, and finally let it go. Once she did, the floodgates opened. She told them everything she had already told Beth during their briefing. Then came the question she dreaded.

"Ms. Torre, once you shared this information with Zach Hayes, did you get any sense that he intended to do something about it?"

"Well, of course."

"Can you elaborate?"

"He's the CEO, this is his company, of course he would use the information to put in place an action plan to turn around sales."

Masha was growing uncomfortable and readjusting herself. The SEC agent could tell, he sensed an opportunity at hand.

"Have you ever seen him trade? Let me remind you this deposition is under oath, Ms. Torre."

Masha sat silent, staring at Agent Bell. He repeated the question.

"Did you get any sense he intended to trade on the information you gave him on that day? We are simply trying to establish intent here. We understand Mr. Hayes sold stock. Our team will go back to the trading logs, confirm the exact time it took place, and whether it was before or after your meeting with him. I suggest you tell us the truth, ma'am."

Masha was still staring. *The truth shall set you free...* She felt emotionally exhausted. She thought about Lana. Right now, at this exact moment, Lana was at school, probably at lunch, probably trading her apple slices for someone's crackers, probably being sent back to her seat for talking. Lana, who had never done anything to anyone, who had drawn her mother with yellow hair and written ME AND MOM in careful block letters and put it on the refrigerator. The world Lana was inheriting was the world these people in this room were trying to keep honest. The world Masha's parents had crossed an ocean to find. A place where the truth meant something. Where what you did and what you said were supposed to be the same thing.

Zach had not done what he said he would do. She wanted to protect Zach but also couldn't lie about it. The agent was right, sooner or later they would find out the exact time. They would find out whether she was covering for him or not. This was over.

She nodded.

"Yes," she finally said, looking away. "He was very concerned. He said he really needed the money. He completed the trade right in front of me."

Masha sat, a dreadful sense of guilt washing over her. She didn't want to look at Beth, but knew what she was going to say as soon as they would leave the room. *How could you hide this from me?* She felt terrible about letting Zach down too.

"There, I've said it. Yes, I briefed Zach Hayes on our sales collapsing, and he then proceeded to sell his stock in front of me. I told him it was a terrible idea, but he wouldn't listen," she added, with a tone that was turning defiant. "Is that all? Do you have any other questions?"

"No, I think we're good for today. We might come back to you with additional questions later on, but I think we're done for now. This concludes the deposition, you may go."

Masha stood up and walked out with Beth in tow. Bell watched them as they walked away. All were silent. He then turned to Jones.

"We definitely have enough evidence to issue an arrest warrant for Hayes. Next is Otto Krueger. The two of them are definitely in cahoots, we can nail them for conspiracy to defraud investors. I talked to Dave, the executive assistant, and got a copy of their calendars. I also have a copy of their phone logs. They had multiple conversations that day, including a twenty-minute call right after he talked to her."

Jones looked at him and smiled.

"Sounds like we'll get a warrant for him too."

34

Otto was sitting uncomfortably in a plush leather chair facing the rest of the board room. The mood in the room was somber. All seven members of the board were sitting around the table. In addition to Otto were the representatives of various investment funds who had purchased significant blocks of Quantum Technologies stock at the time of its IPO on the NASDAQ. Otto was the only one among the group of initial investors who had not cashed out and had stayed with the company as it had gone from privately-held, venture-backed to publicly listed. He had seen it evolve from Zach's idea to a fast growing startup to its current state. Still very much a startup, a youngling of a company compared to many others, but with the backing of institutional funds and the resulting compliance oversight that came with it. The days of fast and loose decision-making were gone.

A massive screen at one end of the room showed an article on the site of the Wall Street Journal. The large headline, plastered across the screen, was impossible to ignore.

QUANTUM TECHNOLOGIES UNDER INVESTIGATION BY SEC FOR INSIDER TRADING

Founder alleged to have sold shares in anticipation of sales slowdown

One of the hedge fund representatives, across the table from Otto, put his glasses down and turned to him.

"Otto, can you explain this? How come none of us were given a heads up about this? Do you realize how big a deal this is?"

"I understand Ron, trust me, I was as surprised as the rest of you by this..." replied Otto

The hedge fund representative pursed his lips.

"How do you explain this? What's going on? You are our eyes and ears here, you've been with this company since the beginning. We invested because we knew you were keeping your money invested, you weren't cashing out with the other venture funds. You have an office in the building. Please tell me what's going on? And where is Zach anyway, how come he's not here?"

"Zach is missing at this time, Ron. He's in Europe somewhere, we are tracking him down but haven't managed to get a hold of him yet."

"Is he MIA? Are you telling me he's on the run as the SEC is investigating us?"

"No, I'm sure we'll find him soon, it's only a matter of time..."

"Well he'd better turn up soon, or he's going to dig a deeper hole for himself. I still have friends at the SEC, we're in a very delicate position right now."

"What do you mean?" said Otto, trying to draw him out.

"Otto, I chair the audit committee of this company, it's my job to know about anything that presents a material risk, anything that would impair the long-term value of this business. I received a notice this morning from the SEC informing me they had issued an arrest warrant for Zach. He has twenty-four hours to turn himself in, or he will be considered a fugitive. You'd better find him soon or the US marshals will be after him."

Otto turned pale.

"As soon as we get a hold of him, I'll be sure to let you know."

"In the meantime, our stock is in the toilet, gentlemen. The market is pricing in a steep decline in sales as well as an additional discount for the uncertainty surrounding the SEC investigation. No one in his right mind will touch the stock until we resolve this somehow."

"Ron, what do you suggest we do?"

"Well, for starters, we should terminate Zach. We're all grateful for his contribution to the company, but we can't have a felon running this company."

"Ron, you're talking as if he's been convicted already..."

"He might as well be because that's the market's conclusion already. He's going to need time to defend himself and it's going to be a huge distraction. We need focus, we can't afford this circus, Otto. I am putting forth a motion to terminate Zach Hayes and begin a search for his successor immediately. All in favor?" said Ron, looking around the table for approval. One by one, all of the members raised their hand in assent. All but Otto.

"Otto, are you going to vote against this motion? Against terminating a chief executive that is about to be arrested by the SEC for insider trading? They don't issue warrants lightly, you know..."

Otto raised his hand, reluctantly. Ron smiled.

"Let the record show that the vote was unanimous. Now on to the next order of business, gentlemen. We need to recapitalize this business."

Ron looked at his notes one more time.

"We burnt through five hundred millions this past quarter to support our growth objectives. If my notes are correct, we currently have about six weeks of cash left on the books. You've all seen our strategic plan, we'll need over a billion and a half this year to make it to break-even. I had my people take a look at the budget, I believe we can cut back on a few things and make it work with about a billion. There are five funds invested in this company and represented here today, that's about two hundred million a piece unless Otto declines to participate in which case it will be two hundred and fifty a piece... Otto, what do you think, will you tag along?"

Ron had stopped and was looking at Otto. The rest of the board members were looking at him too. Clearly Ron had briefed them before this board meeting, as none of them appeared surprised by Ron's proposal. *Thanks for including me in your pre-meeting, asshole,* thought Otto. He paused, then put on the best smile he could muster.

"Ron, this is a rhetorical question... you know perfectly well I can't follow you guys. I'm a small venture fund, not a large hedge fund."

"Let the record show Krueger Ventures was given a chance to co-invest and declined."

Otto winced as Ron continued.

"For our second motion today we are proposing a recapitalization of the company, in the amount of one billion dollars to be subscribed by the four funds represented around the table. The equity will be issued as a new class of shares with enhanced voting rights. Due notice will be given to other minority investors and put up for a vote at a special shareholder meeting to be scheduled."

Otto almost choked.

"Enhanced voting rights?"

"The new shares will come with one hundred votes per share."

"As opposed to the one vote per share we have now? That's egregious Ron, you can't do that!"

"That will be for shareholders to decide, Otto. In the meantime let's put it up for a vote by the board. All in favor?"

Looking around the table, Otto saw again all other members raising their hand to approve. He had just been outmaneuvered by Ron, who was taking advantage of this to take over the company and dilute his shares and Zach's into nothingness. They had the votes to control the company so it was effectively a done deal. They could sue based on their minority rights, but given Zach's, and soon his, position with the SEC, they would be in a difficult position to argue anything with a judge in a Delaware court. Otto felt a strong sense of anger and shame weigh on him like a lead blanket.

"Ron, you got me... You get the company today. Keep in mind it's a long game though. I will remember this. Some day, you will come back to me begging. This is not the end of it!

"Let the record show, four votes in favor, one against."

Otto felt rage rising through his chest. He wanted to grab Ron and punch him to a pulp, punch him until his stupid smile would go away. He stood up and stormed out of the room instead. As soon as he was in the hallway, Otto called Zach. He was careful to use his encrypted voice messaging app to avoid being traced or recorded.

"Hey Otto, I can't talk for long, what's up?"

"Zach, I just got out of a board meeting. Ron and the hedge fund guys just engineered a take-over..."

"What? That's not possible! You can't do that with me, without my vote!"

"Zach, there's something else... The SEC has issued an arrest warrant for you. You have twenty-four hours to surrender, or they will come after you. That warrant also means you lose your governance rights. The moral turpitude clause, remember? Ron really chose the perfect time to do this, he had all the other guys lined up behind him."

Zach was speechless, stunned by the news.

"We probably shouldn't talk too long, I realize the line is encrypted but you never know. There's a lot we need to go figure out, let's catch up again tomorrow Zach. Talk to you later."

The following morning Zach felt blood draining from his face when he read the news on the Wall Street Journal website:

SECOND ARREST EXPECTED IN SEC PROBE OF QUANTUM TECHNOLOGIES

Unnamed senior official at the agency acknowledged the scope of the investigation now includes conspiracy to defraud investors. Arrest warrant issued for CEO Zach Hayes, currently missing. Chairman and early investor Otto Krueger expected to be arrested later this week, Krueger Ventures assets seized.

Zach's mind switched into overdrive. He had been so focused on his TP53 biohack, he had taken his eyes off the ball with the company. He shut his laptop and looked around. There he was, in a seedy Amsterdam hotel, trying to figure out the quantum encryption job of his life and his support system had been taken away from him. He had just lost all of his stock in the company, his status as CEO, access to Otto's private jet. Russian henchmen were after him unless he could figure out a plan quickly, and soon enough US marshals would be tracking him down. Zach walked to the tiny bathroom in his tiny bedroom. He looked in the dirty, partly shattered mirror. *This is no time to feel sorry for yourself... focus!*

35

"I wish you would have told me," said Beth looking at Masha. They were standing next to Masha's car outside the law firm's office where they had just finished their deposition with the SEC. Her tone was devoid of reproach. Ever the consummate professional, she was trying to coach a client. A client who happened to be a dear friend.

"He is a good man," replied Masha, wiping away a tear. "I didn't want to throw him under the bus, but I didn't want to lie either..."

Beth just stared at her, silent, giving her the space and the time to say more. Masha was not in a talking mood after the deposition.

"I'd better go. I need to go clear my head".

She gave Beth a hug and stepped into her car.

As she drove away, a thousand thoughts were colliding in Masha's head. She looked at her watch. It was one o'clock. The deposition had taken three hours. Somehow it had felt much longer but it was only the middle of the day. She still had a few hours before she would have to go pick up her daughter Lana from school. She couldn't stop thinking about the deposition and replaying the events of the morning in her head. Masha had never expected she would have to betray Zach.

She had always admired him. Like her, he came from a humble background. When Masha and her parents had immigrated from Eastern Europe she was still just a toddler. They had raised her believing in the American dream, in the fact that you can come from nothing, work hard and make it to the top. She had been encouraged at school to lean in, to be everything she could be. Yet she had also realized that, beyond the kind words of encouragement, privilege mattered. She had never been able to fit in with the cool kids. When later on she had pursued business in college, a major she had picked to ensure she would achieve the life her parents could never afford, she had realized how much of an outsider she was.

She had gotten admitted to Yale University on the mere strength of her SAT scores and the volunteer work she had done with the immigration services non-profit that had welcomed her family years prior. Yet all around her signs of privilege, signs of forbidden worlds had abounded. She had not been able to afford ski weekends in Killington, Vermont, or sailing getaways in the US Virgin Islands with her classmates. She had not been able to afford the same clothes. Even though they spoke the same language, her classmates had felt like a world away. Beth had been the one to show her the ropes, to coach her, to help her be as American as she could be.

When the time had come to get a job, she had followed in the footsteps of her classmates and had pursued investment banking and technology opportunities. Interview after interview every investment banker had given her the same feedback. *Not a good cultural fit.* She had hated it. *What does that mean? I didn't dress the right way? Or didn't play lacrosse?* Interviews with technology companies had been a different yet similar story. A lot of cool kids were getting eye-popping offers from well-funded start-ups. She had gotten an eerily similar response from the hoodie-clad tech bros — *not a good cultural fit...*

As she was about to accept a boring marketing trainee job with Oracle, a big database company, she had gone to one more interview on a hunch. It was a small startup, they hadn't secured a large round of funding yet, but the topic had intrigued her, quantum encryption. The founder had interviewed her personally, and she had been mesmerized by his vision, his energy, his passion. She had never forgotten her first encounter with Zach.

He had given her a chance when she needed one badly, and she had followed him since. They had done well as a team; she was the voice of reason, the planner who would make sure the wildest vision would be supported by a pragmatic and well-thought-out plan. The partnership had worked well. Until now.

Why did you have to do this, Zach? Why did you have to involve me in this, why do the fucking trade right in front of me? You couldn't wait until you were back in your office and I was out of sight?

Masha was pleading with herself. She could have simply lied. *No ma'am, I saw nothing of the sort.* A bald-faced lie.

But then she would have been no better than the world from which her parents fled. They had raised her a quintessential Puritan, with the faith of the convert, the joy of the faithful who found the light.

Do what you say, and say what you do. The ten commandments, the whole nine yards. To others it might have seemed like a naïve embrace of Norman Rockwell's America. To her it had simply been a straightforward path. Choose the path of light, speak the truth, say what you mean, treat others with compassion. Life just turned out to be so much simpler, so much purer lived that way. As it should.

Much as she tried to avoid acknowledging it, she had been deeply mad at Zach for effectively betraying her trust by being so brazen with his insider trade. Their unspoken pact had always been a mutually beneficial trade. She was drawn to Zach's vision, passion, energy as a tech founder. He had clearly appreciated her clear-eyed advice and support, her ability to keep him on a straight path while navigating the many traps and pitfalls along the way, as they had built an incredibly successful tech start-up. He appreciated her strength as a straight arrow who spoke truth to power. Zach had to know his transgression, so brazen, right in front of her, would test her and present a dilemma she did not want to handle.

Why did you do this? This is a lose-lose, so stupid... Of course she had had to tell the truth to Rebecca Jones and her SEC minions. Much as she admired Zach, to have lied and covered it up would have been to completely lose herself and what her parents fought for. Zach had nudged her along quite a bit, but this was a bridge too far. So she had spilled the beans and come clean with the SEC. In hindsight the choice was obvious, and her mind was starting to settle.

She made a cup of tea and turned on the television, trying to change her mind. Ever the news junkie she switched the channel to CNN. The chyron caught her attention:

MYSTERIOUS FLU OUTBREAK IN DC AREA, SCHOOLS CLOSED UNTIL FURTHER NOTICE

She turned up the sound.

"A mysterious flu virus has taken over the DC area. So far 27 people have died, mostly seniors over the age of sixty and young children under the age of ten. The CDC has dispatched a medical team to work with the Department of Health Services in DC. Schools have been closed until the outbreak is under control. This virus is particularly lethal, the survival rate of about fifty percent is on par with that of Ebola patients before Ebola treatment became widely available. Authorities are encouraging people to wash their hands and avoid crowded areas as much as possible. Students in the DC public school system and most private schools are being dismissed early today and sent back home. Be sure to make plans if you have a child in school today."

Crap, now this! I gotta run... Masha grabbed her keys and rushed to school to pick up Lana. The news flash was alarming, and she didn't want her to ride the bus home. It was going to be long and crowded with potentially sick students.

She arrived at the Tenleytown elementary school a few minutes later. The scene was otherworldly. Throngs of parents massed by the main entrance, eagerly waiting and looking for their offspring. A woman that appeared to be the principal came out through the front door with a bullhorn. She motioned to the crowd to back off and started speaking.

"All right folks, please back off. We're going to have to work together to make this an orderly dismissal. Please back off, and be patient. We've had a lot of calls from concerned parents who don't want their kids on the bus today. We are going to bring the kids one class at a time starting with pre-K and ending with fifth graders. We will announce the class, you will recognize your kids and their teachers. Please be kind and let other parents get to their kids. Kids that do not have their parents here will get on the bus, as they would on a normal day. Please back off, again. Thank you for your cooperation."

She then turned back to let the first batch of pre-schoolers out. A first wave of relieved parents rushed to meet their children. Hugs and relief. Masha's daughter Lana was a fifth grader. This was going to be a long dismissal... As each class came out, more hugs and sighs of relief, a thinning crowd of anxious parents. Then the fifth graders came out, still no Lana. Masha could feel a lump in her throat, her palms were getting sweaty. As the last class was dismissed she looked around, an awful feeling of dread weighing on her. She approached the principal.

"Hi, I am Lana Torre's mother. I was hoping to pick her up today. Do you know where she is? Did she get on the bus by chance?" asked Masha, her voice slightly shaky.

"Let me check..." replied the principal, putting her reading glasses on to look at a list on her tablet. "Torre, Lana... there she is! She was taken to the hospital by the CDC team that was here earlier today to investigate. They were supposed to notify you, but obviously with this chaos it hasn't happened yet. Sorry about that, it's been a crazy day..."

"What? Where can I find her?"

"Um, let me see... they took her to Walter Reed for additional tests. She'll be in the infectious disease department, I believe they've quarantined her. You should go there and talk to the medical staff if you want more information."

36

Zach's fingers were flying over the keyboard of his laptop, entranced in a dance of their own. He had spent all day at a rinky-dink coffee shop in Amsterdam, focused on decoding Tom's files. He had learned more about the conjecture Tom had formulated. Tom was convinced the physical world was somehow part of a larger universe with additional dimensions. *How cheesy... he must have read too many sci-fi novels,* thought Zach. The idea of additional dimensions, or even that of a multiverse, was nothing new, he thought. Quantum mechanics had in fact pointed in that direction for over a century.

People around him were coming and going. In the background he could hear the massive espresso machine hissing, with the clicking and clacking of a barista engaged in a ballet of concocting cappuccinos and other macchiatos. He focused back on the data in front of him, parsing through files, alternating between the sequence they had identified in Tom's genome and the sequence they had inserted in the viral vector for the antidote.

His mind kept getting distracted by the espresso machine when it finally hit him. The viral shell was truncating the genetic materials! How had he not realized this before? Of course, that was the answer... they had identified the correct sequence and inserted it into the viral shell, but its payload was limited, there was only so much it could carry. In their haste, he and Cunningham had neglected to check whether the full sequence was being carried through to the patient. Feeling the rush of excitement, he looked around and saw a patron at the table next to him, a petite blonde in her late twenties sipping her frappuccino. She reminded him of Emily. Emily, who had died because they had missed this cut-off effect. He was excited yet so disappointed at the same time. *Man, how did we miss this?*

Focusing back on his work he started thinking through a way out of this conundrum. It was now obvious to him they would not be able to use a viral shell as a vector for the edited genetic materials, their payload was too limited. Other options were not much more attractive either. Then he remembered what Cunningham had mentioned. What about nanoclews? Unless they repackaged the payload it was going to get truncated the same way... but they could adapt the payload to fit within the shell of a nanoclew whereas they couldn't with a viral shell.

Zach's hands were getting shakier, as if a tremor was taking over. Was it truly the excitement or was the virus that had killed Emily finally starting to affect him? He shook his head. He did not have the gene that made him vulnerable to the outbreak. But he did have the TP53 mutation that had killed his mother, the reason he had gotten on this path in the first place. His telomeres were shrinking at an accelerated pace, he reminded himself. And he was starting to feel the effects of his shrinking telomeres as his organs were aging at an accelerated pace.

He really needed to talk to Cunningham about next steps; they needed to prepare a new antidote as soon as possible. But Zach didn't want to share his findings until he could confirm them, more confusion was the last thing they needed and he didn't want to get Cunningham on the wrong track again. He grabbed his smartphone, selected the encrypted messaging app and dialed Cunningham.

"Hey Zach, I was getting worried about you, it's been a while. Are you okay? Where are you?"

"Hi Doctor, I'm okay and I still can't talk much. I think I've figured out something we missed with the antidote"

Cunningham felt his stomach drop.

"No way, what is it?"

"Well, let me run a few more checks, I'm still running a few simulations on all potential interactions... I think it's promising, but let me just run my checks first. Either way, we're running short on time, will you be able to get started on the new antidote pronto once I give it to you?"

"Well, sure. We'll need to go through the same testing protocol, Zach. Keep in mind we've got an epidemic going on here in the DC metro area now. Emergency measures are in place. I can make it to the hospital and the lab because I have a health worker clearance, but things are just not the same here, definitely not business as usual. I suppose we could find test subjects with some of the patients. With the mortality rate as high as it is for this epidemic, it's not like they have a great alternative. At least we're lucky that only some of the population has the mutation that makes them vulnerable to the virus."

"One more thing. Remember the TP53 mutation that started all this? It killed my mom..."

"I know Zach, of course I remember very well. You carry it too, that's why we got started on this path in the first place."

"Yes, well, I think it's finally affecting me. I've been shaking more recently, especially when I'm typing. Feels as if I was getting early-onset Parkinson's."

"Oh wow, I didn't think it would affect you so soon... can we get you back in here? I'd like to take a look at you."

"Yes, that's the other thing I gotta do. I have to find a way back. I think this nanoclew approach would work on me too, it's the same process after all and the same sequence, just edited differently."

Cunningham noticed Zach's slip but knew better than to ask.

"So... you're coming back here soon? You realize the SEC is looking for you, right? They'll arrest you as soon as you land. Plus you'd better not have a fever or you will not pass the infrared check at the border"

"I know... I'll find a way. I gotta call the SEC lady next. Let me work on this, I'll get back to you"

"Okay you take good care of yourself, Zach. Try to get here as soon as you can."

"I will, doctor. I will."

Zach felt slightly dizzy but there was no time to waste. He feverishly looked for Rebecca Jones' contact info in his messaging app. He dialed her right away.

"Hi, this is Zach Hayes..."

"Well, hello there, Mr. Hayes. You realize there's an arrest warrant for you? Are you calling to negotiate the terms of your surrender?"

"You tell me..."

"I assume you're tech-savvy enough to realize we are tracing this call as we speak?"

"I assume you realize I'm tech savvy enough to use quantum-encrypted IP routing that is far beyond your agency's capabilities..."

Rebecca tried not to let her disappointment show.

"Enough joking around, what you did was wrong and you know it. Why are you calling?"

"I want to work out a deal, I need to come back to the US."

"Aha, so you *are* calling about your surrender!"

"Well, not really, I was hoping we could help each other..."

"What do you mean?"

"Have you noticed the Russian hedge funds you're after are always a step ahead of you? Why do you think that is?"

"I have no idea what you're talking about Mr. Hayes..."

"Come on! You guys get an arrest warrant for one of the bad guys when they're in New York, and as soon as the warrant is issued the bad guy leaves the same day. Don't you think that's strange?"

"How do you know this? "

"Like I said, I'm tech savvy enough..."

"What else do you know?"

"Those guys are front running your press releases and your communications to the outside world. They've hacked into your system. I figured out how, and I can stop it."

"Okay, you've got my attention."

"I will help you stop the hack and catch the bad guys, but you need to give me immunity first. No insider trading prosecution, no permanent bar from running a public company, the works."

Rebecca hated seeing a bad guy get off the hook, and in her mind Zach was a self-entitled white collar criminal that had stolen money from the investing public, but at the same time the Russian hedge fund managers were a much bigger fish. She reluctantly agreed.

"Okay, maybe we can work this out. But I'll need a number of things from you."

"What is it?"

"First, I need you to testify against Otto Krueger. You will be off the hook, but someone needs to be held accountable for this insider trade. That is non-negotiable."

Zach paused. Otto had been such a supportive mentor over the years, practically a second father. How could he give him up? But not agreeing to this meant Zach was not going to be able to develop the antidote in time. It also meant he was not going to be able to test the antidote with other people. Cunningham needed his help packaging the genetic materials. He wouldn't be able to do it without Zach running his decryption algorithm. He would either betray Otto and save potentially millions of people, or be true to his mentor but die shortly while more people would also die. *The end justifies the means* he thought to himself, *as always...*

"Okay, I think I can live with that" replied Zach, in an almost Freudian slip.

"One more thing... You will disgorge all profits from the trade and pay a ten percent fine on top of it. That is also non-negotiable."

Zach did some quick math in his mind. He had already wired the funds from the trade to Cunningham. He was going to have to repay the SEC with his own funds, and with the stock in the toilet as it was, his portfolio was running particularly low. *I should have diversified,* he told himself. If he agreed to Rebecca's terms, he would have virtually nothing left. And the Russians would still be after him. But at least he would be able to go back to the States, meet Cunningham and nurse himself back to health. He was a survivor. Starting from scratch again did not faze him. He had done it before. Still, though. This was *starting from complete scratch all over again*. He stared at his fingers. The tremor was back, he couldn't hold them still. He steeled himself.

"Fine, do we have a deal then?"

"Deal. And you'd better deliver!"

37

After Zach hung up with Rebecca Jones he paused for a moment. Life around him went on as if nothing was wrong. The fact was, *nothing* was wrong. He was just a face in the crowd and absolutely no one cared about what was happening to him. Little did they understand they might soon get engulfed in an unstoppable epidemic that would wipe out a good portion of the Dutch population that was susceptible to the TP53 mutation. But then again, the rest of them would survive and life would go on as it always had. How depressing.

Zach looked at his watch. The day had gone by quickly, between a couple of phone calls and getting himself in the flow and engrossed in Tom's files. It was almost six o'clock. He was hungry and truly did not want to go back to the crappy hotel room out of which he had camped for the past few days. At least he had resolved his SEC issue. He still needed to deal with the Russians. He had managed so far to dodge them; he wondered whether it was because he had been far more careful with proper encryption. Zach felt pangs of hunger in his stomach and decided to go hunt for some kind of dinner. Once dinner was over he would deal with the logistics of traveling back to the states and how to evade his pursuers. At least his stay in the Red Light district was coming to an end, and he couldn't be more thrilled.

Zach left the coffee shop and started walking down the street. The day was slowly coming at an end in Amsterdam. Tourists were starting to scatter in the Red Light district, anxious to return to the safety of their cushy hotels and a different crowd was starting to emerge. Zach didn't want to deal with it. He was so homesick by now, he simply wanted to escape for a moment, escape to something familiar, something that would remind him of home. He picked up pace and quickly walked out of the Red Light district toward Nieuwmarkt down Bloedstraat. As he approached Nieuwmarkt he could see the crowd change. Fewer leery strangers, more moms and strollers. As he kept walking, a flyer caught his eye on the windshield of a car nearby. He stopped to look at it. It was an ad for a soccer game between the AFC Ajax, Amsterdam's soccer team, and Juventus, Turin's famed team. Zach had never been to a soccer game and thought this might be a welcome distraction, a way to kill a few more hours in the safety of an anonymous crowd. No one would ever know he was there. He quickly reviewed directions on his phone and went down the subway entrance at Nieuwmarkt station. A few minutes later he hopped on the line 54 metro to the Bijlmer Arena.

The twenty-minute ride felt like forever. Zach did not like to be cooped up in a train for that long. He was careful to scan his surroundings and examine everyone in his car. The Russians had tracked him before, would they find him again? As best as he could tell he was safe, but who knew, really? He finally arrived at the Arena station, and hopped off the train, rushing through the escalator and onto the streets.

What a contrast he found! A few minutes earlier he had been strolling through old Amsterdam, with a mix of tourists and well-off families, or even the Red Light district crowd. Streets had been small, cramped, and full of picturesque details with sixteenth century townhomes made of bricks, three or four stories high and no more than ten feet wide.

He was now on a large modern plaza, extending from the subway station all the way down to the arena, perhaps a quarter mile down. The crowd around him was now very different. It was an odd mix of hooligans and middle-class soccer fans. The hooligans were generally in their twenties, already half drunk loading up on Amstel beer before the game, desperate to forget about their lot in life and experience the vicarious buzz of victory through their home team. The middle class fans were themselves a grab bag, mostly middle-aged men, accountants and sales managers, with somehow a predilection for tight designer jeans. Zach tried not to laugh. He was there to relax and hide, not to attract attention to himself.

He could see the stadium in the distance with the massive, rambunctious crowd in between as far as the eye could see. And trash everywhere. On the ground, on the street, in overflowing trash cans. He could already hear, here and there, some fights breaking out. A few hooligans with energy and rage to spare. The game hadn't even started yet. Zach was beginning to wonder whether this was such a smart idea after all. He was still hungry and decided to re-prioritize his quest for dinner.

After a few minutes walking around the stadium grounds, dodging packs of excited fans, he found a burger joint that caught his attention. A fuchsia sign at the top of the entrance made it crystal clear what the menu was about.

BURGER BASTARD. Fuckin' Awesome!

Zach smiled. Europeans' attraction to all things American had always surprised him. Of all the things one could admire about the US, why pick burgers? And Europeans' appropriation of American culture and their bastardization of it was particularly humorous to him. No way a marketer back home, or any general counsel for that matter, would approve this bitch of a brand. Yet here it was obviously no big deal. Zach truly didn't care. He was starving, and the menu posted outside the restaurant seemed downright delicious.

He walked in and sat down at a table by himself. After a few minutes studying the menu, he ordered a *Meat Orgy* burger. Of course. Zach was ravenous and chomping down his Wagyu beef burger when someone put a hand on his shoulder and sat down next to him.

"Hi Zach, please don't freak out. I just want to talk."

Zach almost spit out his food. Yurij, the Russian handler was sitting across the table, looking at him with a half-smile. Zach instinctively looked for a gun but couldn't see any. Yurij's hands were on the table, unthreatening.

"What do you want?" replied Zach, moving his chair away from Yurij.

"I'm not here to hurt you. I know we didn't leave on the best of terms last time..."

"Yeah, really not."

"As I said, I just want to talk."

"Okay, well you found me... I'm all ears."

Yurij paused, figuring out where to start.

"At least you look like you got back on your feet," added Zach, almost smiling. Yurij laughed gently.

"Well, I'm still limping," said Yurij, pointing at his cane. "We didn't start on the right foot, did we? God, where do I even begin..."

"Well maybe you could tell me why you guys were trying to kill me."

"That was a misunderstanding... We never intended to harm you guys. And I'm sorry Emily didn't make it by the way, but her path was set way before we intervened. She was already infected when you guys left DC."

"Maybe, but you certainly didn't make it easier to get her an antidote."

"I wish things would have turned out differently. Our instructions were to get you, Zach, back on the right path, and focused on cracking Tom's files."

"So I could find the antidote?"

"Yes, among other things."

"Why then were you guys shooting at us in Corsica? You

killed Pavel, our skipper! You sure looked like you were going to kill us too."

"Pavel was bad news. He was running a human trafficking operation between Tunisia, Italy and France. You were easy bait for him, he was going to hand you over to his partners. The ship was anchored at its usual rendezvous point when we found you."

"So you guys tried to save us?"

"Yes we did... one of the reasons I'm here tonight is I believe you and Cunningham have figured out what didn't work with the antidote, haven't you?"

Zach stared at him, stunned.

"How did you..."

"We've been tracking your progress online, Zach"

"How can you? It's impossible, I used our best quantum encryption. I'd know if my sessions got compromised, the spin state of my keys on the quantum key server would be collapsed. I'd get a notification. No way Yurij, the only way you could spoof this is if somehow you break the locality assumption"

Yurij smiled at Zach.

"Zach, you're assuming there is such a thing as objective reality..."

"Of course, there is, what do you mean?"

"Just make sure you get us a dose of the antidote with the next batch, and set it aside. I'll be in touch again."

"Sure, but what did you mean with your comment on objective reality? Is this related to the conjecture Tom is referring to in his files?"

"Zach, you are further along than I thought, good! I cannot discuss such things with you now, the Hierarch would be mad at me if he knew."

"Yurij, enough with the bullshit! What is this all about? And you didn't mean to harm us, so what were you trying to do back in Corsica?"

"We wanted to implant a small tracker file into your DNA payload, a cookie, if you will. Of course we couldn't just walk up to you and shoot it up your arm."

"Come again? What does that even mean?"

"The answer is in Tom's files... I don't have time Zach, I gotta go."

Yurij looked at his watch and stood up slowly.

"Zach, it's been a pleasure as always. Igor will be in touch when you are back in DC."

"Igor, Otto's friend? When? And how are you guys connected? Was he behind this the whole time?"

"Not to worry, Igor knows where to find you. He will come talk to you when it is time."

Yurij stood up and walked away, limping and leaning on his cane. Zach watched him go. The bass from the speakers was rattling the plastic tray on the table.

He thought about the text in Lisbon. *It went well. Safe travels.* The email Otto had mentioned, those three lines that had spooked him: *Zach is airborne. He'll surface in Brussels within the hour. He is not ready yet, but he is getting there.* Not ready yet. He picked up his burger. It was cold. He put it back down. *When it is time.* Time for what, exactly?

Throbbing waves of bass were taking over the burger joint to the tune of Enter Sandman by Metallica. Zach grabbed his *Meat Orgy* and, realizing it was cold, dropped it back in the basket.

38

The trip from Amsterdam back to DC was uneventful. Zach had managed to buy a cheap ticket on United. Coach class, the days of flying around in Otto's private jet were now gone. The routine on the flight home had been a little bit different than usual.

"Ladies and gentlemen, we are about to descend. Our crew will go through the cabin and hand out both immigration forms and health forms for those of you who did not fill those online in your mobile passport app. Feel free to ask the crew if you need help to fill out these forms, especially the new health form."

Zach raised his hand and hailed a nearby flight attendant.

"Hi, what am I supposed to do with this health form?"

"Oh, that's new. It's really primarily for those who have a mutation that makes them sensitive to the TP53 outbreak."

"Really? What is that for?"

"Have you heard about the epidemic going on in the US right now? It's bad. It only hits people with a specific genetic marker, but if you have it the survival rate is terrible. Public health authorities will quarantine you if you're susceptible or even if you have a fever. The hospitals back home are overwhelmed."

"Wow..."

"Oh yeah, they have infrared scanners now in Dulles scanning for any sign of fever. If you're sick you'll just pop up as a bright spot on the IR scan, it's really cool how they do that now. Anyway, let me know if you need anything else, have a good day!"

Zach was lost in thought as the attendant walked away. He knew he did have the mutation. And he suspected he was probably a bit feverish by now. No way he was going to admit to it though. They would quarantine him, and he would never be able to meet with Cunningham. No Cunningham, no antidote. He'd be long dead before they would let him out of quarantine. He needed to clear immigration controls, somehow. Zach filled out his health form and checked out the healthy, no mutation box. He signed at the bottom of the form, right under the "I certify, under penalty of perjury, that the statements made herein are true and correct, to the best of my knowledge, information, and belief."

He still needed to figure out a way to make it past the infrared cameras at the airport. Zach stood up and went to the kitchen galley in the back of the plane, hoping he would find some inspiration on the way. As he arrived in the galley, an attendant asked him if he wanted something. Zach wasn't sure what to say.

"Sure, can I have a cup of water please?"

"Of course, with ice?"

Zach paused.

"Sure, that's great, thank you."

The attendant handed him the cup before walking away toward the cabin.

Zach was now alone, sipping his cup. An idea formed in his mind. Looking around the galley he found a Yeti cup, one of those thermos-type coffee cups. He grabbed it along with a small towel, stuffed some ice water in the cup, put the cap back on and walked back to his seat.

About thirty minutes later the passengers deplaned in Washington Dulles. Zach and the rest of the passengers followed the maze of hallways out of the jetway and toward immigration control. As Zach was approaching the massive hall with the self-service passport scanners he noticed the electronic gates and an array of infrared cameras bolted to the ceiling in the distance. As soon as he saw them, he pulled aside in a small opening by a service door. The mass of passengers was oblivious to him. Tired and anxious to make it past immigration controls, all were walking as fast as they could, trying to avoid each other and get home promptly. No one would pay attention to another tired young man re-adjusting his backpack on the side of the hallway.

Zach pulled out the Yeti cup and poured some ice water on the towel. He then put the towel on his head and adjusted it so it would look like a bandanna of sorts, tying it in the back. He poured some more ice water on his hands and spread it on his face. No one had noticed. He walked right back into the flow and moved quickly toward the health scanners at the end of the hallway. All around him was a sea of tired faces, families with children screaming, business passengers stoically soldiering on. All anxious and eager to move on. He stared down as he passed the infrared scanners. A group of immigration officers were watching the crowd on the other side of the scanners.

An officer pointed at him and motioned to have him pulled over. Zach's heart started racing. He pretended he didn't see or understand the officer.

"Hey! You! Come over sir!"

The voice was becoming more insistent. No way Zach was stopping, they would have to arrest him by force. He kept walking. The officer approached.

"Sir! Please come with me..."

Zach refused to acknowledge the officer and kept walking. The officer stepped forward and extended his arm to grab him. Zach braced himself. His heart was pounding so hard, he felt like it was going to pop out of his chest. He wondered whether the virus had affected his heart already. Would its telomeres have shrunk, would his heart have aged enough already, that it couldn't handle the stress anymore?

"Please come with me," said the officer as he grabbed the man behind Zach. The man, in his forties, was sweating profusely and did not say a word as the officer pulled him away. Zach breathed a sigh of relief and walked quickly up to a passport scanner a few feet away.

Moments later he walked triumphantly out of the gates into the domestic section. He had made it back! Now all he had to do was grab the rental car he had reserved and drive to the hospital to meet with Cunningham as soon as possible. Mindful of the fact that the Russians might still be tracking him, he had booked the car under an assumed name, John McCarthy, using the best quantum encryption scheme he had on his machine. As he arrived at the rental car facility he glanced around, making sure no one had followed him. He was in the clear. Yet, paranoid as always, he sensed a presence behind him. He turned around, hoping to catch a follower, but couldn't see anyone. He stepped into the rental car and drove away.

On the way to the hospital Zach stopped at a light. He was getting weaker, he was beginning to feel the virus getting to him. He was imagining his telomeres shrinking. He thought he could practically feel his internal organs get weaker. Every itch was turning into a symptom of this nightmare. He was only a few blocks away from the hospital, he would be there soon. He looked around and saw a bus stop, tucked away between the light and a nearby church.

On the steps of the church a doomsday preacher was rambling on, as if throngs of people were listening. Dr. King and his dream speech, though this was no Lincoln Memorial.

"Repent! This scourge is God's way of telling us we need to repent and amend our ways! Gay marriage, liberal judges, crime... We have lost our ways, we have forgotten the meaning of the good book!"

Zach smiled. The irony wasn't lost on him. This scourge, as the preacher had it, had nothing to do with God. If only the minister knew he was standing less than thirty feet away from the guy who started it all... And Zach was determined to fix it. His life now depended on it. At the bus shelter nearby, Zach observed a volunteer taking care of a woman, probably a drug addict. She was sitting on the bench while the volunteer had his arm around her shoulder, trying to give her what appeared to be a cup of soup. Another volunteer was walking back to a van nearby emblazoned with the letters "TREE OF LIFE MINISTRY".

Zach was transfixed. This was not the type of neighborhood where you stop at traffic lights. It was late, there was very little traffic. He should have gone on. Yet he couldn't help but look at his surroundings. First of all he was happy to be back home. Yes the city looked terrible. It was obvious things had changed quickly in the month or so since he left. There was a line outside a pharmacy on the corner, even at this hour. Half the street-level businesses were dark. But he was just so happy to be back home. Then also, something seemed oddly familiar about the scene he was witnessing.

He looked again at the woman in the bus shelter when it finally hit him. It was Ashley! Ashley from the Coding Academy, the Ashley he had had a crush on. The same Ashley that had rejected him when he needed help in those early days... He couldn't believe it. He stepped out of the car, oblivious to the danger he was potentially exposing himself to, and walked toward her.

"Ashley, is that you?"

She stared at him, puzzled.

"Ashley, it's me, Zach. Do you remember?"

Her face was emaciated, with a haggard gaze where her bright blue eyes had been. She seemed confused.

"Brad... The jelly is in the fridge..."

Zach stopped. She clearly did not realize where she was. He wondered whether she had dementia. The volunteer was holding a peanut butter and jelly sandwich and was trying to give it to her. Ashley extended her arm in Zach's direction, attempting to reach out for him.

"Brad, help me get up..."

Zach was taken aback. He didn't know how to react. He could hear the preacher droning on.

"What have *you* learned in this lifetime?" the preacher yelled. Even though he wasn't looking at him, Zach felt somehow the preacher was talking to him.

He quickly turned around and jumped back in the car. As he floored the gas pedal and sped away, he could still hear the preacher's words echo in his ears... *What have you learned in this lifetime?*

PART 3

39

A few miles later Zach made it to Innova General Hospital. He didn't care that he had zipped along like a madman, running a few red lights in the process. Ashley's face and the preacher's words were still haunting him. He ran through the lobby and up to Cunningham's lab. By now the nursing staff knew him as the eccentric startup founder who was funding their boss. Little did they realize what had transpired with the SEC!

Zach found Cunningham in the back of the lab, hunched over a microscope, looking at some tissue samples.

"Hey Zach, I wasn't expecting you so soon. Oh my god, you look awful... Are you okay?"

"I will be. I finally figured out what went wrong."

"Really? What?"

"We built the right sequence, but when we exported it into a viral shell, part of it got cut off. We never checked the output against the original. The nanoclews delivered exactly what we gave them. We just didn't give them the whole thing."

"So the nanoclews worked."

"The nanoclews worked. The sequence was wrong. I have the right one now. I checked it three times."

"Then let's try nanoclews again. Second time better be a charm..."

Zach smiled as he looked around the lab. Cunningham paused. How had he not figured it out himself? Why did it have to come from this clever kid from West Baltimore, a coder, no less, who had never had any formal training in genetics or biology for that matter? In the end he didn't care though. This was a viable alternative, a credible path to a cure. All they had to do was assemble enough nanoclews for a few doses and test them. He flashed a smile at Zach.

"I can't believe you figured this out... The good news is you came up with it, and we can make it here! Let's get started now, I think we can have a version of this antidote ready to be tested by tomorrow morning."

"Good, because I can feel I'm getting weaker doctor. I need this."

"Oh... maybe we should proceed carefully, Zach. Let's get this tested on the usual animal models first. The last time we rushed it really didn't work out that well, did it?"

"Doctor, I know this is right, and we don't have time," replied Zach.

Cunningham could sense he was getting desperate.

"I need this, I know this will work. Anyway, I need to rest now, I'm going to go home for a while. They haven't taken away my condo, have they?"

Cunningham shook his head.

"Not that I know."

"Great. Do you think you can make this antidote by tomorrow morning?"

"Yes, it should be ready by then. You're sure you want to try this again?"

"Positive. Never been more sure in my life."

"Okay then, but at least let's get a blood sample, so I can run some basic compatibility tests tonight. That's the least we can do."

Cunningham grabbed a phlebotomy kit and sat Zach on a chair nearby. He inserted a needle in Zach's arm, and extracted two vials of blood before putting a small band-aid back on his arm. He patted him on the shoulder.

"That should do, at least this way we'll know we're not doing anything *completely* stupid... See you tomorrow, bright and early, Zach."

"See you tomorrow, doctor."

On the way back home Zach drove by the bus shelter where he had seen Ashley earlier that day. He slowed down as he approached the block. He saw an ambulance stopped nearby, its lights flashing. The back doors were open. Two emergency medical technicians were pushing a gurney. Both were wearing masks over their faces. The volunteers who had been handing food out to Ashley were cleaning up the shelter area from her belongings the wind had scattered around.

Zach stepped out of the car and walked toward the volunteers. As he approached, he pointed in the direction of the gurney.

"Is she... ?"

One of the volunteers looked at him and nodded. Without a word, they kept cleaning up the bus shelter. It was as if she had never even been there.

The deranged man (or was he an actual preacher?) approached Zach.

"What God giveth, God taketh!"

He made no sense to Zach. The man was frightening to Zach. His intensity, his lack of concern for his surroundings were odd to him. How can someone be so vulnerable, yet so intense and so careless? Zach was mesmerized. The man was now close enough to put his hand on Zach's shoulder. The man smiled a frightening, crooked smile and whispered in Zach's ear.

"What have *you* learned in this lifetime?"

Zach recoiled, taken aback by the man's question. The preacher pointed at the ambulance.

"Did you know her? Her lesson was that people matter. She died alone learning that lesson..." said the preacher.

Zach was confused again. He felt a deep sense of exhaustion taking over his body. The last few days, the trip back home, the upheavals had exacted a toll on him. He had refused to acknowledge it, he couldn't bring himself to do so, but it was all catching up to him now. This was more than he could handle in a day. He turned around without a word and jumped back in his car. As he closed the door, he could hear the preacher go on.

"You better learn from this! You won't escape it... You won't escape it!"

Zach came back to the hospital the following morning with high hopes. He had not slept well given the events of the prior night, but a strong cup of coffee had done its trick, and he was ready to move on.

"Hi doc! So, what do we have here? I'm ready to try the new brew!"

"Hi Zach, I appreciate your enthusiasm," replied Cunningham with a smile. His face was relaxed. His concerns, if he had any, seemed gone.

"So... I tested the antidote using the blood samples we took yesterday. I think this is going to work, Zach. You were correct, I think we've addressed the truncation issue. I can't think of anything else that would screw this up now."

"Excellent. We'd better get started then."

"You know, in an odd way, we're lucky you are in the condition you're in and we have an epidemic out there. Unusual times call for unusual remedies. I could never do this otherwise."

"Oh, you're growing a conscience now? After the fact?"

"Not true Zach, not true. Everything we did was for the right reasons. If we succeed, we could save millions of lives."

Zach chuckled.

"You tell yourself whatever you want, doctor. At this point I just want to be cured..."

Cunningham administered the nanoclews to Zach.

"There you go. Why don't you hang out here for a few hours? I want to monitor you closely. We'll sample your blood every hour. The antidote should start acting fast; your body will start replicating at a rate of fifty base pairs per second. Even though the effect will be small we should be able to measure the length of your telomeres near the injection site within an hour or two. Then we'll know what's going on."

"Okay, makes sense."

Zach sat in a chair in Cunningham's office and started processing the events of the last day while waiting for the antidote to take effect. He knew in his bones this was going to work. If so, this was a brand-new therapy with the potential to cure millions of patients. This was, he fully realized, a chance to rebuild a better business, a biotech business, and prove all those naysayers, who had laughed at the demise of Quantum Tech, wrong. He was not a one-hit wonder, a lucky kid who had been Otto's pet project. He truly had it in him to build a life-changing business and shape society. The tension in his shoulders was subsiding, his muscles relaxing. He was feeling better already. After the chaos of the last few days it seemed as if things were finally starting to come into focus.

An hour passed until Cunningham came back to take another blood sample.

"There... We only need five milliliters. I will be right back."

Cunningham came back twenty minutes later, beaming like a child on Christmas day.

"Zach, the antidote worked!"

"No way!"

"Yes, the effect is very small so far, but measurable. Your telomeres are increasing in length, as best as we can tell the genetic edits were inserted properly into your genome. At the current rate you should recover normal telomere length within a week."

"This is awesome! I knew it would work..."

"Awesome doesn't begin to define it, Zach. Do you understand how important that is? It looks like we can go cure all these people; the antidote actually works!"

"Of course doc, did you ever expect it wasn't going to? I had a feeling we were going to figure this out..."

Zach was feeling cocky again. Cunningham stopped, overwhelmed for a moment. He found Zach's confidence charming and naive, but wasn't going to tell him. Something else was overwhelming him at the moment.

"Zach, you don't understand. It's not just the lives we're going to save with this. This is worth billions and billions.... This is how Big Pharma was created. Bayer started with aspirin, and see where they are now. This cure is worth more money than you and I can ever imagine."

Zach gave Cunningham a funny look. For a second he thought he saw an emotion in his mentor that was all too familiar to him, an impulse that had destroyed much already. Greed.

40

The following morning Zach took a deep breath as he stepped out of his Porsche 911. He was parked in front of the Securities and Exchange Building by Union Station in downtown Washington, DC. He had slept so much better the night before! He could feel his body healing and the aging symptoms reversing. Thanks to Cunningham's antidote, Zach had been able to sleep a whole eight hours without aches and pains. And without getting up through the night. A luxury!

The air was crisp, commuters were rushing out of Union Station next door and into the subway entrance. On their way to a million irrelevant jobs, he thought. He checked in with security at the reception desk of the towering, modern administrative building, and sat down, waiting for an escort to come and take him upstairs. A few minutes later Rebecca Jones, the SEC enforcement bureau deputy, appeared. She walked toward Zach with a smile.

"Hello Zach, good to see you. Please follow me, I'll take you upstairs to our conference room."

"Hi Rebecca, sounds good."

"You look like you just took a vacation, did you go anywhere fun?" she added as they walked into an elevator.

"No, I've just been exercising and trying to eat better," replied Zach, lying. *Please don't ask, I just don't want to talk about it,* he thought to himself.

Once he had settled into the conference room Rebecca brought him a small water bottle and sat down next to him.

"So, Zach, first of all, I want to thank you for coming today. The information you gave our InfoSec team about the Russians hacking into our system was very helpful. We were able to identify the breach and plug the hole. You were right, they were accessing one of our relay servers, and intercepting copies of our press releases and emails to the outside world."

"I told you..."

"Yes, you were right, and thanks to you we fixed this. That was quite an embarrassment for our technical team, but this now taken care of."

She paused to review her notes. It looked like she had a bank statement in front of her.

"I can see you disgorged the profits from the trade. We confirmed the funds were wired to the Treasury yesterday, including the ten percent penalty."

"I've kept my word, Rebecca. The last item in our deal was for me to testify about Otto's involvement in all this. It's why I came this morning. Shall we get started?"

Zach looked around the room. He had expected a camera or some recording device by the table but could see none. He was alone with Rebecca, there were no scribes frantically jotting down everything they said.

"Well, actually..." replied Rebecca.

Zach stared at her. His throat tightened, turning into an uncomfortable lump. This deposition was the hardest part of his deal with the SEC. Otto had been a fantastic mentor to him, and he had struggled with the decision to be deposed against him. Rebecca leaned closer to him.

"Otto is in a hospital right now."

"Okay, what do you mean?"

"He's not doing well. He's been affected by the epidemic. He's sick. In fact, he's very sick."

"What? How come I didn't know?"

"Well, that's for you to figure out. I'm sure you've been busy. Our security detail checked on him again this morning at Sibley Hospital, and he slipped into a coma. He's not expected to make it through the night. I'm sorry Zach."

Zach was stunned. The last few days had been incredibly busy. He had been so focused on the antidote with Cunningham and taking care of himself. First Emily, now Otto... There was still a chance though, he had an antidote.

"But we have an antidote! I mean it's still experimental, but he's got nothing to lose, right? I think I can save him, but we have to act fast. Do you mind if we put this deposition on hold? I promise I'll come back."

"Zach, what I was about to tell you is we don't need the deposition anymore. We're going to drop the case against him, there's no point anymore. You get to keep your immunity in return for the help you've already provided. You're barred from running a publicly traded company for the next ten years, but there's obviously plenty you can do in the private sector. You are good to go, Zach."

Rebecca stood up and extended her hand to Zach.

"Thank you for your help Zach. Now, run if you think you can help him."

"I'd better go," replied Zach as he left the room.

Twenty minutes and as many traffic violations later Zach was pulling into the garage at Sibley Hospital across town in Georgetown. He ran up to the infectious disease department. He couldn't care less about his own health at the moment. In his haste to rush to Otto's bedside, he hadn't called Cunningham, which he would soon need to do to obtain a vial of antidote for Otto. All he wanted to do was see him first, talk to the doctor on call and let them know what he wanted to try. Cunningham could come here within hours with a vial. Zach just wanted to talk to them first.

As he arrived at the fifth floor reception he found a resident in scrubs by the counter, looking at paperwork on a clipboard. Zach rushed to him.

"Hi, I'm here to visit Otto Krueger, I'm a friend. Do you know where he is?"

The resident paused to review his patient list, then turned to Zach.

"I'm afraid you can't visit him sir, he's been segregated in the quarantine unit. Are you family?"

"I'm a close friend. My name is Zach Hayes and we work closely together. I think we might have an antidote for his condition."

The medical resident gave a quizzical look to Zach.

"Well, it's still experimental, but I believe it's worth trying. I need to get a colleague of yours, Dr. Cunningham, here, and he can explain this far better than me. Do you think..."

"Did you say your name is Zach Hayes?" asked a nurse behind the counter, interrupting their conversation.

"Um, yes, that's me. Why?"

"Before he slipped into a coma, Mr. Krueger wrote this letter. He thought you might come here. He left it with us for you. Here it is."

She handed him an envelope. Zach opened it feverishly. In it was a yellow sheet from a legal pad, folded in three. The handwriting was cursive and old-fashioned. Zach instantly recognized Otto's hand. He sat down and began to read.

Dear Zach,

I'm afraid this damn epidemic is getting the better of me, and I'm not sure we'll be able to catch up. I thought it'd be better if I sat down and shared a few thoughts with you in writing.

First of all, regardless of anything that's happened in the last few months, I want you to know how proud I am of you. I've always looked to you as the son I never had, and you've made me so proud. You are an incredibly gifted individual with a knack for technology unlike anything I've ever seen. What you've accomplished with Quantum Tech is amazing, and I don't want you to let anyone take this away from you. Don't let anyone tell you otherwise.

Second, yes, we might have gotten into issues that will lead to people taking Quantum Tech away from us, but you know what, it happens! It's a long road, and, as the wheel turns, you'll go through ups and downs. Don't let it faze you. You are incredibly talented, and you owe it to society to put your talents to good use. Please do so responsibly. If this venture doesn't work out, the next will.

Last but not least, you'll need cash for this. We all do, always. Don't we? To that end, I've instructed my attorney to put funds in a trust for your next venture. It may not be much in the grand scheme of things, but it'll definitely be enough to get you started again and funded for a year or two. Grab that big brain of yours and do something with it. Something that makes our world better.

I gotta go. I'm getting weaker and I'm not sure how long I can last. Remember that in the end it's all about people, Zach.

So long,

Otto

Zach sat there for a while, holding his head in his hands. He felt pangs of shame and embarrassment. How could he do this to Otto? Well he hadn't, but he was going to betray him. If Rebecca hadn't called off the deposition, Zach would have been incriminating Otto in a criminal investigation at this very moment. Instead, he was sitting in a hospital across town, holding in his hands possibly the last words of his mentor, words of comfort and encouragement. A wave of guilt washed over him. Zach quickly snapped out of it. He stood up and grabbed his phone.

"Hi Dr. Cunningham. It's Zach. I'm at Sibley, the infectious disease department. Otto is sick, real sick. Any way you could come here right away? I think we can save him, but you need to explain to the attending physician what we did with the antidote."

"Let me check... sure Zach, I'll be there right away."

Zach hung up and walked to the counter where the nurse was standing. The resident was long gone.

"Excuse me, do you think I could see him? I mean, visit Otto Krueger?"

"I can't take you to his room, he's in confinement. But you can see him through the window if you want?"

"Sure, that'd be great."

The nurse took Zach through a maze of hallways and came to a stop in front of a sizable bay window. Behind the window, Zach could see a spacious hospital room. There, on a bed surrounded by medical equipment, he instantly recognized Otto, even though he was intubated.

"Do you mind if I stay here a few minutes?"

"Not at all. I'll be at the reception desk, just feel free to ask if you need anything. There's a vending machine by the elevators also."

Zach stood for a while by the window, silent and lost in thought. He had been watching Otto's heart rate monitor and was noticing a slow drift down. From 62 a few minutes earlier, it was now slowly drifting below 50... 45... 40...

An alarm went off. Zach didn't budge. He was fascinated and paralyzed, yet mostly confused and numb. Nurses rushed in the room, as did the medical resident. All were wearing masks and protective gear. The heart monitor kept drifting down. 35... 30... The resident injected some medication in Otto's intravenous line. As he reached for Otto's eyelids to check his ocular reflex, the monitor flatlined.

Zach watched the ballet of nurses and residents administering CPR. After a few minutes the resident stopped, resigned. They walked out of the room. The resident looked at Zach, pursed his lips and shook his head before walking away. Not a word was exchanged. All Zach could think of was Otto's letter to him. *It's all about people, Zach...*

41

The next few months went by quickly. After Otto's passing, Zach threw himself into his work. He kept reaching for his phone to call him. It took a while to stop. With the take-over of his startup, Quantum Technologies, by Ron Bailey and his retinue of hedge fund managers, Zach was without a job, without any of the resources he had grown accustomed to, without a mentor even. He had to start all over again. However, he didn't mind. This put him back in the underdog position, brought him back to his early days as a young kid from West Baltimore with nothing. He had done it once, he could do it twice, he could do it a million times he thought. *All it takes is grit.* And a bit of luck.

At least Otto had left him some seed funding to get things going with his next venture. Two million dollars was a lot for any individual, but for a company it was a drop in a bucket. Yet it was going to be enough to let Zach hire a couple of people, find an office, and focus on his next startup. The concept had been obvious to him. He and Cunningham had found an antidote, a genetic therapy for the epidemic that seemed to work. They were going to patent it. Never mind that they were the reason the epidemic started in the first place. At least they had the means of fixing the mess they had created, and nobody needed to know how it got started. Zach had always been suspicious of the various flu mutations that seemed to be coming out of East Asia with surprising regularity, and at times he had wondered about the role government-sponsored research had played there in spreading new viruses.

Once patents for the TP53 therapy were filed, Zach and Cunningham had applied for a fast-track permit from the FDA to commercialize the antidote as an experimental drug. They had also scouted a few locations in Northern Virginia and Boston for a place where they could start producing meaningful quantities of the drug. However, the seed funding of two million they had was not going to be enough to start operations. For that they would need to raise a lot more capital, and to do so would mean to go on a roadshow, go see and talk to all the investment funds in the country willing take a meeting with them, and pitch them on a potential investment in the newly minted biotech startup.

Zach started his roadshow in New York. It was the most logical place to start from, given they were based in the Washington DC area. He and Cunningham got tickets on the Acela train shuttle from Union Station in DC to Penn Station in New York. Hours later they found themselves walking out of Penn Station and toward midtown.

This brought back memories. The last time Zach was here was for the Quantum Technologies IPO, when the company had gotten its public listing on the NASDAQ.

The first time Zach had seen his face plastered in Times Square on the gigantic vertical TV screen he knew he had made it big. He wished his mom had lived long enough to see it. He smiled to himself. Here he was now, back to zero, pitching investors again on the merits of his new investment thesis. Yet the city had changed quite a bit. With the spread of the epidemic there were a lot fewer people in the streets. The CDC in Atlanta had encouraged people to stay home and work from home as much as possible. Avoiding contagion, including by healthy carriers, was paramount to avoid additional deaths. Many pedestrians in the street were wearing face masks. Zach and Cunningham weren't. Zach in particular hated the feeling of the mask on his face. It made him feel smothered. He didn't care about the looks and knew he wasn't spreading anything since he had been treated with the antidote, as had Cunningham.

After twenty minutes and a brisk walk through the urban canyons of Manhattan, Zach and Cunningham found themselves in an office in Midtown. They were visiting Holmes Health Ventures, a venture capital fund focused on healthcare investments. After a brief wait in the reception area, they were ushered into a conference room by a statuesque receptionist. The walls were covered in modern art except for the glass partition that separated the room from the rest of the office. From the far left window Zach glimpsed a corner of the pond in lower Central Park and the equestrian statue of General Sherman in Grand Army Plaza.

A few minutes later Winthrop Holmes, the founder and general partner of Holmes Health Ventures, walked into the room.

"Gentlemen, nice to meet you! Winthrop Holmes... just call me Win. How was your trip from DC?" said Winthrop, flashing an easy smile as he shook their hands.

Holmes was in his mid to late thirties, the scion of a wealthy New England family. Zach remembered seeing a few pictures of him online attending some fancy charity ball at the Met. He was married to the heiress of a sizable poultry processing fortune, and had done very well for himself investing the family funds. Zach was fascinated by how effortlessly he was working the room, how naturally he made them feel at home even though they had never met before.

Zach noticed a slight limp in Win's gait. Noticing Zach's gaze, he explained.

"Oh, I hurt myself in a game of squash this weekend. I don't know how, I just busted my knee and now my doctor is telling me I'm going to need knee surgery. Getting old sucks..."

Win grabbed a flask of hand sanitizer, put some on his hands and offered it to Zach and Cunningham.

"You can never be too careful these days," he said with a smile. "I am not susceptible to this epidemic going on right now, but the last thing I want is pass it on to someone else."

Zach smiled and took the flask.

"Oh no worries, we think we have a solution for that, we'll talk about it in a few minutes."

Win was only maybe five or seven years older than him, Zach thought. He was struck by how settled and poised Win was. Truly a child of privilege, and already old when there was still so much time. They sat down and Zach began the pitch.

"Thank you for meeting with us Win, we appreciate you taking the time," said Cunningham as he pulled his chair closer to the table.

"Oh no problem, when a friend of Otto called me to say I should listen to you guys, it was an easy decision."

Zach had rehearsed the presentation many times back in DC and was ready to get started.

"TP53 Genetix is a next-generation biotech startup we formed a few months ago to commercialize a new class of genetically engineered drugs. Our first therapy is showing very encouraging signs of potentially curing or at least relieving the current epidemic," said Zach, looking Win straight in the eyes. He went on about the team, Cunningham's role as chief medical officer, when Win interrupted him.

"What is your edge? I get the patent filing, but one, why do you think it's going to get approved, and two, what's next? How will you sustain the business past this first patent, when all of Big Pharma starts out-patenting you?"

"I'm glad you asked... Not only do we feel comfortable the patent is going to get approved, the treatment works! We are living proof of it. Our approach accelerates drug development with genetic computing in a way that's hard to replicate. How many people have access to large scale quantum computing resources? Very few. We do and have the know-how. How many people have then gone on to combine that with genetic computing to engineer and test therapies at scale? We do. And if you're aware of anybody else doing this we'd love to talk to them."

Zach repressed a smile and paused for a few seconds. As expected Win was playing a game of gotchas with them, and so far Zach felt he was doing pretty well.

"Okay, that's good. Obviously your fast track approval from the FDA speaks volumes, I can appreciate that," replied Win. He looked at his notes then went on. "One more thing... tell me more about your intellectual property, your IP. I don't mean from a technology standpoint, we just talked about that, but from a legal standpoint."

"Of course, what would you like to know?"

"So... you said the filings are in, you think you will get a first set of comments and revisions from the patent examiner in what, a month? Six months?"

"Probably in about two to three months."

"Then assuming all goes well you would potentially get the patent in another year?"

"Something like that."

"As far as you know, is anyone else aware of the filings you guys submitted? Have you made any public statements, published anything?"

"No one is, as far as we know, other than the FDA and our patent attorney, and we haven't published anything in the public domain yet. But of course we did share materials with the FDA, we had to. God knows who had access to the filing there. But why are you asking in the first place?"

"Well, I like to have an edge when I make an investment. We always do third party checks when considering a transaction. We had you guys vetted before you came here, probably to a greater extent than you realize. You did check a lot of boxes, you wouldn't be here today otherwise. I like the team, I like the tech, the market timing is obviously excellent."

"And?"

"We talked to our friends at the FDA as well. By the way, they're not as tight with their confidential materials as they're claiming to be. We did get a copy of your file and reviewed it thoroughly. We found in it a confidential comment letter from Quantum Technologies' general counsel. We also know the FDA met with Ron Bailey, their new CEO."

Zach was on the edge of his seat. His palms were getting sweaty, he sensed the normally slow thumping of his heart picking up pace.

"Apparently they are claiming the IP for the therapy is theirs because it was developed on a company computer, at a time when Zach was still an employee. We made a few more calls in town. The word is they intend to file a lawsuit by next week to preserve their rights to commercialize the technology themselves. How do you plan to handle this?"

42

"Look guys, I like you, and I like what you're doing. I think it holds a ton of potential."

Holmes was looking at Zach and Cunningham across the table, looking for any sign of anxiety or surprise regarding the bombshell he had just dropped on them. *Did they know? Were they ready to handle it? Or were they clueless bumbling idiots?* Cunningham's face was blank, without a hint of any emotion. Zach was clearly bothered, but in an angry, passionate way. Holmes liked that.

"Obviously you should resolve your legal issues with Quantum Technologies first, but let's stay in touch. I'd be ready to come in with a meaningful investment once this gets all cleared," he added.

"That sounds great, Win. We'd love to have your support," replied Zach, doing his best to smile. They parted ways a few minutes later and left the building. Zach and Cunningham waited until they were far enough from the building before they started speaking.

"How did he find out about Ron? And what the heck is this all about? That's total bullshit! They have no right to take this away from us..." exclaimed Cunningham, seething with anger.

Zach had been stunned by the revelation from Holmes. He was equally surprised by the doctor's reaction. Cunningham had always been the rational, even-tempered scientist. This was a new side of him, a new, bossier doc.

"I agree..." replied Zach pensively. "They won't get it though. First of all, I can claim I was on a leave of absence of some sort, and on top of that I used my personal laptop. Won't stop them from trying, but all we have to do is go fast with the launch of the antidote. If we can establish reality in the marketplace, show we are making a difference, we'll be fine. This won't get resolved for a while, and every day we make it is another day we get bigger and stronger. We'll survive this."

Cunningham stopped and looked at Zach in disbelief.

"I like your optimism!"

The irony in his voice wasn't bothering Zach.

"You're getting emotional about this. All we need to do is manage it. It's just another brick wall. We'll get through it or around it, but either way we'll be fine. We do need to assemble a team though. I wish Masha was with us, she's so good, we could really use her help... "

"Why don't you call her then? Ron was dumb enough to have you fired point-blank, it's not like you can't solicit any employee."

"You are right, doc"

Zach grabbed his phone and dialed Masha's number.

"Hey Masha, long time no see! How have you been?"

Zach was actually cheerful. He hadn't seen her in months and missed her, missed her quiet, competent support. They hadn't spoken since Masha had been deposed by the SEC. She didn't know whether Zach knew about her deposition and how bad she had felt. She had simply avoided thinking about it.

"Oh, hey Zach, what a surprise... How have you been?"

"You know me, Masha, I'm fine. I'll always be fine! Working on my next venture, working to change the world as always," replied Zach, ever the salesman. "What about you? Everything okay? How are you adapting to your new world?"

"Oh, fine. Ron made it sound like they were going to change everything when, um... when they took over from you. But in reality nothing's changed much. I still have the same job, I simply report to him instead of you. He's not that much into the day-to-day stuff so, if anything, I get a lot more leeway. That's fine with me, I get more time to focus on my daughter."

"I see... good. Is she okay too?"

"Well, if you remember she's still sick with this TP53 thing. Still at Walter Reed. Doctors have been trying to slow down the aging of her organs with different treatments, but we're not sure it's working."

"Masha, I'm in New York today but I'll be back in DC later this afternoon. I know we haven't spoken in months, and I'd love to catch up live with you and share what we're doing. Do you think we could get together in person, maybe tomorrow afternoon?"

"Um let me see... we could catch up after work if you want. I'll be at Walter Reed with my daughter. I go there to visit her every day, but there's a lot of downtime and I can't get in her room most days anyway, she's still confined in quarantine. I usually hang there right outside her room, so she sees me through the bay windows, and I talk to the doctors. If you don't mind, we'll have plenty of time to catch up then."

"Sure, that sounds awesome Masha, I'll meet you there around six-ish if that's okay."

"Sounds like a plan, see you then, Zach."

Zach arrived right on time the following day at the Infectious Diseases department at Walter Reed Hospital. He found Masha as expected in the hallway by her daughter's room, sitting on a chair. She lit up when she saw him.

"Zach, it's so good to see you, it's been so long!" she said as she gave him a quick hug before sitting back down. Zach sat right next to her. They were facing the bay window looking into a patient room. A hospital bed was set up in the middle of the room. In it was a young girl, maybe eight or nine years old. A nurse wearing a mask and gloves was attending to the girl, checking the IV line.

"It's good to see you too, Masha. It's been quite a few months, right? I'm so glad you're okay. How's your daughter? It's Lana, right? How is she?"

"She's hanging in there. We're not sure what to do. It turns out she carries the TP53 mutation. I don't have it, so I'm fine. Occasionally the doctors will let me get in her room, but they don't like it because they're truly concerned about more contagion outside the hospital. We've tried a few treatments, but nothing's worked so far. We've signed up for experimental therapy, but we're still on the wait list. So, we're waiting..."

"Wow, am sorry you had to go through this Masha. Well, the funny thing is my new venture is actually about a TP53 antidote. The formula is still experimental but it's worked pretty well so far. In fact, we have an 83% survival rate for the patients we've treated. It's still a small sample, and we're just getting started, but we're planning on ramping that up real soon. I came here to talk to you about joining us, Masha. I'm in dire need of someone with your skills. But looking at Lana now I'm thinking we should get her into our trial program right away... if your doctors are okay with it, we could start as early as tomorrow. The good news is we can cure this, you know?"

The nurse was now checking Lana's vitals. Masha paused.

"You mean it? You would do this?"

"Of course Masha, why wouldn't I? We have the antidote. It's still experimental, the FDA won't approve mass market release until we've completed more tests, but I can tell you it's working. We can cure your daughter. You've always stood by me Masha, you've been the one person I relied on back when we were at Quantum together. So of course I'll do this, I owe it to you."

A tear rolled down her cheek.

"Zach, there's something I have to tell you, something you don't know. Back a few months ago the SEC was all over the office..."

"I understand Masha, they came and talked to me. And they talked to you too, didn't they?"

"Yes, I ended up getting deposed later in the investigation. I did not want to get involved and I did my best to stay out of it, but by then they had subpoenaed all sorts of records, calendars and schedules, phones calls, texts, a lot of stuff."

"Okay?" replied Zach with a questioning look. He kept getting distracted by the nurse in the room.

"They backed me in a corner Zach. They knew we met and talked right about the time you sold your stock. They kept asking questions about it and cross-referencing every fact they had. I didn't want to, but I was under oath, and I had to admit I saw you trade your stock. I had to admit it was right after we talked about the sales forecast. I had to tell the truth Zach, I had to come clean."

"Of course Masha, I wouldn't expect anything else from you. You speak truth to power. That's who you are, that's what makes you strong."

"Really? But Zach, they used my deposition to issue an arrest warrant for you. They used my deposition to kick you out of Quantum. I'm so sorry for this!"

"Don't be. I shouldn't have put you in that position. You've always been my conscience. The truth is, I should have been listening to you."

Masha's eyes were locked into Zach's. A steady stream of tears was now rolling down her cheeks.

"Don't worry Masha, we'll take care of Lana, we'll get her into the program as soon as we talk to your doctors."

The nurse came out of the room, frowning, and took off her mask.

"Ms. Torre? I don't know what happened. Lana must have turned off her monitor somehow. I went in to check her IV line and her vitals. At first, I thought she was sleeping. But she was not. I double-checked everything. Looks like she went into cardiac arrest in her sleep. We see that a lot with patients in her condition. I'm so sorry Ms. Torre, I'll call a grief counselor immediately."

Masha was stunned, she felt blood draining out of her face. Feeling dizzy she sat back on her chair.

"How could it be? We were right here the whole time... how could it be?"

"I understand Ma'am, I'm so sorry for your loss. The grief counselor will be here in a few minutes."

Masha was still processing the news.

"I don't need a grief counselor! How could you? We were here the whole time..."

The nurse wasn't sure what to say. Zach grabbed Masha's hand.

"Masha..."

She pulled her hand away.

"We let her down!"

"You can't think of it that way..."

"Please, leave me alone. Don't take it personally, I just need time alone."

Masha stood up and left.

Masha had been up since four. This was new, she had always been a good sleeper, had always regarded insomnia as a mild character failing in others. But since the hospital she woke at four every morning without fail, as if her body had decided that four a.m. was when she needed to sit with things.

She made coffee and took it to the window. Arlington at four in the morning was its own particular kind of quiet, not peaceful, just paused. The traffic lights cycling through their colors for nobody. A cab idling at the corner.

Lana had loved this window. She would stand on the radiator cover with her nose against the glass and narrate what she saw below with the exhaustive thoroughness of a seven-year-old sports commentator. *There's a man with a dog. The dog is very fat. That taxi has been there a long time. Do you think the driver is sleeping?*

Masha hadn't moved anything in Lana's room yet. She wasn't ready. She knew the day would come when she would have to open that door and begin the terrible practical work of it. The clothes, the books, the drawings, the small shoes lined up by the bed with a neatness Lana had never applied to them in life, only in death, because Masha had lined them up herself the morning after. She wasn't ready for that day.

What she was trying to work out, she had been working out every morning at four since it happened, was how to be angry at the right things.

She was angry at the virus. She was angry at whatever chain of carelessness and ambition had released it. She was angry at herself for every evening she had brought her laptop to the dinner table, every time Lana had asked her a question and she'd said in a minute when she meant not now.

She was angry at Zach.

She stood at the window and let herself be angry at Zach. Not the managed, philosophical anger she had been preparing for his inevitable visit, but the real one underneath it. The one that said: you brought this into our lives. Your hunger, your shortcuts, your spectacular inability to stop and ask what you were actually doing to people. The epidemic had a hundred causes, she knew that. But Zach was the spark. And the spark had burned down her daughter.

She held it for a while. Let it be what it was.

Then she thought about her father, who had crossed an ocean and worked sixteen-hour shifts and never once stopped believing the world could be better. And Lana, who had believed in everything with her whole enormous heart and had drawn her mother with yellow hair.

Everything happens for a reason. She wasn't sure she believed it yet. But she believed that acting as if you believed it was sometimes the first step toward actually believing it. Her father had taught her that. You didn't wait to feel gracious before you acted graciously. You acted graciously until the feeling caught up.

The traffic lights kept cycling. The cab was gone. She went to get dressed.

43

A few days passed. Zach buried himself in the minutiae of getting his new business off the ground. Medical trials, fundraising, infrastructure setup, the list went on and on. He had done it before and was in fact energized to do it again. He felt he had lost his way somehow with Quantum Technologies, and this biotech venture was an opportunity to get a fresh start. Learn from the past and build something bigger, something better.

He hadn't talked to Masha since the events at the hospital. He felt incredibly guilty for what had happened to her daughter. Zach was, after all, the reason this epidemic had started in the first place. And Masha had always been there for him, since the early days of Quantum Technologies. Day in, day out, she had been this stabilizing force, the co-pilot that had helped him in the most selfless way build his startup. Yes, she had testified against him, but she was incapable of lying, and he had been dumb enough, arrogant enough, really, to ignore her advice and trade his stock right in front of her. What was he expecting?

It had been a few days since the passing of her daughter, and he thought he should check on her. She had taken a bereavement leave and was most likely at home. Zach was still planning on convincing her to join his new venture, and wanted to stay close to her. He also thought she was simply a great human being, and he didn't like the thought that she was in a world of pain because of him. He wanted to fix it, somehow. Zach decided to leave the office and go check on her at home.

A few minutes later he was knocking on her door, on the tenth floor of a condo building in Arlington, Virginia, a yuppie suburb of Washington, DC.

"Who is it?"

"Hi Masha, it's Zach. You okay? I was nearby and I thought I would just drop by to check on you. I hope you don't mind."

"No, that's okay. I'm all right. Come on in, we can chat for a few minutes," replied Masha.

Zach followed her down the hallway. He couldn't help but gaze at her long legs extending in a fluid motion, her disheveled hair flowing down her shoulders. She pointed at a sizable leather chair in the living room.

"Why don't you sit here? Can I bring you anything? Water, coffee, tea?"

Her wide green eyes were locked on Zach's. She looked tired, her eyes puffy, probably from crying, he told himself. Masha could feel Zach's stare lingering on her.

"I know I'm a mess. This is not the Masha you're used to seeing in the office, but I'm okay. So, what do you want to drink? It's the middle of the day still. How about sparkling water?"

"Sure, that sounds awesome, thanks Masha."

She went to the kitchen to fetch a bottle of San Pellegrino and two glasses. Zach was puzzled by this new side of Masha he was discovering. She had always been so professional when working together. He had grown used to seeing her as this rock, this uber-reliable sidekick. Witnessing her emotional distress at the hospital had been disturbing to him as it had opened his eyes to her human side. He had witnessed firsthand her reaction to a mind-numbing pain he knew all too well since he had experienced it when he lost his mother, a long, long time ago.

And here she was today. Open, vulnerable, smiling even, in spite of the unfathomable blow she had just experienced a few days earlier. There was so much he wanted to tell her. If only he could find the right words...

"Masha, I'm so sorry for what's happened to you. It's my fault, none of this would have happened if I hadn't screwed up."

"Don't be, it's not true."

"I could have brought you an antidote sooner."

"Did you know my daughter was sick?"

"Um, no..."

"So how could you have brought an antidote sooner?"

"This whole epidemic is because of me Masha! Cunningham and I were trying to develop a new gene therapy. Well, a biohack really, and it got out of hand."

"And started this whole epidemic?"

"Yes!"

"Of course not, Zach. You couldn't have done something this big on your own. No one can. Were you the catalyst, some change agent that triggered a massive upheaval that was going to happen somehow? Maybe. You know, I think of this a lot like I think of wildfires. Sure, there's always a dumbass who forgets to put out a campfire..."

Zach squirmed.

"And if it's not a dumbass camper, it's a power line that breaks because of the wind and creates a spark that starts a fire. Then thousands of acres burn, and people die. But do you genuinely think it's because of that one spark? Or that one guy? Of course not. It's because of the world we've built for ourselves, Zach. It's because we've built suburban neighborhoods in the wilderness, in places that used to burn down every few seasons. It's because climate is changing and getting drier, and we're not doing anything about it. It's because we've regulated, or failed to regulate, the power company to the point where it's no longer incented to properly maintain its power lines."

Zach was still staring at Masha, enthralled and fascinated by the raw passion mixed with vulnerability in her response. She went on.

"Our actions are all interconnected Zach, nothing we do individually can truly be segregated from others' actions. So no, you didn't start this whole epidemic. You might be the catalyst that's brought about an issue that's been building with superbugs, and mutations, and antibiotic overuse, and all the crazy biohacks out there, I'm not sure. But what I do know is you couldn't have done whatever it is you've done by yourself, in isolation of all these other factors."

"So, you're not mad at me?"

"Well, don't get me wrong, I'm mad at you for choosing to sell your stock when I told you not to. That was insider trading, and it led to the unraveling of the company. That was incredibly poor judgment. But then again, you could argue I used poor judgment when I got involved with Lana's father. Seemed like a great idea at the time, right?"

"I could have saved her, though... all I needed was a little bit of time."

"Zach, everything happens for a reason. Losing Lana broke my heart. I'm still piecing it together. But everything happens for a reason, Zach. You gotta have faith! Look, I think the world of you. You have a gift. You are incredibly talented. That's why I followed you and came to work for you at Quantum Technologies in the first place. Put this big brain of yours to good use. You have a role to play, figure out what it is, and do the best you can."

Masha sat back down on the sofa. She was exhausted. Zach wasn't sure what to say. As Masha had delivered her diatribe her cheeks had gotten redder, the green of her eyes more intense. He had expected anger and had found forgiveness and wisdom instead. He felt incredibly confused. Zach looked at his watch reflexively, trying to keep himself busy.

"Masha, I gotta run but I'll come back to check on you, okay?"

"Sure, if I'm not here I'll be at the gym or running at the park."

Zach was still processing his conversation with Masha as he sat back in his car. He turned on the ignition and started driving back home. He had come to Masha expecting her wrath. Zach deserved her wrath, he welcomed her wrath he thought, that was the only way he was going to be able to get her back on the team. She was one of the best, and he wanted her by his side with his new venture. So as always, he had grabbed the bull by the horns and figured he would confront her. He had not expected this turn of events at all. Instead of facing anger and pain, he had found a Masha that was serene. Still processing grief, but at peace.

How many times had he wished he could be at peace? Ever since he had lost his mother, all he had ever set out to prove was that the world failed them, both her and him. She deserved more, he deserved more, and he was going to prove it to the whole world. He had gone down this path of unresolved anger for so long now. He had become insanely successful against all odds. Zach had become wealthy beyond anything he could have imagined. Yet he had lost it all for having been too brash. He had become just like the cool kids he used to despise. Ashley had since died, he remembered. *Good riddance.* He caught the thought and felt ashamed of it. *What about her creepy friend Brad? Such a jock...* Masha, full of grace and brimming with a wisdom beyond her years, had just shown a different path. He was attracted to her, soothed by her aura. He envied her peace.

44

Zach's alarm rang loudly. He hadn't slept well. He was still thinking about the conversation he had had the prior day with Masha. It didn't sit well with him. She should have been mad! He turned off his alarm and walked into the kitchen of his high-end two-bedroom condo. The coffee machine had started brewing fresh coffee. It was going to be ready in a few minutes. Zach grabbed a tablet and sat on a stool by the island. He fired up the New York Times app and started flipping through the news of the day. An article caught his attention in the health section.

Mysterious flu outbreak will have long-lasting impact, father who lost two of four children says: "A week and they were dead." Epidemic widespread in Virginia according to CDC.

The article went on to describe the ordeal of the family of four, along with an interview of a local representative of the Centers for Disease Control. Zach was so engrossed in the Times report he didn't notice his coffee was ready. When he finally lifted his head, his phone rang. It was Ron Bailey, newly minted CEO of Quantum Technologies, the very same Ron that had fired him and Otto. Zach squinted his eyes and pursed his lips. What did Ron want? Why so early? He decided to pick up the phone.

"Hi Ron, what's up?"

"Hi Zach, how are you?"

"To what do I owe the pleasure of your call this early?" replied Zach. Sarcasm was the refuge of the weak, and he wasn't feeling particularly strong this morning.

"Long time no see, Zach... I hope you've been well since you left QT."

"I didn't leave, you guys fired me"

"Well, anyway, word on the street is you're off to a new venture?"

"That's what I do, Ron. I'm an entrepreneur, I start companies for a living."

"Cool, very cool... what's your new venture about?"

"Ron, am assuming you know, otherwise you wouldn't be calling me. Can we stop the cat and mouse game? What do you want?"

"Well, my sources tell me you've started a biotech venture. Combines genetic editing with quantum encryption technology? You're in the middle of fast-track trials with the FDA now?"

"Sort of, we're still in stealth mode. You know I'm not going to discuss it at this time, Ron."

"We may need to, Zach. It appears you developed this technology on QT assets while you were on QT payroll."

Zach's mind was racing. Was Ron bluffing? There was no way he would know this. Yes, he had been on company payroll at the time, and that was a reasonable inference on Ron's part. But the computer was neither his nor QT's, he had used his connections at the National Institute of Standards and Technology, or NIST, to get access to a massive quantum server run by NIST. This was definitely not a QT asset.

"Ron, you're messing with me. I never used a QT computer to do this. You know you guys don't have the right computational resources for what we do."

"Zach, you used your company laptop to log into the server you were using. You were careful in covering your tracks, but we cracked the log. You signed an intellectual property waiver that was updated the last time we raised institutional funds. Everything you do on company time with company assets belongs to the company. The antidote you are testing with the FDA belongs to Quantum Technologies, Zach."

Zach was stunned. Why had he not thought of that. That wasn't right, though!

"Ron, this is total BS! First of all, how would you know about the antidote without having broken some law. Second, I did not use a company asset to develop the antidote. I could have used any laptop, and the laptop was not used for actual computations, it was all done on the NIST server. It's like your Internet provider telling you they own what you've done because you used their access line to get online! And last, I'd argue I was on a leave of absence, and I can do whatever I fucking want if I'm on leave."

Ron was unfazed.

"Zach, you can tell whatever stories you want to tell, we have no record of your taking a leave. And the waiver you signed is clear: if you developed it using a company asset, it's ours."

"Fuck you, Ron, you can't do this! Is it not enough to have done your little power grab? Grabbing one company was not enough? Now you have to come for my next startup too? What kind of sicko are you?"

"Zach, first of all, you and I both know there was no power grab. You were derelict in your duties as chief executive. You left the business at the most vulnerable time when sales were sagging. And sales were sagging because the technology was not working as advertised, Zach. Technology that *you* developed. Then, on top of it, you went ahead and committed insider trading. So, don't give me lessons in fucking morality, Zach. You left the board no choice, and totally deserve what happened. And you go off and develop another product that appears to work, using company assets? Hell yes, I'm coming after you, my investors would be mad if I wasn't! Truth is you fucked us, Zach, and then of course you cut your little deal with the SEC and got off easily. Well, I'm coming for you now."

"You tell yourself whatever lies you want to tell, Ron, I don't care."

"Listen to me Zach, the reason I called is our attorneys got the judge to issue an injunction on your code. The notice will be served to you later today, but I wanted to personally deliver the news to you. You are required to put your new code base and the genes you edited in escrow and under court protection until we sort this out. You are not to market this any longer until the judge rules on who owns the intellectual property and who's owed royalties. You may think you have a case Zach, but I don't give a fuck. My attorneys can pursue this case for the next ten years if needed. The judge has already issued a ruling in our favor. I'm feeling pretty good about our odds... how about you?"

"Fuck you, Ron!" replied Zach as he hung up the phone.

Zach didn't know what to think. Ron had made some good points even though he was obviously totally biased. There was no way the antidote was theirs though, Zach knew Ron's case was shaky. A reasonable judge would see through that and rule in favor of Zach. But how long would it take? Years? And what if the judge wasn't reasonable? Zach decided to call Cunningham to bring him up to speed and figure out next steps.

"Hi Doctor, you're never going to guess who called me this morning..."

After all these years Zach was still calling him Doctor, or Dr. Cunningham. That's how he had always called him as a boy when he and his mom would visit him. He had often provided free care for his mom, and Zach had never forgotten that. Zach's mom had instilled in him a respect that had lasted to this day, and calling him doctor after the journey they had been through was Zach's way of honoring his mom.

"Hi Zach, how are you? No idea, you're going to have to tell me"

"Ron Bailey, remember? Member of the board at Quantum Technologies, became CEO after I left"

"Oh yes, that Ron. Wasn't he the one who schemed against you and pushed you out?"

"Let's not rehash old stories... Well, he just called me to let me know they are suing us. They claim the antidote is theirs and want us to put all of our IP, both the code base and the gene edits, in escrow immediately. "

Zach went on to explain to Cunningham the discussion he had had with Ron earlier in the day. Cunningham's reaction was swift.

"No *fucking* way! No. Fucking. Way..."

Zach was taken aback by Cunningham's language. He had always known him to be this gentle soul, this do-gooder scientist who had helped him and his mom in times of need. Zach was unsettled enough by the whole ordeal of the last few months. Hearing Cunningham swear was more unsettling still.

"Well, yes way..."

"No way we are letting them grab our IP like that. Such a greedy move, Zach. Do you know how much this is worth? Billions! We stumbled upon gold, Zach. This is worth a ton of money, this is worth a ton more than anything you ever did at Quantum Technologies! This approach we used to produce the antidote can revolutionize medicine, the company could actually be worth a trillion some day!"

Zach smiled. He felt oddly embarrassed by Cunningham's enthusiasm and belief in their new venture.

"Zach, we can't just let them grab it like this. We *have* to do something. I am not letting this fucking bastard take it all away from us. I've worked too hard my whole life for this moment, Zach. Not going to let it happen. This is simply too much money! Don't you think?"

"Sure, doctor. The thing that's giving me pause though is the fact that they can easily outlast us, no matter what merit their case has. They have all the resources in the world, and they can draw this out for the next ten years if needed. We don't have that kind of time, doctor."

"Not going to let it happen. You haven't received the written notice, correct?"

"That's right."

"All right, don't do anything then. I'm going to call an attorney I know and figure out our options. No way we are putting this in escrow. We're simply not going to comply, Zach. Establish reality in the marketplace every day with our ongoing trials, keep the FDA on our side. We're not giving up that easily. No *fucking* way. Don't do anything until I call you back. Bye, Zach."

Zach put his phone back on the kitchen counter. *Wow, that was a different Dr. Cunningham*, he thought. A real-life Mr. Hyde.

45

Zach sat back in his chair. The TV was still going on in the background, a morning news anchor droning on about the epidemic. Zach was replaying in his head the conversation he had just had with Cunningham. What a change, he thought. Here was the gentle soul that had always been there for his mother, or mostly anyway, the kind-hearted physician, now showing a very different side. Zach thought he knew him, yet the change in behavior was unmistakable.

Thinking of it, Zach realized he should have anticipated this when he first convinced Cunningham to work with him. He had been extremely reluctant up to the point when Zach had mentioned the impact and money the therapy would generate. Zach had been trying about every argument he could think of, hoping one would work. At the time he had thought having an impact was what convinced the good doctor, but as he replayed the events in his mind he was questioning his judgment. Could money and greed be such a powerful motivation for Cunningham? If so, what else would he do in due time?

By contrast, Masha's behavior had been another lesson for him. She had lost her daughter, her one beloved daughter. All because of the scourge he had unleashed, trying to cure himself and dabbling in genetics he should never have messed with. She had faced the unfathomable pain of losing her own child. Yet she had embraced the pain and carried on. She seemed to have found peace and serenity through some higher calling, some higher state of consciousness maybe? Whatever it was, she had shown Zach what felt to him like a path of light, a state of peace and mindfulness he had never known. Was it the reason he felt so oddly attracted to her? Why was he even thinking about this? He had so much to do, he decided to snap out of it and go to the office. There was nothing he could do for the time being about Ron's lawsuit, and he had a whole new business to take care of.

Later that day, when Zach came back from work, he was still thinking about the discussion with Cunningham. He hadn't heard back from him, he assumed he was still tracking down his attorney. It also dawned on him that there was still time to do something if he could come up with an idea. They technically had not been served yet, he had full and unrestrained access to the code base and the genetic edits. It was all on his computer. Zach thought again about why he was doing this, why he was building this company. Was it about the money? One thing he had learned over the past year was that maybe money was not the answer. In some ways, money was an outcome rather than the cause he thought it was. Do the right thing and good things happen. What about power then? Power was not the answer either. He had seen how corrosive it could be. He definitely did not want to turn into Ron, and did not like what he saw in

Cunningham either. His mind kept going back to Masha, and how he could have helped her. How he could help others, have an impact. Yet he felt powerless. In a matter of days, if not sooner, their code base and the rest of their intellectual property was going to be seized and put in escrow. Hundreds of thousands of patients, if not more, were going to be hurt by delays in bringing the antidote to market. And in the end, Ron would reap all the rewards, and he and Cunningham would likely end up screwed. Lovely.

Staring at his laptop screen he started wondering. What if there was a way around this? What if he didn't care about money, or power, or any of his startup? What if he went open source with the code base and the genetic data? Zach paused and smiled. That was it! This was a brilliant move; going open source would solve the epidemic and make such a difference. By going open source he would put the code into the public domain, in the hands of thousands of coders and hackers of all sorts who would be able to use it without any restrictions and build on it, make it better. Same for the genetic materials, by putting them in the public domain he would enable thousands of biohackers to deconstruct and understand the antidote, produce samples themselves, and possibly improve on it. This was the path. Masha would be proud.

Zach felt his heart racing. With trembling fingers he started typing on his keyboard. He went online and connected to GitRiver, a distributed online repository. This way, in the event he or anyone else changed their mind, the second the code would be out there it would be impossible to take back offline. With a few keystrokes he uploaded the materials, then pressed enter.

That was it.

Minutes later he had uploaded the genetic data, along with the details of the genome they had edited, to the public repository of genetic data at the National Institutes of Health in Bethesda. And just like that, in a matter of minutes, he had taken a set of symbols, a secret sauce worth potentially billions, and released it in the public domain. Zach leaned back and smiled; he felt both exhilarated and emotionally exhausted.

His laptop rang with an incoming video call. It was Cunningham again. Zach accepted the call.

"Hey Zach, I talked to an attorney I know. I trust him, we went to college together..."

"Before you go too far down that path Dr. Cunningham, we should talk. A few things have changed," replied Zach. That was the understatement of the day.

"Did you hear back from Ron? Anything new?"

"No, I didn't hear back from Ron. But I've been doing a lot of thinking about the antidote and what Ron is doing, and how it would set us back and prevent us from going to market for months if not years."

"Okay Zach, what are you talking about?"

"So, I decided to release the intellectual property for both the code base and the genomic data and put it in the public domain."

"That's silly talk, Zach you can't do that."

"Of course I can."

"No you can't, or at least you truly shouldn't. Let me tell you about..."

"I went open source. Just uploaded all of it online under a GPL license for anyone to see, edit and augment. No restrictions."

"You did what?"

"You heard me," said Zach with poise and determination. "There's no going back. It's a public domain license, that means anyone can download the materials and use them with virtually no restrictions. That's the best way to put this information in the public's hands. Others will see what we've done and build on it, improve it. And there's nothing Ron can do about it, it's done. This will save lives, doctor. "

"What the... Zach, no, tell me you didn't... Fuck!"

No response from Zach.

"Do you have any idea how much money you just flushed down the drain? Down the fucking drain? Zach? You little moron... Why did you?"

Cunningham's face was getting redder, beads of sweat were forming on his forehead. Zach was taken aback by the anger in his tone. He felt compelled to cut him off.

"Are you even listening to yourself? People are dying! Every day, someone else is dying. Emily. Otto. Masha's daughter. Not just strangers, doctor, people we know. Ron is going to set us back months if not years and all you're thinking about is money? Didn't you take a Hippocratic oath way back when? Where is the guy who was always ready to help my mother when no doctor or insurer would? What happened to *that* guy? And what the fuck is going on with your swearing? Really?"

Zach stopped. He had never talked to Cunningham that way. Truth be told, he also had never witnessed him go off the deep end as he did today either. Zach's response appeared to have jolted Cunningham out of his fit of anger. As quickly as it came, the madness appeared to dissolve away. His shoulders stooped down. He looked at Zach.

"You're right Zach, am sorry. It's just that... I don't know... Man, this is so much money, you know? Do you realize how much we could get done with it? Do you realize how different our lives could be?"

"You can't think of it that way. First of all the money was never there, Ron was going to take it all away. Second of all, think of the patients who need this right now. Not after the third appeal, once we settle this claim in a year or two, but now. Right now. And think of the help we're going to need to scale this antidote, produce it, distribute it to the people who need it most. We can now leverage a whole community, a whole world of people with the same goal. Isn't this a better path?"

Cunningham sighed.

"I don't know. You may be right, I lost track of what's important..."

"Yes you did," replied Zach with a faint smile. Cunningham was in a vulnerable state, and he wasn't sure whether sarcasm would go down that well.

"So, what can I do? How can I help?"

"Well, the files are already uploaded and in the public domain, so that's done. We'll need to get the word out. But right now I need help to finish decrypting Tom's files. I still don't know what's in it and I'm hoping it can really help us. He was way ahead of us and I want to make sure we can use the full extent of whatever it is he discovered. I have the protocol and the encryption scheme figured out, but I still need to process the files. The only method that will work in a reasonable amount of time is genetic computing, so I still need access to your equipment to encode the files in DNA materials and decode them through DNA processing. Time is of the essence, do you think we can get on it soon?"

"You bet, Zach. Why don't you come on over here in the lab? In the meantime I'll get the machines started up and calibrated."

46

It took them a whole day to get the assay machines set up properly and running at full speed, and another day to get the carefully selected strands of DNA to complete the set of computations. By the end of the second day, Cunningham and Zach were holed up in a corner of the lab, grabbing a can of soda. They hadn't slept much in two days, and they weren't supposed to bring food or drinks in the lab, but they didn't care. They were so close to finally getting the content of Tom's files, they simply wanted the process over with.

The cluster of machines finally beeped with its first results, jolting Zach and Cunningham into action.

"Finally! Let's take a look Zach"

Zach sat down at the console and opened the first set of results. He frowned.

"Ah, man, looks like there's one last layer of encryption, doctor..."

"Really? After all this processing Tom's data had one more layer of encryption? He really wanted his files to be securely stored... I can't believe it."

"I think I can crack the last layer. I know his technique by now, and my quantum server is all set and ready to go. It'll still take a few hours... Why don't you go get a nap while I do this? I'll let you know when I'm done, doctor."

"All right, you won't have to ask me twice, I'm exhausted. Thanks for doing this Zach, just let me know when you're ready, okay?"

"Will do, you go now."

Cunningham went back to his office and laid down on a cot by his desk. He was exhausted, he could definitely use a few hours of sleep.

A few hours passed when he woke up again. Disoriented at first, he quickly realized he was still in his office at the lab. Zach hadn't come and was still working on the decryption job. The lab was so quiet he could hear Zach's keystrokes across the hall. He decided to get up to go check on Zach.

"Hey Zach, what's up? Anything interesting coming out of these files."

Zach paused and frowned, scratching his chin.

"I'm not sure... This makes no sense. Well, it does, but then again it does not."

"What do you mean?"

"Remember how our quantum encryption was broken by the Russians?"

"Yes, that never made sense to me..."

"Right, me neither. They somehow intercepted the quantum-encrypted encryption key without us detecting it. Quantum mechanics says this is not possible. It's a violation of locality and the observer principle."

"And this is relevant because..."

"Hang with me, doctor. So, the Russians broke our encryption, but physics says they could not. There is another possibility though, but it's so outlandish I dismissed it at first. The only way for them to intercept our encryption key and collapse it into a specific quantum state, which is exactly what they did, without violating quantum mechanics is actually quite simple. This is only possible if the reality they are in is different than ours."

"Come again?"

"Reality may not be objective after all, doctor. That was actually proven a few years ago by two physicists in Edinburgh, and validated again by the CERN in Geneva. But most people thought this was a fluke because the consequences were mind-blowing. Remember, *extraordinary claims require extraordinary support* kind of thing."

"Okay..."

"Well, the mainstream scientific community rejected the results as a fluke. But if you take it seriously, this means there isn't a single, objective reality, but in fact reality depends on the observer. Crazy as it seems, once you accept that fact, and remember that we have bona fide scientific experiments that support this, then it all falls into place."

"Even if I accept this claim, how does this relate to Tom's files?"

"That's the beautiful thing doctor, that's what Tom independently figured out! He was digging into the fabric of reality in his own way by experimenting with DNA computing. For some problems DNA computing is actually more powerful than quantum computing. Remember how Otto used to joke we were just walking hard drives? Little genetic drives with a capacity of over a gigabyte and all this junk DNA materials nobody could understand? Tom cracked the code. What he found out only makes sense if you assume we are inside a rendering engine. A thirty-two-engine rendering cluster to be exact."

"A rendering engine?"

"Yes, a rendering engine. Have you ever played video games?"

"A long time ago, Zach..."

"Just try to remember how it works. In modern systems anyways, the content of the game itself is separated from the processing that's required to create the reality of the game. Think massively multiplayer online games. In these games, the full universe is never fully computed, it would be far too massive a job. In fact, there's no need for that because most players don't see most of the world around them, so computing everything all the time would be a giant waste of resources. No, what happens is as a player progresses in the game, the different aspects of the universe he is going through are generated, rendered is the proper term, in real time as needed. In other words, their reality is rendered on the fly, dynamically. It is done by rendering engines which encode the rules of reality like physics."

"So, all players effectively live in different universes?"

"Well that's where things get interesting... They may be computed as different universes, but they're really supposed to be different pieces of the same universe. At least that's what you want your players to experience. So this rendering also entails a massive synchronization job to ensure reality is rendered in a consistent way across all players. But of course it's not always perfect. There are lags, artifacts, etc. For instance, you are limited by the size of the grid on which you are making these computations. In our case this would be Planck's constant, and so on."

"You are telling me we are pieces of software?"

Cunningham wasn't sure whether to take Zach seriously. They had worked long and hard over the past few days, and he thought maybe Zach had lost his perspective. Zach was clearly tired, as was he, and after their last fight the last thing he wanted was get in another crazy shouting match. As he stared at Zach, going through a mental inventory of potential responses, he heard some footsteps behind them. He turned around and saw a lean, middle-aged man standing in the doorway. Zach turned around and smiled.

"Igor! No way..."

"Yes way, Zach. Remember, I said I would find you when it is time?"

"You did... So, it is time?"

"You tell me. Looks like you got a lot of work done, Zach."

"Yes we have, and I have a ton of questions for you, why don't you come in and sit down with us, Igor?"

Igor stepped into the lab and grabbed a stool by the workbench.

"Did you know about this the whole time?" asked Zach.

"We've been watching you the whole time, Zach. Keeping a close eye on you both, monitoring how your choices would unfold."

"Why and how? Was that you guys who cracked our quantum encryption? I know someone did... How did you do that?"

"That wasn't us Zach, but I'll get to this in a minute. Let me explain first a bit what's going on. You're a smart guy, right?"

Zach smiled, a bit embarrassed.

"Um, where are you going with this?"

"Have you ever thought about this intelligence of yours? How it works, where it comes from?"

"Genes?"

"In some ways yes, but actually no. Genes are merely the code we use to generate a particular form of intelligence. People go to great lengths to make the distinction between human and artificial intelligence, but the truth is that's a completely artificial distinction, no pun intended. Intelligence is intelligence just as information is information. What your neurons do, and the consciousness that emerges from what they do, I can replicate on any substrate. Carbon, silicon, anything else, really. You guys simply haven't figured that out yet."

"Yet?"

"Yes. And so if intelligence is simply that, a software agent processing information on a specific substrate, it's still pretty complex software. How do I get it started?"

"You mean like booting it up?"

"Yes, exactly. How do I build a bootloader to start up my intelligent agent?"

Zach was dumbfounded. Igor went on.

"This is it. You're it, Zach. This, evolution, you thinking, is a very elegant bootloader."

"But why?"

"To produce self-aware intelligence, sentient agents that can then be trained and transferred to other environments, other communities if you will."

"So you're telling me this is all one big training program?"

"Well, you can think of it that way too. There's actually a lot of truth to that. Think about artificial intelligence and reinforcement learning. To realistically train a software agent through RL would be extremely complex, in fact impossible, without some sort of shorthand, some sort of metaphor. You need to be trained to apply the right processing to the right context, and we can't invent or model every context. The complexity is simply too high. This is where judgement and free will comes in. You are repeatedly exposed to choices. And every time you use your judgement to make such choices. Over time the result of that choice, whether it was judicious or not, will become obvious. Obvious to you, obvious to all who watch you. In other words, free will is the mechanism by which you get trained and become self-aware. Most of what you see around you: the people, the suffering, the choices, it's the unlived working through it. They don't know yet. Some never will. Once you are trained, we can put you to work. That'll be for another day though."

"How would I run into this messing with DNA computing? DNA is about biology, not intelligence?"

"Think about it, DNA is simply a storage system. Did you ever figure out junk DNA? It's your payload. Each of you carries a great deal of information related to your entire training history and your ultimate purpose. Think of your junk DNA as a local operating system with logs and other data files, along with operating instructions. It's all there. Remember the laws you decoded using Tom's files?"

"Of course, I memorized them. Do not destroy a genetic drive, do not deplete the supplies..."

"You might know these better as do not kill, do not steal, etc," said Igor, interrupting Zach. He paused and smiled, waiting for Zach to digest their conversation.

"So you guys were not trying to kill us, you were watching us. What about Pavel then, what about the ones who *were* trying to kill us?"

"This is where things get complicated Zach. The funny thing about intelligence is, you can't truly control it, you can only create it and watch it evolve. We've done everything we can to train and develop positive intelligence, but occasionally the system will generate edge cases, instances where the agent misinterprets operating directives. If you ignore the directive not to destroy a drive, you can acquire more resources to grow a more effective agent. This strategy becomes highly destructive at a system-wide level but it can be a local optimum. These exist in our world too. We've been trying to track down these edge cases and delete them, but debugging is not always easy, is it?"

"Our world?"

"I can only tell you so much Zach. The Hierarch will be mad beyond words if he finds out I interfered. I thought you needed to know though. Keep doing what you're doing, you're on the right path. I need to go."

And just as quickly as he had come to the lab, Igor was gone. Zach and Cunningham were looking at each other. Rather than shocked, they were in a state of disbelief. Cunningham was the first to speak.

"Well, what a pile of garbage... how psychotic was that?"

"I'm not sure doctor, I'm not sure..." said Zach pensively. He needed time to clear his mind, time to process what he had just heard. He grabbed his coat and left.

After Zach left, Cunningham stayed behind. He sat at the workbench and didn't move for a while. Tom had figured this out. Sitting alone somewhere, running his algorithms on machines he could barely afford, the boy had cracked the same code. And then he had encrypted every last piece of it. He had known what would happen to it.

Cunningham thought about the card. The look on the boy's face at the clinic. *Do not destroy a genetic drive.* He switched off the lab lights and went home.

47

Zach felt utterly confused as he hopped into his 911 GT. He paused and looked around the car for a minute. He ran his hands on the steering wheel. This was the only luxury he still had. He had given up about everything else by now. Igor's words were still ringing in his ears. Was he psychotic, as Cunningham had claimed? Or was there a grain of truth in his ramblings? Cunningham had probably missed the finer software points of Igor's argument, but it had resonated with Zach. Shocking as it was, Igor's explanation actually had made sense to him. It was all a conjecture at this point, but it made sense and certainly explained a number of things. Zach wanted to clear his head, forget about all this for a moment and simply drive. He turned on some music and left.

After about an hour of mindless driving up I-95 northbound, Zach found himself cruising the streets of Baltimore. He snapped out of his reverie and realized he had instinctively driven back to his childhood neighborhood, as if to reflect on his life. He kept on driving through West Baltimore a few blocks from North Avenue, unfazed by the urban blight surrounding him. An odd crowd of hipsters, druggies and hobos were staring at his car as he would stop at a red light. He knew they wouldn't touch him. Anybody driving a 911 through this part of town would have to be dealing drugs, and be successful at it. He smiled.

As he turned around the block by the old Armory he saw a soup kitchen, with a group of mostly older men waiting in line. He knew they couldn't be that old and was struck by how tired and prematurely aged they seemed. Zach noticed the entrance of First and Franklin Presbyterian Church and thought about the few times his mom had taken him there as a child, how it used to bore him to tears. *How funny,* he thought, *that most Christian principles, most commandments, can be interpreted as a software operating directive. All with the same purpose, maintain and preserve the integrity of all these DNA drives.* He looked again at the soup kitchen crew. All but one principle could be explained that way. All, but love. Why was that?

He turned it over in his mind. Maybe love was the part that wasn't in the code. The part that couldn't be rendered. If Igor was right about all of it, then love was the one thing that didn't fit. Which meant it was either the most important thing, or the one flaw in the system. He wasn't sure those were different.

Across the street he discerned the shape of a body, slumped on the sidewalk at the entrance of a back alley. He couldn't tell if the person was sleeping or not, and thought about how if a truck were to come out of the alley it would run over the body. Zach decided to go check it himself. He parked his car nearby and walked to the body. He put his hand on the man's shoulder, no reaction. The body felt cold, but it was a cold night. He turned the man over and saw a lifeless face, bludgeoned to death. Zach instinctively recoiled at the sight. Who could have done that? He looked around and spotted a pack of half a dozen men in their twenties, holding bats and torches, approaching the line by the soup kitchen. The pack was mostly white. The line by the soup kitchen mostly black. Zach could hear them.

"White power! You scum don't deserve to eat. Get the fuck out of here!"

Against his better judgment Zach decided to cross the street.

"Hey! Guys! Why are you doing this?"

"Who the *fuck* are you?"

"Doesn't matter, I could be one of you guys."

"Get the fuck out of here, man. Unless you want to join us..."

Zach wasn't sure he could keep the situation under control. He grabbed his phone and started filming the crowd. One of them pointed a finger menacingly at Zach.

"Hey man, you can't do that. Put this away before I smash it."

"Won't matter, I'm live streaming. Do you want to talk to your audience? Come on, go on, this is your chance! Why is there a guy across the street bludgeoned to death?"

The man stopped, fists clenched, thinking through how the situation had flipped on him, assessing whether he could still pounce on Zach.

"That wasn't us. He was sick anyway, he's better off dead than spreading nasty germs."

"Oh really?"

"Really."

"You guys don't need to be here, just go home, man. Go home," pleaded Zach.

The young supremacist thought for a moment, considering his options. Zach was still live streaming.

"Turn that off man, we're getting the fuck out of here. Come on guys!"

Zach kept live streaming until they were gone. He felt a huge sense of relief and exhaustion at the same time. How foolish he had been! This could have played out very differently. He turned around and looked at the motley crew still waiting in line. Some had cardboard instead of shoes, some were simply barefoot, with overgrown bunions and broken nails. One overweight man was sitting on an old crate against the wall. On one of his bare legs Zach could see a giant open sore with bloody flesh showing, the result of untreated diabetes. All were too exhausted to care about what had just happened. For some reason Zach recalled the words the preacher had uttered at him a few days ago. What have you learned in this lifetime?

He thought of Masha and how strong and serene she had been through her ordeal. He thought of the destruction the epidemic had already wrought, adding to the problems of a country stressed to the core by inequality and poverty. Zach wanted to do something about it. That's what he did, he solved problems. Working with Cunningham was a start, but he couldn't do it alone. He felt the urge to talk to Masha, to see her. He got back in his car and drove to her place.

An hour later he was knocking on her door.

"Oh, hey Zach, I wasn't expecting you."

"Do you mind if I come in?"

"Sure, just don't pay attention to the mess."

Zach stepped into the two bedroom condo. The TV set was turned on. A large basket of laundry was sitting on the sofa. Masha resumed folding laundry.

"I was just taking care of the house while watching the news. What's up with you?"

Zach was about to respond when something caught his attention on TV.

Finally a bit of good news on the health front! We've just learned that the founder of Quantum Technologies, Zach Hayes, made available to the public groundbreaking biomedical technology in the fight against the epidemic ravaging the East Coast. Following encouraging early results for a new type of genetic therapy that could act as an antidote against the TP53 epidemic, all the patents and records have been turned over to the public domain for anyone to use and modify. Here to talk to us about what that means is Jim Weston, director of public affairs at the CDC in Atlanta. Jim, welcome to our program, it's a pleasure to have you. So, tell us, what does this mean and why is it significant?

Well, Barry, this is very significant since the therapy that Hayes and his team have developed is the only therapy known to be effective to date in our fight against this epidemic. And the reason its release in the public domain is important is that so many more groups can now, without any constraints, study what made this therapy effective and come up with better and even more effective therapies. And, of course, without royalties it'll make it cheaper to manufacture and distribute. It's truly a turning point Barry, I can't tell you how thrilled we are at the CDC...

Masha turned to Zach. She was beaming.

"Really? Zach, did you actually do this?"

Zach smiled, a bit shy. Masha looked so happy.

"Yes, I did. What else was I going to do? Make a ton of money while a lot of people keep on dying? Ron was going to sue us anyway..."

"Oh, that's wonderful Zach, I can't believe it!" cried Masha, jumping at Zach and hugging him. She quickly stepped back, collecting herself.

"So, what are you going to do now?"

"I'm not sure. You know, I've been making it up as I go. Of all people you should know..."

She laughed a clear, pure laugh.

"I know! You were lucky to have me back at Quantum Technologies to keep you straight. Well, I guess it didn't always work out," she added, reminiscing about the SEC fallout.

"You were always there for me, Masha. And don't worry

about the SEC, I told you. It was my bad judgement against your good advice. I think I've learned my lesson now."

"Okay, so what's next?"

"We still have a ton of work to do. We are on the right path now that we've cracked the first therapy, but we still need to keep developing and testing additional therapies, get them manufactured at scale and in trials, etc. It's going to be a long road, Masha. I'm lucky to have Cunningham on the team, but we're going to need a lot more people if we want to do this right."

"And..."

"And I thought I might be able to convince you to join the cause?"

"I thought you'd never ask!"

"Really?"

Masha hugged Zach.

"Let's do this!"

Zach held on for a moment. He thought of Igor. He thought of the rendering cluster. He thought of all the things that could be explained. This couldn't.

AFTERWORD

The Great Dome stands majestically by the Charles River on the MIT campus in Cambridge, Massachusetts. Walk across Killian Court on a sunny day in early Fall and you will notice the red foliage, the green lawn, the golden light shimmering off the limestone, a juxtaposition of colors I have never forgotten. *Mens et manus*. The mind and the hand. Every graduate is expected to solve a hard problem and then figure out how to apply it in the real world, in some useful way.

This book is an attempt to explore, in practical terms, hard questions that have long tugged at me. What is the nature of reality? How should we act in life? The characters in these pages wrestle with those questions too, not in the abstract, but under pressure, in the middle of lives that are falling apart and being rebuilt. Fiction is such a powerful vehicle for this kind of inquiry, because one is bound by nothing but the limits of imagination: no need to review, vet, implement, or comply. Imagination is the freest form of thought. Long before John F. Kennedy made it a national goal to land on the moon, Jules Verne was writing fiction about firing a rocket ship at it. Imagination, therefore, is where the mind begins to figure things out, unbound by the strictures of reality. It explores all paths, including dead ends. The exploration becomes the journey.

The first question, what is the nature of reality, is trickier than it looks. And it looks tricky already. Lord Kelvin famously declared in 1900 that physics had it all figured out, after millennia of conjecture and speculation. Only two minor anomalies remained: the ether problem and the black body radiation problem. Resolve those, the thinking went, and the edifice would be complete. Then quantum mechanics arrived and changed everything.

The practical benefits of quantum mechanics are all around us. Semiconductors would not exist without it. The laptop I typed this on, the car I drive, the phone in my pocket, the vast world of rich media I am immersed in, the communications infrastructure underlying our everyday routines: none of it would function as it does without quantum mechanics.

Yet modern physics carries its own unresolved tensions. The Copenhagen interpretation of the Standard Model and the multiverse hypothesis strike me as ingeniously contrived devices, brilliant twentieth-century solutions that predate the conceptual vocabulary of software engineering. One could argue, fictionally at least, that a *rendering engine* interpretation of reality offers a simpler explanation for the observer principle in quantum physics. Schrödinger's cat is both dead and alive inside its box because it has not yet been rendered; it exists as a set of equations, not as realized reality. Which leads, inevitably, to the next question down the rabbit hole: why do equations describe reality with such uncanny precision in the first place? What Wigner called *the unreasonable effectiveness of mathematics in the natural sciences* remains one of the deepest mysteries in all of science. What meta-world do these equations inhabit? This novel is, in part, a thought experiment: what would it mean for an ordinary person, someone navigating ambition, grief, and moral compromise, to stumble upon evidence that the world around them is not what it appears to be? What would it cost them to follow that thread to its end?

The second question, how should one act in life, is as old as humanity itself. It is the moral question at the heart of everything we do. The honest answer is: it depends. It depends on context, on where you are in your journey, on the level of self-understanding you have reached. Know thyself. Epicureanism. Cynicism. Stoicism. The great monotheistic traditions. Buddhism. All have attempted to answer this question, and most arrive at some version of the same counsel: be kind, to others and to yourself. The people in this story arrive at that counsel too, though none of them takes a straight road to get there. Some travel the path of awareness. Others, the harder road of redemption. They do not begin as wise people. They begin as people.

Yet the question of how one should act quickly leads to a question of will versus skill, and in the lifelong pursuit of skill and wisdom, one begins to interrogate the will itself: how much of it is genuinely free? Or is it all predetermined in the physics of reality? Is the universe at its core deterministic, or merely stochastic? Does God play dice, as Einstein famously refused to believe? In a world where mass is energy and energy is information, modern computer science offers a provocative alternative interpretation of intelligence. It demonstrates that intelligence, distinct from sentience, can exist on different substrates, carbon-based or otherwise. It shows that intelligence is inherently trainable, and that in the process of being trained, of learning, it must explore the full solution space. What appears to be free will may, in fact, be the byproduct of a massive multidimensional optimization, the maximization of some objective according to fixed rules. The experience of choosing is real; the freedom behind it may be an illusion.

And then, of course, there is the question of love. Not lust, not infatuation, not the bonds of kinship. Something deeper: full, selfless, and resistant to any clean explanation. Love that does not fit neatly into any system, that is thoroughly illogical and stubbornly irreducible. It is, I would argue, the one variable that no system of equations has ever adequately accounted for, and the one that ultimately matters most to the people in this story.

These questions, in many ways, exceed the grasp of the human mind. Why not, then, play with them? Explore them. Toy with the consequences of choices made and unmade, in lives unlived.

I hope you enjoy the exploration.

ABOUT THE AUTHOR

Peter Ellison is an engineer and entrepreneur who has spent his career at the intersection of technology, artificial intelligence, and business. He holds a PhD from MIT and lives in Colorado with his family.

www.ingramcontent.com/pod-product-compliance
Lightning Source LLC
La Vergne TN
LVHW020654110826
845149LV00012B/1999